"SAUL, ARE YOU WITH THE UNDERGROUND?"

I didn't jump; partly that was because I had been nerving myself for this moment for so long, but mostly it was because the underground hadn't existed in twenty years—he might as well have asked if I was in the Girl Scouts. "How did you get that idea?"

"You don't talk about the skyboys much, but you sure listen hard when other people do, especially when they've got a complaint. You aren't a skyboy spy, or if you are, you're a smart one, because you've moved so slow that by now people want to ask you into the church. Since there's nothing around here to spy on, you've gone to too much effort to be one of them. So, to be blunt, I think you're one of us."

At that I almost did drop my glass. "You're with the underground?"

"This will certainly be one of the best hard SF novels of the year, and Barnes is a writer to watch."

—Orson Scott Card

ISAAC ASIMOV PRESENTS

THE MAN WHO PULLED DOWN THE SKY

JOHN BARNES

W🌐RLDWIDE®

TORONTO · NEW YORK · LONDON · PARIS
AMSTERDAM · STOCKHOLM · HAMBURG
ATHENS · MILAN · TOKYO · SYDNEY

THE MAN WHO PULLED DOWN THE SKY

A Worldwide Library Book/August 1988

ISBN 0-373-30303-3

First published by Congdon & Weed, Inc.

The Tail Wags the Dog

by Isaac Asimov

One good way to work out the future is to study the past. I've always thought so. A science fiction writer who deals with a future political situation *must* consider the past. He has no other guide. Besides, there's no reason to suppose that human beings ten thousand years ago, or ten thousand years from now, have not been, or will not be, guided by the same emotions, irrationalities, and, on all-too-rare occasions, iron logic, that rules them now.

Thus, when, a great many years ago, I started writing about the fall of the galactic Empire, I felt that I had no better guide than Edward Gibbon, who had written "The Decline and Fall of the Roman Empire" (which I had read twice).

We are now on the point of establishing settlements in space; on the Moon, for one thing, and in artificial worlds placed in orbit about the Earth, for another. If one wants to describe a world of this sort, one can scarcely avoid thinking of the time when European nations established settlements on the shores of other continents. That was a task which, in the 16th and 17th centuries, offered the same degree of technological difficulty, considering the then-state of the art, that the settlement of space does today.

What, then, happened back in the ocean age that is past that can guide us in the space age that is about to come?

The most dramatic story of all involved the British colonies on the eastern shores of North America. Not only is it particularly dramatic but it is the best-known to Americans because those who lived that story are our cultural and historical, if not necessarily biological, ancestors.

What happened was that the colonies revolted against the mother country and won their independence. They set up an overall federal government to which the individual colonies/states gave up some of their sovereign rights, spread out across the continent and grew steadily more populous, strong, and technologically advanced. Eventually, they became the most powerful country in the world and, in particular, advanced from suspicious but weaker adversary of Great Britain, to friendly partner and ally, to somewhat contemptuous master. Nowadays, as members of the British Labor Party bitterly remark, when Reagan says to Thatcher, "Jump!" Thatcher replies, "How high?"

This took two hundred years, but the pace of events tends to increase with time. Can we imagine that space colonies can also break away from Earth, quickly grow more advanced technologically, and, particularly in view of their dominating position in the sky, in a very short time come to dominate the Earth far less benignly than the United States dominates Great Britain?

My own feeling is that this is not likely. I reason it out as follows—

The settlement of space is a task that is extraordinarily difficult, expensive, and risky. (The recent Challenger disaster and the problem of finding the funds with which to replace the Shuttle and put through the modifications and improvements that we are committed to is a sad example of that.) I don't think that either the United States or the Soviet Union can carry through the proper settlement of space by themselves, especially if they continue to spend an enormous fraction of their money, time, efforts, and emotion on preparations for possible war with each other.

Either, then, the United States and the Soviet Union learn to cooperate with each other (and with the rest of the world) in order to move out into space, or else humanity simply won't move into space in any practical way. They will merely convert near space into another theater of war and bring closer the destruction of everything.

However, I have no intention of trying to force my views on anyone else. For one thing, I may be completely wrong.

So, for an alternate view, in which humanity moves into space in a big way and manages to continue its bad old habit of intrigue and war (and a very exciting and thrilling view, too) read *The Man Who Pulled Down the Sky* by John Barnes.

PROLOG: EROS 2089

It was much too good a real window to waste on an access tunnel. The high towers of Kraals Twelve and Twenty-Seven, hanging from the dark bulk of Eros overhead, swept against the stars. I thought about my xfathr, Kiril, and his stories about the early days before they'd set the asteroid spinning.

That almost made me cry, which I didn't have time for. I looked around; Mendenhall was listening intently to his earphone. The rest of the creche was waiting, tense and scared. Except Mendenhall of course, we were all seventeen, but could have passed for fifty just then. Kwanza and Kari were holding hands; I envied them that, and really wished today wasn't my turn to be sergeant. Ihor scratched and stared into space—maybe his thoughts were running the same way mine were.

Kireiko appeared to be asleep. I tagged her gently with the tip of my boot; she gave me a wink, a smile, and a wave, but she looked like she was about to vomit.

Mendenhall snapped his comm unit closed. "Okay. Let's get it over with; it's time. All ready, sarge?"

"Yeah, boss."

"Okay. By the numbers one more time. Sergeant Saul here and Kwanza make the entry. Kari's through next with the HE. The rest of us follow. Sarge gives the signal for the bugout; if he can't, Kwanza does, then Kari. Subject, of course, to my override.

"Latest word is that these last holdouts are from the 27th Gagaringrad Volunteers."

All of us nodded; Kari's smile had a tight, ugly look to it, and I knew she was thinking of the hospital massacre.

"One more thing," Mendenhall added. "If this works, I think I can promise you all a good grade for the semester."

It was a pretty good try under the circumstances, but his jokes had never worked all that well in the classroom either. "Let's go," he added.

It was no more than two hundred meters up the shaft, but it seemed to take forever; the gravity fell off as we climbed upward, of course, and we'd been scrambling up and down access shafts almost from birth, but somehow it was more effort than usual. Ahead of me on the ladder, Kwanza was dripping sweat from under his armor.

We got to the first ledge. Kari planted her charges—a quick, precise job, like everything she did. "You want to check that, Saul?"

I went over it carefully, once, then twice. "The contacts look good and your continuity light's on. Okay, spray."

Kireiko covered it with plasteel; now it looked enough like a simple patched breach to be overlooked. "Okay, on up," I said, my voice more strained than I'd have liked—but then, it was the first time I'd been sergeant since Suzanne had died. Anyway, everybody moved; after a little more climbing, we were on the ledge we'd picked for the break-in.

"Directional explosive" is misleading; the polarized faces of the molecule-thick layers send ninety-plus percent of the explosive power into just one plane, but a split-second later the sonic reflection gets you anyway. When Kari had arranged the charges in a neat square on the bulkhead, Kwanza and I climbed a few meters up the shaft and the rest of the group went down a few.

"Now," Mendenhall said.

My ears rang and the pressure wave flattened me against the ladder. I kicked off and dropped to the ledge—twelve meters isn't bad at one-eighth gee.

The section of bulkhead had blown inward, as intended, straight into F Large, the last cosmorine holdout in any kraal on Eros. They'd held F Large from the first day of the invasions; they'd gotten used to thinking of this bulkhead as safe. That was all that saved Kwanza and me, because, instead of bursting rudely in on the noon meal as we'd planned, we were facing the backs of two companies drawn up for an assault.

We did what we could with the time it took them to turn around. We sprayed the place with flechettes; as the toxin took hold, cosmorines slumped everywhere. Kari was up beside us, flinging the concussion charge, and a moment later our ears rang again. For an instant there was some confusion and panic, and it looked like it might work anyway.

But we hadn't bagged enough officers, and these weren't raw recruits. Flechettes rained back through the breach, pinging off the back wall, sticking in our armor. Kari saw what was up and grabbed the panic line, sliding down the shaft on it. Kwanza and I followed about three meters apart, me first, hoping he wouldn't land boots first on my face.

It was a full fifth of a gee at the bottom of the shaft; we were coming down pretty fast as we jumped clear to join Kari.

I still don't know what happened up there. Mendenhall was next onto the panic line; he dropped out within two seconds of Kwanza and me.

Then Kireiko and Ihor plummeted out of the shaft, feathered with flechettes. They made a sick double thud as they hit the deck.

It wasn't really worth checking to see if they were still alive, but I jumped forward. Mendenhall grabbed the edge of my backplate and hauled me back; just in time, because two grenades dropped out of the shaft. We all backpedaled through the nearest port, slamming it shut before the explosions shook the bulkheads. After a minute, we could hear the cosmorines clambering down after us.

Mendenhall was barking into his mike. "Enemy breakthrough, two companies, back and bag gone wrong. Urgent; three companies required to secure and defend Maintenance Space R, R-for-Rocket, on Deck Twenty-eight. What? Repeat please? Request three companies—repeat please..."

He turned back to us, his face incredulous. "They're claiming there's a surrender in progress. We've been ordered to return to main HQ."

"No," Kari said, her eyes filling with tears.

Kwanza shook his head as if he'd just been hit.

"Who surrendered?" I asked.

"They did. Combination of high cost and lack of public support, I'd guess. Let's go—the men dropping in behind that port don't know yet, probably."

We were all silent going down the corridor. "So we won," Kwanza finally said.

Mendenhall shook his head. "If you think that, you haven't been doing your homework. Political independence is just the first step. We still depend on them for most goods; some of it isn't stuff we can replace."

The picture of Kireiko and Ihor, dead behind us and probably being cut up for trophies by the cosmorines—and of Suzanne, blown to bits two weeks before—pushed into my mind. "We've already lost things we can't replace."

Mendenhall nodded, smiling coldly. "True. But we can go on living. Once the Orbital Republics figure out the power they still have, we might not be able to."

"Shut up," Kari said. "Class dismissed."

He glared, but then Kwanza started to cry, and I joined in, and so did Kari, and we were all standing there hanging onto each other. Mendenhall stalked off in disgust.

We never did make it back to HQ. They just mailed us our discharge papers.

4 October 2108

FROM: Dr. Clement Mendenhall, Chairman, Special Project on Economic Security

TO: Office of the Facilitator

CLASSIFICATION: Maximum secure. Direct relevance to Confederation Security.

SUBJECT: Impact of volatiles trade on Confederation balance of payments; implications for military security and political stability of the Confederation.

Per your instruction, I've prepared the following tables to show the scope of the problem. I regret to repeat that there are no political or organization solutions to this problem in sight.

As everyone knows, cargoes of volatiles—water, ammonia, carbon dioxide, and methane ices—are moved by solar sails. Other alternative methods of transit considered in the past have been ballistic trajectory and mass drivers.

- Ballistic trajectory has been ruled out because it requires very large accelerations in the early and late parts of the flight; with the exception of water ice, the frozen volatiles being shipped do not have the structural strength to take the acceleration without the addition of a large and expensive skeleton.

- Although mass drivers would seem to show more promise, the continuous slow accelerations required for transporting volatiles demand either that the mass driver eject very large amounts of material at low velocities (thus throwing away up to 85% of the cargo) or that it have very large quantities of power

AVERAGE TRIP TIMES IN DAYS
(Includes time to reach escape velocity)

Destination	Earth	Source of Volatiles Jupiter (Io/Europa)	Saturn (Titan)
Apollo	50	690	460
Eros	46	682	451
Mars (Phobos)	57	702	473

MINIMUM RETURN REQUIRED PER VOYAGE
(expressed as fraction of principal,
based on prime rate of 9/1/08 = 4.5%)

Destination	Earth	Source of Volatiles Jupiter (Io/Europa)	Saturn (Titan)
Apollo	1.006	1.087	1.057
Eros	1.005	1.086	1.056
Mars (Phobos)	1.006	1.088	1.059

continuously available—thus requiring enormous photocell banks, which are, of course, a great deal heavier than thin mylar sails. To compete effectively with solar sailing, the mass driver would thus need to be much more efficient at converting incident solar energy to kinetic energy of the vehicle. At present no photoelectric power system attains more than 18% of the propulsive efficiency of solar sails.

The physical problems associated with solar sailing may be summarized briefly.

1. There are four potential sources of volatiles currently available. Earth, Io, Europa and Titan. Only Earth's orbit lies within that of Apollo, Eros, Phobos, or the asteroidal cities.

2. The propulsive force on a solar sail is inversely proportionate to the square of the distance from the sun. Thus a ship beginning its voyage from Earth accelerates at about .03 g; the same ship starting from Saturn, 9.5 times as far from the sun, accelerates at only .00033 g.

3. Io and Europa are satellites of Jupiter; Titan is a satellite of Saturn. Thus shipments from these worlds must get out of the two deepest planetary gravity wells in the solar system—again with much lower accelerations available.

4. Finally, distances increase as you get further from the sun. From Eros, it is sometimes as little as 22 million km to Earth; it is never less than 561 million km to Io or Europa, and never less than 1203 million km to Titan. These much greater distances, again, must be covered at much lower accelerations.

To this must be added an economic consideration: due to continuous banking and radio EFT, interest rates are equal throughout the Republics and the Confederation. The importance of this is that all volatiles shipments must be financed before the volatiles can be extracted, assembled into barges, equipped with sails, and launched. This can be done either by arrangement of a self-liquidating commercial loan or by prepayment of the receiver; in either case the anticipated returns must exceed the amount of the principal invested—**plus interest compounded throughout the voyage**—for the voyage to be profitable. Thus, there is a minimum cost for which a shipment can be sold if a profit is to be made.

The attached two tables should make the situation clear. Note that because of Jupiter's very high escape velocity, a ship from Io or Europa must actually use its sails to decelerate into a rendezvous orbit with Apollo, Eros, or Phobos. This effect is so large that trip times from Saturn are considerably lower—which should be a familiar fact, since it was the original justification for the settlement of Titan. Note also that margins need not be large for marginal effects to be large. As long as the Republics continue their standing markup of 4% over production cost, they will continue to reap enormous profits—about 22% per annum return on investment—while Titan, Io, and Europa are barely able to stay in the market through our carefully concealed subsidy programs.

I must again reiterate my position in our meeting of 2 October. Although the settlement of Titan, and the closing of Adonis, have reduced our balance of payments problem with the Republics, they have not and cannot eliminate it. The Republics continue to make enormous profits while dramatically underselling our domestic sources. We must relocate our entire population to the Jovian and Saturnine systems, break the grip of the Orbital Republics on Terran resources, or resign ourselves to the status of economic colonies.

To the Minister for ExtraConfederation Relations's remark that war would be an unmitigated disaster, I can only repeat: disaster is relative. Given the choice between war, with its high probability of our defeat, and relocation or resubjection, with their certainty of defeat, we must take the best of a set of very bad options. In anticipation of your probable decision I have begun a study of possible strategies for victory at an acceptable cost.

1

I hate getting the zero gee classroom, but I always end up there anyway. It has advantages for a grad seminar—arranged in a sphere, everyone can talk directly to everyone else. But for freshman Political History, a straight lecture course, it's simple misery; you get three or four creches in tight little knots scattered around the sphere, usually at the maximum possible distance from the instructor. I end up in the center of the sphere, trying to lecture while slowly tumbling end over end—not really in keeping with my dignity as a professor.

That particular day in 101, we were doing the period between the Home Rule Declaration and the Collapse of 2034. Class was about over, and I was facing the usual parade of dumb questions: "Why did the dirtsiders keep trading with the Orbital Republics when it was ruining them? Why didn't the UN step in? Did it have something to do with dirtsiders being superstitious?"

That last was especially dumb because it was Standard Winter Solstice and the anthro department had a display of crucifixes, Santa Claus statues, menorahs, and other such out in the hall.

The worst question of the lot, I'm sorry to say, was from Goddard al-Ghirad. He just couldn't see why the UN permitted borders to be in inconvenient places. "But they *knew* Earth was going broke with the borders where they were."

This after ten minutes of arguing.

I tried to fob him off with an enormous assignment—for extra credit, read Mendenhall's *Historic Problems in State-to-State Trade*—and get discussion moving again, but he wasn't giving up. "All right, one more question, Mr. al-Ghirad."

"Well, uh, gospa—don't some people say that that book was, uh, influenced by Pratt?"

"Yes, they do." I swallowed my irritation; after all, his home kraal was in Titan Orbital, and they're pretty traditional in the new stations out toward the frontier. "They are free to say that, just as we are free to read Pratt to see what we can get from him. That's because we live in the Confederation—not in Port Armstrong or Gagaringrad. One thing I hope we can teach you here is that freedom is something more than our side's favorite slogan—that it is something we do rather than something we own."

A couple of the Libs in the class applauded, which gave me a warm feeling, but you don't keep a political job by offending people. "I think, however, that Pratt would not have liked the book much. For those of you who haven't read any of Pratt, he's very much a normative economist as opposed to a positive one—that is, he analyzes the morality of the system, not its operation. Dr. Mendenhall's book is a positivist dissection of some historical situations—the Viking era, the slave trade, the Opium Wars, the Third World crises of the last half of the twentieth century, and, of course, the events leading up to the Great Collapse. I think it would strike Pratt as essentially irrelevant. Pratt was a good enough economist to understand why those things happened, but he was mostly interested in deploring the fate of the losers." I forced a smile at al-Ghirad. "Which should be a relief to you. You seem to be interested in the same questions. You don't suppose you're coming down with Prattism, do you?" Even the al-Ghirad creche laughed.

I went over the high points once more quickly; it was time to dismiss them anyway. "Remember to work through Chapter 12 tonight. It also wouldn't hurt to go over the session faxes available in the department office."

As they swam out, I waited around for the transcriber to print out the faxsheets of the lecture, figuring that I might as well save any possible material for that Gymschool text I was supposed to be writing. Somebody was floating behind me; whatever it was, it would keep a minute while I got organized.

"Admirable defense of principles, Saul. You're probably a good influence."

"Dr. Mendenhall," I said, startled.

"Something urgent's come up," he said. "We need to talk in my office, right away. I hope that doesn't sound too much like an order, but I'm afraid that's what it is . . ."

I nodded, slid my papers into my pack, strapped it on, and pushed off after him. He got a lot more zero gee practice than I did—his office was on the same deck as the rotation joint—so it was hard to keep up with him, despite his age. Even after we got through the rotation joint and started using our feet, it still took some effort to catch up—it was rush hour, five percent gee is a little light for walking, and students are careless about the ped lanes.

The whole way down Varsity J Corridor I kept wondering. I hadn't been having sex with undergraduates, taught anything controversial, or offended any potential sources of money. Whatever else I had done was theoretically beneath his notice. Why did the Chancellor want to talk to me?

He'd been my thesis advisor, of course, and before that I'd served under him in the Provisional Revolutionary Army back during the war, but there had never been anything more than a mutual, familiar respect between us, so I didn't think he had just decided to have a chat for old times' sake.

As we rounded the corner into 14th Tunnel, he flashed a smile at me, the toothy kind that came right before he sprang the trap in oral exams. "You know I like to be obscure, and I'm going to. You are either in more trouble than you've ever been in, or you're not in trouble, or both. Depends on point of view."

He didn't say another word for the five more corridor intersections to his office; he opened the door and Kari was sitting there.

She was obviously as surprised as I was; we hadn't seen each other since the creche dissolution three years ago. We both managed an awkward hello.

Mendenhall simply ignored our embarrassment; maybe he didn't notice it. "Would you like coffee, or did you get enough of it on Earth?"

"I never turn it down," I said, pulling myself into a seat.

"I'd kill for a cup," Kari added.

"I may hold you to that." Mendenhall fussed with the coffee; to avoid Kari's eyes, I looked around the office. It was pretty much the same arrangement he'd had when he'd been a prof—a desk and chair, with an old keyboard-type terminal on a stand behind his desk. Confederation University didn't have or need much in the way of administration; most of what it took he did by going quickly through his inbox every morning, entering his decisions at the terminal as he went.

He filled the coffee cups and handed them to us; I waited for the low-grav waves in mine to settle out. Kari, as she always did, opened hers too soon and lost a couple of blobs onto her shirt.

"This stuff was a lot cheaper when I was a kid—I got hooked before my wallet knew better. I think you'll like the blend." Mendenhall sat down without using his hands, the way permanent low-grav people do; I was startled to realize how old he must be if he was on PLG.

He drew a deep breath. "This is harder with you two. I've known you longer. Do you remember the Significance Game, back when you took my sophomore methods course?"

Remember it? It had been the bane of our lives. The rules were simple—suddenly in the middle of his lecture, Mendenhall would point and bawl out your name. He would announce some hypothetical event; your job was to demonstrate, under his interrogation, that the event was worthy of your attention. "Well, *I* think it's interesting" was *not* an acceptable answer.

"Sure," I said. "What—"

His finger jabbed at me. "Pareto!"

Then we all burst out laughing; Kari especially, and somehow the embarrassment disappeared with that. I had stood up, spread my feet to a comfortable width, and let my hands drop to my sides with my head up—the exact posture he preferred us to take for the game—but an absence of practice, and muscles conditioned to Earth-normal, had sent me a good forty centimeters off the floor.

He gestured me back into the chair. "Well, your reflexes are as good as ever. Let's see about your mind.

"Here's the problem: they're shutting down Kraal Two on Apollo. The reason is what you'd expect: short supply of volatiles, even with maximum feasible conservation. You are appointed advisor to the Facilitator. You don't have to tell him that it's significant in its own right. From his standpoint, it forces him to a decision. What is it? What do you tell him to do?"

"Hire Dr. Mendenhall and do what he says."

"Good, your training took. However, more seriously..."

Kari jumped in, as she always did. "How many people do they have in Kraal Two there? There's some spare room here and on Phobos—"

"Kraal Two is less than half full—we've been encouraging the teams there to emigrate, so there're only two thousand people left—not a drop in the bucket for any one settlement, but we could scatter them around the Confederation easily enough. No, if it were just resettlement, I wouldn't have you people in here; so let me rephrase the challenge. What *significant* action does this force our government to take?"

As always, Kari's little trick had bought me enough time to think and come up with at least an approach to answer. "I don't know," I said. "It's a tough little dilemma. Relations with the Orbital Republics are tense, and I hate to depend on them for volatiles; on the other hand maybe the trade would help relations, and after a while they might be willing to renegotiate. I do have that right, don't I—shutting down Kraal Two will place the rest of Apollo in violation?"

"I'm afraid so. It's the last remaining civilian facility there. And the Treaty of Von Braunsberg specifically forbids garrison-only bases on any body inside the Martian orbit."

I sat and thought. "We *can't* give up Apollo."

After a moment, Kari asked, "Why not?"

I guess I must have looked surprised. She smiled wistfully. "My research never was team-central, Saul, and I've been over in Team Levi-Strauss for a while now. Straight politics and economics just aren't my field."

"Well," I said, "In a sense the problem is just plain astrogation. The Republics occupy Earth orbit, plus they have their bases on the moon, right? Theoretically we have all of the solar system beyond the lunar orbit, but in practice we only occupy a few asteroids, plus the major moons of Jupiter, and most recently Saturn's moon Titan. Those moons are our only domestic source of raw organics and water—the 'volatiles' you hear about in the news. If the Republics ever attack us—and remember, even now, they've never completely given up their claims on us as colonies—those moons are what they'll go for.

"One reason they don't dare to attack us is because we have most of our forces based on the asteroids that orbit between the Earth and Mars—Apollo and Eros, since we had to give up Adonis two years ago. If they were to go after our resources, we could attack their home cities almost instantly—so their fleet has to stay back to protect them."

"Why do you think they'll attack us? They trade with us."

Mendenhall grinned. "Let me tackle that one; I literally wrote the book on it. We're at a huge economic disadvantage in our trade with the Orbital Republics, but the military situation is a standoff. If they get the upper hand militarily—by making us withdraw from our forward bases—then they'll be able to threaten us into trade concessions. And in a generation or so, we'll be broke, and back under their domination in practice, even if the diplomats preserve our political independence. Basically, what it works out to is that if we don't have bases inside the Martian orbit, the Confederation is doomed, and we'll be right back where we were before the Independence War."

"And we're in danger of losing Apollo?" Kari asked. "Because the treaty—"

"Forbids us to have exclusively military bases inside the Martian orbit. We're supposed to have some civilians there as hostages." Mendenhall was grim.

"We can't just give up Apollo, and then say no more?" Kari asked.

I shook my head. "If we do that, Eros is next, for one thing. We're almost as bad off for volatiles as Apollo is, and we'll be broke in a few years, too. We could try to get the outer colonies, especially Titan and Europa, to donate volatiles—but they aren't going to want to do that. Shipping sunward is just too uneconomic—you can't outrun compound interest.

"We might award bonuses to comet-wrestlers, of course. But I don't know what level that would have to be at, subsidy programs always get attacked, and besides I just don't like the root wastefulness of hauling all that stuff sunward when there are better sources closer. We could open Mars to exploitation, but the xenobiologists would scream—and rightly so. It's stupid to wipe out the only other example of life we've got, before we understand it, for a transient political thing.

"So—I don't like it, but it looks like we don't stop backing at Apollo. We move the garrison and fleet back here to Eros temporarily, but what we really do is keep backing up, give up all the trans-Martian asteroids. This won't play well with the public, but—"

Mendenhall waved his hand. "Good try. But let me fill in some details. To subsidize comet-wrestlers enough to completely supply all the trans-Martian cities, we'd have to roughly quadruple the processed-mass tax."

I whistled; he nodded. "Exactly. It would kill half a dozen industries—and we'd have to either subsidize those or rely on the Orbital Republics for those finished goods. The other detail is the point at which we'd become self-supporting in volatiles, if we moved the populations of the sunward colonies outward.

"Mars was a poor guess, Saul, even if you include Phobos on your abandonment list. The Asteroid Belt is bone-dry, too, and ultimately it doesn't pay to move volatiles even one kilometer sunward, because even with mass drivers you can't decelerate the ice blocks into a lower orbit in anything less than a year or two. They're too big and they won't hold together. And the mass driver is too expensive anyway—doing it with solar sails, the way we actually do, it takes several years to bring in one ice shipment. Even if the prevailing interest rate was below one percent and inflation was zero, that wouldn't pay. And in an economy growing as fast as ours—"

"Inflation and high interest rates are built in," I said. "This is all obvious now that you mention it. Most of it I already knew but hadn't put together. Why haven't I heard of this before?"

"Because there is just one university in the Confederation, the government didn't want people to know how bad things really were, and every bit of research done at Confed U is carefully watched. Personally I've turned back eight projects that were headed that way. If I may return to the main point, the Belt cities would have to go, too. Ceres, Ceres Orbital, Juno, Vesta, and Psyche don't leak quite as fast, and the energy price of volatiles isn't as steep there. But it's enough to kill them in another ten years, especially because part of what keeps them going now is a hidden subsidy: economic competition with sunward stations that are even worse off. With that gone, they'd fold up fast.

"The border would be all the way back at Jupiter."

"Ganymede, Io, Callisto—those would be the front line stations?" I couldn't believe he meant that.

He shook his head. "Everywhere would be. They won't sortie from the Earth-Moon system as long as they have to worry about ballistic-drop shots into Earth and the Republics. But out there—if war came in the wrong set of planetary positions— well, it could be a long run from Jupiter to guard Titan. Think about how big that separation gets, say, in ten or twelve more standard years, and how unlikely we'd be to see them coming without forward observation. And imagine Titan—one orbital and two little surface settlements—having to put capital accumulation into defense. It was bad enough when we had to abandon Adonis."

I raised my hands. "Okay, you've got me, again. Like every other time we played the Significance Game. What do I tell the Facilitator to do? We can't just raise taxes and build military bases in the Belt or coerce the volatile-rich worlds into subsidizing the dry ones, because the Constitution won't let us. Militarily we can't let go of Apollo. But if we don't we go broke, teach the Apollonians to live on iron and vacuum, or declare war. Which, I might add, the smart money says we would lose."

He flipped the window from an Earthscape to outside view. The Earth and Luna were a brilliant double diamond in the sky, slowly crawling across the empty black as Eros spun. "Are you so sure we'd lose? But let that go. Kari, you do semiotic demography. All this trouble could be avoided if the Orbital Republics were just willing to give us an even break, to stop pushing their natural advantages to the limit. What are the prospects for their taking a kinder view of us within the next few years?"

She made a face. "Zip. For at least two big reasons—the extended lifespan and the drift in the signifieds. No, we can't expect concessions from them at all."

"A war would cost them a lot, too, even if they won," I said. "Would they overlook that?"

"I'm on my home territory now, Saul." She smiled; I grinned back, and there was a little moment of old times before we both realized and looked away, embarrassed. "The extended lifespan problem is straightforward," she went on. "There are still a lot of veterans of the early days alive and influencing the culture—even most of the original settlers from back in the 1990s. And all of them hate us. The time for that to die down to manageable levels, in the old days on Earth, might have been thirty years or so from the Independence War—so we'd only have needed to hang on 'til about 2120; but with the extended lifespan it could go well into the 2200s.

"That's bad enough, but the drift of signifieds is worse. Barring some major social dislocation, the trend runs against us for at least four more lifespans—call it a thousand years. Of course, in that time there will have to be some dislocations, but we can't count on them turning up in time or being in our favor."

"Uh," I said, "excuse my being dumb, but what's a drift of signifieds?"

"Well, let's see, you just had basic semiotics, right?"

"Even that was a long time ago."

"Okay, remember that things and concepts are called signifieds, and the words and symbols that stand for them are called signifiers? Well, the drift of signifieds is what happens when the signifier stays the same but the signified changes. The British monarchy, or the Roman eagle, or the Communist red flag are all examples. The symbol stayed pretty much the same, but what it meant changed a lot over the long run of history.

"The normal path of the drift is for the signifieds to move closer to reality over time. Of course, since reality also moves, the signifieds never quite catch up. Like the red flag, which began as a symbol of pure anarchic revolt and ended up as one of ascetic obedience, because the movement that adopted it began in rebellion and ended in conformity."

I nodded. "I think I understand the process. Why is it important?"

"Because the way the signifieds drift tells us something about what social values are likely to be a generation or two in the future. And the drift of signifieds in the Orbital Republics points to aggression and dominance increasing in value for several more generations; a lot of the terms and symbols that used to stand for tolerance and individual liberty will become symbols of aggression and violence.

"Mostly it's the effect of sending so many of their young males down to the Protectorate all the time. Colonial powers—especially ones with pretensions to democracy and equality—often drift that way.

"And of course, the more they drift that way, the more they get into fights with their neighbors, and the more they get militarized, and the faster the drift goes. In some historical cases that vicious circle ran unbroken for centuries."

She stopped and smiled at me again. "Okay, end of Semiotics 101. But the answer is, Saul, that the generation in power in the Republics would rather fight us than compromise. The next several generations will be even worse. So in that sense, I guess war is just about inevitable if things go on as they are."

"And that," Mendenhall said, "is why I brought you both here, despite all the embarrassment involved. You will notice that both of you, for quite disparate reasons, tend to believe a war with the Republics is in the wind."

"I hope not, because we'd lose," I said. "They have several times our population and resources. And a lot more troops."

"Yes . . ." He smiled. "Ninety percent of those, though, are in the Protectorate Administration on Earth. Cosmorines only in name, in many cases."

"They've had the training. More than our kids get. And politically speaking if you had trouble getting Titan to go along with shipping volatiles way below cost, imagine what it would be like to talk them into an aggressive war."

Kari snorted—a short, ugly noise. "War is popular. No matter what the political system, declare war and the first thing citizens do is rally to the state. Peace gets popular only when a side is worn out, losing, or both."

"You really believe that?" I asked. "You're sounding more like Pratt than ever."

She started to snap at me, but Mendenhall broke in. "I'm inclined to agree with her, Saul. And believe me, the only thing I share with Pratt is the ability to see that if something has happened for every case you have a record of, it's likely to happen again. You're both still fun to work with . . . I'm looking forward to that, anyway."

"Working with . . ." Kari began.

"I presume you've realized that all this is not merely an exercise in theory, as much fun as it might be if it were."

"I'm beginning to see," I said. "Are we at war?"

"Not yet. In fact, Kraal Two doesn't close for some months yet. But it will. They'll be picking up a load of volatiles at aphelion in a couple of weeks, but that won't last them even with rationing. It's not a big load in the first place, and they'll be dry a month after perihelion. So we are about nine months away from the outbreak of the Second Space War, or whatever the historians are going to call it. We know that. The Republics don't, thanks to a certain reticence on the part of our Bureau of Reporting and Statistics. As you've pointed out, we're a bit outgunned, man for man and ship for ship.

"So it's war. The key question is, how can we win anyway? And the answer is, if we're ready and they're not, by catching them flat-footed, before all their resources get into play. So as of now you're mobilized—if you want to be."

"I hadn't realized I had any options."

"You can wait and be drafted two months before the actual outbreak. Or you can go to work for me."

"For you?"

"My official title now is Head of the Directorate of Irregular Operations. In plain language, I'm the chief spy and saboteur. There's something you can do for me, unless you'd rather be ranking officer on a boarding craft, which is what you'll be doing otherwise."

I shook my head. "Something's wrong in the files, then. I retired as a buck sergeant nineteen years ago. A boarding party gets commanded by a captain at least."

"Other things are wrong than the files. How many combat veterans do you suppose we have? The Independence War was almost a reproductive generation ago and the population was a lot smaller then. We've had a baby boom ever since, but very little of it's combat age yet. The ratio of militarily relevant population—a revealing little number we came up with, people between sixteen and sixty over total population—is actually worse than it was during the Independence War. We need all the old vets we can get.

"Besides, your name is famous. These kids grow up on stories about Kiril and Masako Pareto, and your desk drawer has a good-sized pile of medals of your own in it. You'd be good for morale—they need you almost as badly as I do, Saul.

"I suppose in that sense I'm being selfish. And you wouldn't be a captain. More like a colonel I'd guess. For me you're going to be a Naval ensign at low pay, mostly to hide you from any prying eyes that might get into the data banks.

"But, dammit, I need someone with your background. Let me amend that—I need everyone with your background, or anything remotely close to it, and that comes down to about thirty-five people in the Confederation."

"My background?"

"Combat vet. Political commitment to the Confederation. And believe me, no matter what they claimed about not watching you, my predecessors made an extra-special point of knowing which way everyone leaned politically. And most important, Earthside experience."

"What's that got to do with it?"

"It's where you're going. That's where we need you."

I was shocked. I don't make the point of wearing my patriotism on my sleeve the way that the Children of Independence do; but sit the war out spying on Earth? The absolute back of the backwoods? True, I had written more history than I had made, but all the same—

He smiled at my expression. "Surely you're not still so young you're afraid of missing out on a war?"

"It's not that, gospa. It's just that—well, I don't want any special favors. If my students went off to their deaths while I relaxed on Earth counting water shipments—" I shrugged and shook my head. I didn't want him to think that I wasn't grateful for the chance—

He glared at me. "What I want you to do is far more dangerous than boarding under fire, and couldn't be done half as well by anyone else."

The old man let me take that in for a moment, waiting for the instant of maximum confusion, just as he always had.

He smiled thinly. "You yourself mentioned that ninety per-cent of their cosmorines are on Earth."

"They could all be back up in the Republics within a couple of days. Even if the fleet managed to surprise them, before you got one of the Republics occupied you'd have the other eleven crawling with cosmorines, and a counter-assault within a week."

"But if even the reserves are down there—so that any at-tempted counterattack would have to go up the gravity well—"

"They wouldn't leave themselves that unguarded," I said firmly.

"They did in 2076."

"Yeah." Then I saw—there was a sinking feeling in my stomach, and at the same time I wanted to jump up and pace the floor.

I glanced at Kari; she was nodding too. "You're right," she said. "They did. That's the job, then? Get a rebellion going, big enough to make them send the reserves down from orbit?"

"That's the assignment. Officially. Unofficially, your feel-ings can take you where you want to go with it . . . and I will be privately pleased, let me add." He pushed the FAX button on his terminal and something rolled out on the scroller. "This will be one of the texts for your training course, such as it will be, since there aren't many living people who've ever done this sort of thing. I don't think Saul will need to read it, though."

I looked down at the title page he had printed out. *"The Role of Ideology in the Administration of Earthside Economies: A Study in Well-Intended Repression,"* I read. "So as a bonus, are they finally going to publish my thesis?"

"In a couple of months. It was good work, Saul. We all went to bat for it, you know—but the government of the time—"

Hadn't wanted to offend the Republics; I knew that. Now, of course, the goal would be to build up indignation over the oppression of the Earthsiders. "I'll take the job," I said.

"Me, too," Kari added.

We shook hands all around; he promised we'd hear some-thing the next day.

Out in the corridor I asked Kari if she'd like to go for a snack; she agreed, and we headed for Roget's.

As we sat down among the potted geraniums, Kari said, "He really pulled out all the stops on you. Patriotism, personal loyalty, even your thesis . . ."

"You volunteered too."

"Yeah. I didn't want to get the same treatment." She cut a big bite out of her sweetbar—I noticed mango-tamarind was still her favorite. Most of us who've been Earthside prefer flavors we didn't encounter on Earth; after you get back the synthetics all taste like drycake for a while. She chewed slowly, looking away from me, and finally said, "I didn't know we'd meet today."

"Me either."

"How's Kwanza?"

I shrugged. "Oh, pretty well."

"Are you guys seeing anyone?"

"Not right now. It's hard to find new creche partners. And I think we kind of miss you."

Her jaw set. "Team Pareto threw me out."

"Kwanz' and me voted for you."

She looked down at her food, slapping at it with the fork. "I know, I miss you guys, too. I think my new creche is going to expel me. They say my work isn't central to Team Levi-Strauss, either."

"That's terrible," I said, meaning it.

"Want to form an interdisciplinary creche? Team Leonardo or Team Franklin or something?" She tried to smile, to make it look like a joke.

They don't allow those, of course; but she knew that as well as I did. I leaned forward and kissed her cheek. "I think Kwanza and I would be glad to have you move in unaffiliated; we could nominate you for Permanent Guest and probably get it."

"Thank you." She looked up. "I might be able to work things out with my creche, still. I can't promise."

"We're not going anywhere. You know where we are."

"Do you really think you can get me Permanent Guest? Team Pareto didn't like me much even when we were officially a creche in the team."

I shrugged. "We'll trim the sails once the ship's off the catapult."

"Are you sure Kwanza feels the same way?"

"Well, yeah. We're both pretty hetero; it's tough with just each other in the bed. Sometimes he'll hire a girl, or I will, but it's just not the same."

Then we were both quiet, just eating; sometimes we'd both look up, and want to speak, and end up just smiling or looking away. Finally she said, "I wonder if Mendenhall threw us together on purpose."

"It does seem like him," I said. "Probably to make sure we'd both accept. Of course, he didn't grow up in the creche and team system, you know. He actually lives in a room all by himself. So it's hard to figure out anything he does."

She nodded. "Do you still hate him? For what happened to our creche?"

"Mixed feelings. He was almost a second xfathr when I was working on my doctorate."

"For me, too," she said. "He's always treated us decently, I guess. I just wish I understood what he's really after."

And after that we decided to hang around and then have dinner together, and I gave Kwanza a call so he could come up and join us. We all got slightly crazy and decided to splurge, so we ordered the meat platter: one rabbit leg in plum sauce, half a broiled guinea pig, and a stuffed tilapia, in exchange for about a day's wages. Worth every millicredit, too—it's the dish Roget shows off with, and the vegetables that come with it are all real, too. I'm told there are creches, mostly the younger ones coming along, who actually prefer the synthetics and eat the Standard Issue more often than they have to, but I refuse to believe that of anyone.

Somewhere late in the evening, Kari decided to go home with us "just for the night." As we staggered back to quarters, arms around each other and all three of us giggling uncontrollably, I began to think that maybe between Kari and the war my life might get shaken up, started on a better path. Kwanza and I had both been going stale in the three years since she'd left; maybe if Kari came back, and we had some of our old kind of adventures, we'd quit feeling so old and pointless.

Looking back, I can see that I was being a prize idiot.

2

The cover story they came up with was that I was going out to Ganymede for heart surgery. The advantage to that was that my alibi covered both me and Kwanza, since of course he'd go along to the hospital if I were seriously ill. In fact, if they built up the heart attack story enough, it would probably cover a lot of the senior members of Team Pareto.

All of us except the youngest creche were going, of course—the mixture of formalism with field work that we specialized in was exactly what Mendenhall was looking for. "For the sake of the team, we'd better win," Kwanza said, as he filled our glasses.

"If we don't, there won't be many left," I agreed, sitting up in bed beside him. "There wouldn't be much of the Firths or the Veblens, either. I'm just hoping Kari will get through okay—"

"Always the romantic," Kwanza said. "Remember what she was like in a knife fight, back in the last war?"

"Yeah." All of a sudden I thought of Kireiko, Ihor, Suzanne. "Vanished toves," he said, and we drank another of a very large number of toasts. Kari had left that morning—her cover story was that she had a teaming offer on Callisto. The last three weeks, since her application for Permanent Guest status had been accepted by the team council, had been almost like old times; now the place seemed emptier than ever.

"Got a whole five liters to deal with," I observed, refilling the glasses. "We probably ought to save a liter each for the trip."

"Yeah. That way, we can still be standing for Roget's, late tonight."

"Good idea, old tove. How long are you going to be by yourself? Have they worked it out yet?"

"Yeah. Four days 'til I ship out—"

"Four?"

"That's what they tell me. It's not so bad. We'll both spend several weeks in drop boats, you know."

"With drugs, though. People can't stand being all alone like that without—"

"I can." He was looking at the window, which was tuned to Gulf of Alaska, early morning. "I haven't taken the drugs the last two trips."

I didn't know what to say; I must have looked pretty stupid. "No drugs at all?" I finally asked.

"I guess I wanted to find out what loneliness was like..."

There was a lump in my throat. "Well, how was it?" I managed.

"Different. Your thinking gets...clearer for a while. There's kind of a peace to it." He shrugged. "I just wanted to try it. I guess I like it if it's not too often. After all, people in the Republics insist on it."

"Sure, they think a room of your own is a necessity, and I can see that it might be nice to be able to shut the door on an argument. But after a while, with that substitute for settling the issues, I'm not sure I'd want to room with you." I thought I was being perfectly reasonable, but when I stopped talking I realized I was almost choking.

Then he held me for a long time. "I like being alone, I guess, now and then, but I do come back," he said finally. "I'm your xbrothr. We share work."

I finally returned the hug, and then we had another toast to each other, and suddenly we were just talking about the whole idea of being alone, as if it were an abstract thing that had just come up. My xfathr always said if you get two societists and a bottle together, you'll get everywhere except to a conclusion.

"Look at it, for a moment, from a Prattist viewpoint," I said. "Institutions make personalities. People who have always had space all to themselves tend to be greedy and self-centered. Hell, look at the way people stand quietly in line here and the way they squabble and jump the queue even in Tsukubanichi—which is relatively speaking the civilized Republic.''

"Actually," he said, "people in the Republics seem to get along rather well—especially in the face of institutions that, as you say, force them into conflict. Of course their shrinks spend a lot of time treating 'diseases' that are really just plain loneliness, but that's not something that's immediately apparent. Maybe if you locked one of them up with several other people and minimal physical privacy, the way we live, *he'd* crack up.''

"You're not suggesting that living in your own cage is normal! Drycake, Kwanz', we use solitary confinement as a punishment.''

He finished his glass, filled it, topped mine. "Sure. And ninety-plus percent of human history, we all slept in one communal sprawl like baboons. But the way they do it in the Orbital Republics isn't much different from the way most people in the West lived after 1970 or so—and the ones who couldn't usually wanted to.''

"And," I said, "*Interaction of Market and Personality Structures* was published at Harvard in 2003—right in the middle of all of that.''

"Pratt again! If that poor idiot kid doesn't, I'll have to turn you in myself. You, old tove, are halfway to collectivism.''

"So's the Confederation!''

"You know it, and I know it—but if we let these kids know it, we're out of a job. They really believe all this stuff about the 'perfection of post-liberal democracy' that they give them in Gymschool.''

I took a long drink myself and smiled blissfully. "You're hedging, Dr. Pareto.''

"It's what I do best. You should take my seminar in advanced hedging next semester. Seriously, though, Saul, what are two nice societists like us doing with this kind of a job?''

I shrugged, got up, and flipped the window to Sault Ste. Marie, mid-morning, not far from where I was scheduled to come down. "They're not going to have much to look at out here for a while," I said. "I bet the ORs turn off the flow of scenery when the fighting starts.''

"Now who's hedging?''

"True." I sat down. "Kwanz', I'm not sure I can do much of a job of explaining. I guess it's just that I can't see freezing in the dark while the ORs tighten their grip on Earth; our society needs to win that war. I'd rather not fight—"

"'—but by Jingo if we do,

"We've got the ships,

"we've got the men,

"We've got the money too,'" he sang. "Has it occurred to you that if we freeze in the dark, we'll still be together?"

"Sure. And if we win, we will too."

"Don't be too sure. Think about it. What's the best way to keep property communal, historically speaking?"

"Not to have too much of it," I said. "I see. You're afraid the team and creche system would break up like the Israeli kibbutzim in the 1990s or the Free Kolkhoz did twenty years later. When there's a lot to go around, people don't see why they shouldn't own it."

"Yeah."

I shrugged. "Well, I'll grant the possibility. But we're not rich yet. I'd rather we were free to decide to decay into privatism than have the right decision forced on us."

"Drycake, Saul, that problem's the tip of the iceberg!" He threw his empty glass against the wall; it bounced around and landed in a corner. "What is he up to?"

"Who?"

"Mendenhall. What is it that he's trying to pull?"

"Kwanza, I'm still not sure I know what we're talking about."

"Well, ultimately, if we win the war, the Confederation will get swallowed. We don't have the population to rule even spaceside humanity directly. Two-and-a-half million of us to 170 million in the Republics. So that means we'll have to set things up one-man-one-vote and then depend on some kind of coalition with Earth, which has a completely different set of interests, assumptions, beliefs..." He raised his arm in mock salute. "The problem, in other words, is that it's just not practical to be a patriot anymore. We either lose the war and the ORs send us out to freeze in the cold, or we win, and get swallowed up and outvoted in the second federation of the solar system. So all our patriotism is not likely to do us any good."

"I never thought it would. But given the choice between a long-range threat if we win, and one right now—"

"Sure. That's what I try to tell myself. But it doesn't wash. There are alternatives to this, I'm sure of it, but with all the training time in the last month I haven't had time to work on it. Import substitution, for one thing. If we just played nice with the ORs for a couple of years and built up some trade advantages, we could pay for the volatiles. Or within the Confederation, we could just set up a simple futures market in volatiles; that might very well make shipping sunward feasible—expensive, of course, but feasible. And besides, it would drive capital out to the frontier stations where it's needed most. Why does there *have* to be a war with the Republics and a revolution in the Protectorate? What's Mendenhall *really* pushing for?"

I nodded. There was a lot of sense in all that—but it seemed a little late for him to worry. "How long have you been thinking this way?"

"Some weeks."

"Did you talk with Mendenhall?"

"He just said there were things I hadn't figured in, and then very politely threw me out of his office."

"With all those doubts, why are you going at all?"

"Plain restlessness, partly. We were a pretty special generation—the ones that were fighting age for the Independence War. And now we're just fodder for the economy. I'm tired of it, and so are you. We had ourselves a glorious war, and now we think we have a taste for adventure and glory."

It made some sense; I made a toast. "To war, for not being dull."

His tone was friendly but absolutely firm. "I am not going to drink that toast." He swung a seat down from the wall and sat down, facing me. "That's what I was getting to. There have been short, glorious wars in history, some of them even important. But very few, and practically none since 1914, Saul. You'd know that if you just read your own syllabi. And think about what we're doing, where we're going!"

He was tensed up again, beating a hand against the wall. "Drycake, Saul, we're going to reinvent people's war! Think about what a guerrilla war against a colonial regime has al-

ways meant, all the way back to the Maccabees. Why do you
think Gandhi almost starved himself to death; trying to get his
own followers to quit resorting to butchery! Let's not kid ourselves about all this. We're going to take a peaceable, decent,
hardworking group of people who have been innocent victims
for decades—"

"And help them stop being victims!" I said, finishing my
glass. "And that you can toast."

"Yeah." He let a long sigh get out, though, and after he
drank he said, "The problem is, they also stop being innocent.
I can handle that, I think. Most of my field work has been
economic anthro—counting ships and shipments, tracing trade
flow and the distortions around the GXSs. So the world
changes. More data to gather and more papers to write. Big
deal.

"But for you, tove . . . that thesis of yours was the work of a
muckraking idealist. What's going to happen to you . . ." He
shook his head. "If I was superstitious, I'd pray that I will have
the strength to refrain from saying, 'I told you so.'"

Then all of a sudden he burst into a dirty song, and I joined
him. We noticed the bottle of wine was close to empty, so we
toasted the rest away to something or other and went down to
Roget's to sit among the students and get some more drinking
done. Old Roget, the patriarch of the team himself, came over
to have a glass with us, looking his usual worried-sick self.

"What's the tragedy for today?" I asked him. "Worried
about a vacuum shortage, or what would happen if everyone
in the kraal farted at the same time? Let's see, if they all did it
within twenty seconds that would be two-point-five hectofarts
per second—"

"I wish it was that simple," he said. "No, the problem is that
E Large is empty. The Athletic Society moved over to Kraal
Eight."

"I didn't know Team Roget administered it," Kwanza said.
"I'm sure you'll get another tenant, though . . ."

"We don't. We don't even hold shares in it. That's not the
point. The point is that we got D and the government has A, B,
and C; the University has F. As long as the Athletes were in
there, there was no other place around that anyone could open
up another bistro. Now some young, eager creche from Team

Crocker or Team Hilton's gonna take E Large, and there'll be competition.''

We were drunk and we couldn't help it—we burst into laughter. He gave us the usual hurt expression, and somehow that made it funnier—this was a perfect example of a Roget worry. There probably wasn't a team in the Solar System dumb enough to open a restaurant in a kraal that already had one, but it was hard to get that out through the laughter. Kwanza whooped and slapped my back—

All of a sudden I felt the little needle go in.

A convulsion hit me, and I jerked to my feet, thinking I had to get away, that somehow inexplicably Kwanza had gone over to the other side and I had to warn Dr. Mendenhall. The room spun crazily around me.

There was a sudden pain in my chest; I gasped for breath and fell forward across the table, helpless. I felt Kwanza slide another needle into my thigh; almost instantly I felt better, but very sleepy and slow.

Roget and Kwanza were whispering—I couldn't hear what they said, but suddenly there was a loud ringing as an ambulance capsule got there. I felt two attendants grab my shoulders to turn me over, and then I didn't feel anything for quite a while.

I WOKE UP all at once, feeling well-rested and vaguely happy— that's what the right drugs will do for you. I rolled out of my bunk to stagger into the privy I could see to my right.

Instead, I found myself floating across the cabin, and then free fall reflexes took over and I swam back to the privy. My first thought had been that somehow the kraal had broken loose and fallen away from Eros, but then I realized I was in a drop boat, I made use of the can, splashed my face a little in the bubble hood, and came out to look around. The previous evening was coming back to me, but it seemed too peaceful now to believe that. Maybe it had all been a bad dream . . .

There was a tape, labelled ''PLAY THIS,'' floating in the sundry cage. I shoved it into the slot.

Kwanza's face came up on the screen. ''Hi, tove. Just thought I owed you an apology and explanation. The boss wanted your heart attack cover to look real. Best way to do that was to make sure it didn't look like it could be an act. But I'm sorry I had to be the one to do it. Roget wants me to apologize for him, too.

"Good luck. By the time you get this we'll both be in drop— I lied about my departure time, too, more boss's orders. Be sure you erase the tape before landing."

I was about to click it off, but at that point Mendenhall turned up on the screen. "Just three quick notes, Saul. One, you have a backpack TBN transceiver; use it when you get down and at least once every ten days after that.

"Two, you'll be meeting your usual contact for the Lakes. The whole Human Heritage Research Foundation's been turned over to intelligence work for the duration, so any contact you'd usually make is okay. Also, if for any reason the operation is called off, or we lose and you're stranded, the Cleveland Ruin contact is holding false papers and Orbi-Transit fare for you—you'll just return as you usually do, subject as always to how easy it is to bribe customs.

"And three, make sure you get back, because win or lose we are going to need people like you after this is over."

I said half a dozen nasty words to the screen, which made me feel a lot better, and then I set the dials for a breakfast and pulled out the sloshbag for a wash.

As I got into the sloshbag and put the respirator over my face, I was grumbling, but I realized that if it had really been up to me this was how I would have picked to leave—one minute laughing in Roget's and the next on board and on my way. Besides, the four gees it spins up to in the launch centrifuge is better to take anesthetized—I usually do.

Still, my "heart attack" had been a little scary.

The warm water filled the sloshbag and I began to wiggle and squirm in it, enjoying the feel. It's not like a real bath—a drop boat doesn't have the room or the power reserves to support that, and of course there's nobody else in there with you. But it will get you about as clean as you can hope for in six liters of water, and the squirming around in midair, rubbing the floating bubbles of soapy water onto your skin inside the soft, warm bag, is a lot of fun and a good way to relax. Some people who've made drops claim they spend almost all their un-drugged time in the sloshbag. I guess I have a touch of claustrophobia, because after a while I feel a little too crowded to stay in there—it's dark, for one thing.

Finally I clicked the drain cue, collapsing the bag in a tight hug as the water was vacuumed out; a moment later the ethanol squirted in, and I wiggled around again to get that spread around—some of the popular text channels and vid documentaries have novel ideas about how this gives us a "perfectly sterile environment" on the way back, but in fact, going either way, it just prevents accidentally releasing stray drops of water into the cabin, where they can be a nuisance. Besides, Earth isn't really any dirtier an environment than the stations are—more biocules, maybe, but the pathogenic ones are just as common in space cities, where there's nothing but hosts for them.

I opened the bag and got out, pulled the respirator off, and swabbed my face with the damp cloth. The temperature had already been brought up close enough to body temperature to be comfortable to just sit and dry in; the antidepressants were in the sundry sack, but I decided I'd try loneliness—if Kwanza could stand it, I could. I took breakfast out of the oven and put the Callisto Theater production of *Macbeth* on the viewer.

In the next weeks I learned that I, too, could enjoy loneliness—the long trip is the best chance you ever get to catch up on reading, writing, thinking, and whatever hobbies you have, and there are really no responsibilities to consider. If the ORs are going to intercept you—and that's unlikely because of the amount of space involved and their understandable lack of fear of a few scientists—you're going to be gone before you know it; otherwise, there is nothing to get concerned about until the landing bell sounds.

3

When I finally turned off the exterior camera, Earth was nearly filling the screen. Coming in over the pole as we do, HHRF researchers get what just might be the most spectacular view in the Solar System—though saying so will get you into a brawl with anyone from Titan Orbital. From a few hundred kilometers up over the South Pole, with the window turned to wide angle vision, the Earth stretches out all around you—South America dead ahead beyond the Palmer Archipelago, Africa to your right, Australia with its silvery Inner Sea almost below you—and, of course, the huge expanse of water stretching out in all directions. Beyond that there's a strip of blue fading to black, and then, like a necklace around the earth, the Republics above it.

Just as it's hard to imagine that Antarctica was covered with ice only eighty years ago, it's hard to imagine what the night sky of Earth looked like before the Republics were built; at night, from most places on Earth, at least four of them are always visible, unmoving against the slow-turning stars, each minute disc as bright as Venus. From my view, high over the pole, there were nine of them—the three sunwardmost were lost in the dazzle. Unlike previous landings, when the drugs had kept me in a pleasant but unobservant stupor, this time I could hardly tear myself away from the window; the second warning bell actually sounded before I turned off the window and started landing procedure.

After a last check to make sure things were locked down tight, I swallowed my pills and strapped in—for trips like this, we still did re-entry just like they did it in the first days of the space age, and out the shitport with the gees.

The ride down was bumpy, but I'd been good about exercising and it wasn't any worse than usual—coming in fast like that, with no wind-down orbit in what amounts to a controlled plummet, involves a lot of tricky deceleration that I'm glad the computer takes care of.

After a while of feeling my chest cave in and my face peel back, the drugs took hold and I blacked out. When I woke up the drop boat was rocking gently in Lake Huron. By the time I had my kit pulled together, I could hear people on the outside surfaces. Either the Protectorate Administration was a lot more on the ball than usual, or Esterhazy was being his normal, highly efficient self.

After a last check to make sure I had everything, I set the submerge for four hours, plenty of time for Esterhazy to get it unloaded, then slung on my pack and TBN and opened the upper hatch.

The *Queen of Long Point* was bobbing gently next to the drop boat. Esterhazy was on his poopdeck, running back and forth and swearing at everyone on general principles. He waved and bellowed out "Saul!" loud enough to wake God.

I clambered around the chute tower to slide down the sloping surface of the drop boat; someone threw me a rope. I was pleased to discover I hadn't lost the knack of swinging up from the lower platen onto Esterhazy's deck, though I'd made neater landings.

It was a really fine May evening, but I still found I needed to dig out a jacket first thing; people think that because Earth is warmer now it's tropical everywhere, but the whole change of climate was just three degrees Celsius on the average, and it gets cold at night on the Lakes. The *Queen of Long Point* was rocking gently and the crew was joking and clowning around as they got the cargo bays on the drop open and removed the payment—mostly specialty steel, but also pharms and some electronic stuff. This was going to be a profitable haul for the old pirate, I could see.

I felt his hand clap on my back and, in keeping with my dignity as a distinguished scholar, managed not to fall forward onto my face. He was a big man; his shoulder length hair was a deep auburn-red, coarse, heavy and straight, his eyes were a light gray with flecks of green, and he carried himself like an ancient Viking king—which, at the drop of a beer mug, he would happily tell you he was descended from, despite his family name.

"So, what's it to be this time? A bold quest for some musty old volumes in the ruins of the Duluth Public Library? Economic census of acorn growers in Michigan? A count of all boats whose names begin with T in the Canal? Or an odyssey to the North Pole to see if there's any truth to the ancient myth of Santa Claus?" As always, he was trying to get a rise out of me; actually he had always taken a great deal of interest in my work—I suspect because it helped him to identify future good places to plunder.

"Deep cover," I said quietly.

He nodded soberly, exuberance suddenly gone. "You don't need to tell me more. I got word a few months ago from the, uh, Chancellor. And a man who's travelled with the Fleets before is due down any day. I might have guessed you'd be part of it, too." He turned to holler orders to the crew off-loading the cargo; apparently their answer satisfied him. "You'll be using your usual cover, then?"

"If you can call it a cover anymore. I was really flattered by the offer from your cousin."

He grinned and clapped me on the shoulder. "You wouldn't have been if you'd seen the girl he was offering. Besides, the courting-rights tender was bound to get to you too late—"

"Yeah. It took just over a year, and the Subversion Control people at the Republics Post Office had cut it to ribbons anyway."

"Well, Harry knew, of course, that you wouldn't have been able to accept the offer in any case. After all, how would you get her home? But he really wanted to show his wife that he had tried literally every possible approach—short of the skyboys."

I nodded. "They're still enforcing that Native Relations Act?"

He grimaced. "Oh, yeah. One of their men who had run off and joined the bandits in the Chi Ruin area got caught a few months ago. They shipped him up to Gagaringrad for rerationalization and they executed his wife. His kids are in the Spaceman's Orphanage at Niagara District Office."

"You sound like you know the case."

"We're going to try and rescue the kids after we drop you off. The orphanage is guarded by Native Forces, so we can bribe our way in cheap enough. I do have it right that you're headed for the South Erie?"

"Yeah. I think they just picked it at random."

"You! Careful with that crate! Those chips are worth five new ships!" Esterhazy turned back to me with a grin. "That's my oldest boy, Calvin. I have to pick on him to get the crew to like him. If I hold on a few years they'll like him enough to make him captain when I'm gone—and three generations of Esterhazys have captained the *Queen of Long Point*. My father did the same thing for me."

He dropped one of his massive, bearish arms around my shoulders; I noted the scars where more cancers had been removed, and thought to myself that I would have to get used to the idea of someday coming here and finding no Esterhazy. That's one problem with having Earth friends—most of them die by age 40, after less than a fifth of a normal lifespan. "Let's get out of the sun," he said.

The *Queen of Long Point* was an old ship, of course, but she was well-tended; I noted that the squeaking step on the ladder down to the captain's cabin had been repaired since last I had been on board. Esterhazy's cabin was probably the most comfortable place anywhere in the universe, once you got used to being in it with Esterhazy. Like any Sea Gypsy captain, he had reserved the highest cabin in the poop for his private domain where he could live pretty much as he wanted; by tradition, Sea Gypsy officers never have permanent homes ashore—there would be no point in it, since the Women's Fleets don't maintain any regular schedule and husbands and wives meet everywhere.

"Where's Anna?" I asked.

"She went overland and joined the Women's Fleet at Cape Cod this year. I'm expecting her back in about two years. She was going to see if she could negotiate a cargo of spices somewhere—Zanzibar if the fleet went that way. Good idea, the Lakes Women's Fleet's been just hanging around fishing in Ontario this season."

"Good catch?"

"Too good! Last we met up with them they foisted a quarter-hold full of dry fish on us that took us a month to get sold off. Anyway, out of sympathy they gave us a few kegs of Catawba. Like some?" He grabbed the decanter and started pouring without waiting for my reply.

Esterhazy's little kingdom was warm—he had wintered in Superior too often to have it otherwise. There were layers of rugs on the floor and where there weren't books on the walls there were heavy wool hangings in brilliant colors, mostly running to crimson and navy. The furniture was simple, of course—by preference he slept in a hammock rather than a bunk, so there was only one large table and half a dozen chairs and stools.

"An honest profit and a fair wind home," he said, handing me a glass. It was wonderful stuff—better than any of the space-made because it had a distinctive taste. I've been told I'm biased, but to me most space-made wine has a certain sameness to it. I think that comes from just-slightly-too-perfect control of the conditions—hydroponic grapes are picked on a timetable marked in quarter hours, and processed by yeast that is gene-engineered to the last digit, to prevent any bit of the precious ingredients not turning out right. As a result, there are no poor wines in space—but, in my view, there's nothing idiosyncratic enough to be great, either.

We each slowly and reverently finished our glasses before speaking again.

Esterhazy sighed, got up, and switched on the overhead light. The warm yellow glow of the handmade bulbs made the place seem overwhelmingly peaceful and comfortable, and I let myself succumb for a moment to that sentimental feeling that I was home.

He sat again, looking at me as if he were thinking hard without reaching a conclusion. Finally he said, "I made a mistake up there. I shouldn't have mentioned your destination."

I shrugged and waved a hand. "No one was around. A very minor breach of security."

He shook his head. "Not what I was thinking of. The crew will know where you're going, of course, when we drop you off, but I'd like to keep it secret 'til then—you'd get too much volunteered help, and have to turn it down, which will upset them.

The place was *not* picked at random. That particular office is... well, you'll see. But I don't think that you'll have any trouble with what you're supposed to be doing.''

I might have pressed him, but it was getting dark, and I still wasn't reacclimated to a full gee of gravity, so after some more small talk, I went to the guest cabin and got undressed. The gentle rise and fall of the *Queen of Long Point* put me to sleep as soon as I stretched out.

I GOT UP an hour early that day; it was partly that I wanted to get on with things, partly just that I had taken to rising early during my week on the *Queen of Long Point*. The marshes were cold before dawn, but I switched on the stove and had a good, big, warm breakfast in the cabin. In the day since Esterhazy had dropped me off, I still hadn't named this johnboat; that was atypical for a Sea Gypsy, so before doing anything else I had worked up the *"Spirit of Monroe"*; with my usual nod to my team totem, I had pulled out the papers to be Saul Fox.

After breakfast, I pulled up the anchor and got myself underway. The Sea Gypsies call any riverboat with a square stern and a flat bottom a johnboat; this one was bigger than the name suggests, just over eight meters but drawing only about forty centimeters.

With the sun up, it began to get warm; the north wind held, though, so I was able to tack my way upstream. The little boat wasn't steerable with too much sail, of course—that flat bottom and shallow draft gave it an unpleasant habit of yawing all over the place. But with her one lateen mainsail and a small jib I jury-rigged for the occasion, I could make decent progress up the wide, sluggish river.

The river itself was kind of an object history lesson, a product of the Troubles. The big increase in rainfall had caused what had been barely a big creek to spread out across its whole floodplain, and the rise in Lake Erie had dammed it. Stream piracy had joined it to the Maumee about two hundred kilometers upstream, and the triangle between the rivers had reverted to the tangled, mucky wilderness it had been when the European settlers got there—the Black Swamp.

You'd think no one would live there, but the soil was rich and wherever it could be kept drained there were farms—nowadays this was probably the most densely populated area in North America. That, of course, had drawn the attention of the Protectorate Administration, and the District Office had been set up in Rogers City, the biggest town in the area.

To some extent I was going over all this as I worked the *Monroe* up the river, but mostly I was just enjoying the morning. One thing you could say for the kill-off of most of humanity in the 1990s and again in the 2030s—it had been a good thing for other animals. There were huge flocks of ducks, deer along the shore, even a couple of otters playing on the bank. Once I heard a rumbling screech that told me there was a cougar around somewhere.

Maybe three hours later the first ramtowers and windmills started to show up, indicating that I was hitting the edge of the settled area. Usually a Sea Gypsy gets announced by flags and attention rockets as he goes, and I was a little surprised that I wasn't, but then I realized it was Sunday and just about prime church-going time.

A few minutes later, a small boat came around the bend toward me; I gave them a hail and hove to.

The father of the crew—which seemed to be all girls—waved back. "Morning! You staying around here or heading on up river?"

"Staying, I hope, if there's work. I'm carrying a forge."

At the old man's command, they pulled in close. "There'll be work. You want to tie up at my pier, about a half kilometer upstream, off on your right? I'm Jesse Snyder. You a Methodist?"

Actually some of my people had been leaders in the Great Rationalization, but that's not something you say to an Earthsider. "Baptist," I said—the singing was my favorite part.

"You're in luck, then. Take the road from my pier across my place and turn left at the old Interstate. The church'll be to your left a ways down the road. It's less than two kilometers all told, and they start late. See you sometime this afternoon." He waved, then motioned to the girls—I counted six of them at the oars, all light blondes—and they shot off downstream.

I made two more tacks around the big bend and found his pier. As I was tying up, I saw the pier was solid and obviously inspected regularly, and the ramtower was freshly painted; the whole place stank of comfortable prosperity. Remembering a little theory from our "training," I sort of doubted that Jesse Snyder would be my first recruit.

With the sails stowed and everything secured, I put up the gangplank and got off, heading up the road in the direction Snyder had pointed.

There were several ramtowers in sight; the river winds quite a bit, so farms are wedged in close together to share the valuable river frontage that means assured electric power. The flags didn't announce any particularly unusual events—a birth at one place, two towers flying willing-to-trades, and a mumps quarantine.

The path up to the main road went through a grove of walnut trees; every thirty meters or so there was a brushpile to encourage game, and probably there were traps and snares in the grove—not set on Sunday, of course.

It had been cool in the shade of the tall walnuts, but as I came out onto the road it was warm and getting hot. At least there had been plenty of rain in the last couple of days to hold the dust down. Until you've lived on an unenclosed planetary surface, it's hard to imagine how many different ways there are to be uncomfortable.

After a couple of hundred meters the dirt road joined with twentieth-century highway, broken and cracked but still recognizable. I turned left. There were a couple of families walking ahead of me; I was going to catch up and introduce myself, but before I did, we came up on the church.

The Baptist church was whitewashed rough-cut plank, clapboarded on a simple vertical frame. They had started a steeple, but no bell hung there—of course, the price of having one forged would have been more than a farm produced in a year, and none of the OR charities was going to make donations to a church. Still, the building itself was in good shape, so it was a fairly well-off congregation.

The greeters were a pleasant young couple; he looked a bit younger than she did. "I'm Manuel Proxman, and this is my wife, Mary," he said. "You're a Sea Gypsy?"

"Yeah, just come up the river looking for work. I'm tied up at Jesse Snyder's pier."

He winced, then caught himself and said, "Well, there should be work all summer around here if you want it. I'm just upstream of Jesse, on the other side. There's a ford there in the dry season. Be sure to drop by some time soon."

"We don't get much company," Mary put in.

"I'll do that," I said. I went on into the sanctuary.

The church was hung with elaborate cloth banners of Bible scenes. I'm told that they fetch incredible prices in the ORs, where they're hung in galleries like paintings. Down on Earth, they're one way to keep a church from being drafty; but Earthsiders just can't make anything without decorating it as much as function will permit. The pews—the wooden benches the congregation sits in—were carefully finished and carved; the rough work had been done on the pulpit but the fine carving had barely been started. I estimated the building itself must be ten years old or so, and it might be another twenty years before it was officially "finished"—after which renovations would begin immediately.

I'm not terribly suggestible and I've had all the usual barriers against superstition ingrained from birth, but I had to admit that there was something pleasant and restful about the place. I was sitting off in a corner where I could watch unobtrusively, and it was interesting just to watch all the greetings and hugs being exchanged among neighbors. A thought came to me—I was going to like it here.

Manuel and Mary sat down at the other end of the pew from me, giving me a friendly little wave, and then, with the boom of the door being closed, the service started.

A big, muscular old man with white hair—maybe the oldest Earthsider I'd ever seen—strode to the pulpit and opened the big Bible there. He looked out a little blearily and I mentally marked him down for a set of spectacles.

He asked us to stand up, and then he prayed for a while. If you've never seen it done, it's probably the strangest thing that happens in a church; the preacher has a long talk with something up in the rafters while the rest of the congregation stands stiffly and examines its hands or shoes. Then we sang a couple of songs—as usual, the Baptists were a good place to go for that—and "took the offering," meaning they passed a basket and people threw millicredit coins into it; the money goes to support the church. I know none of this is very dramatic, but after all the stories that they tell us in the Gymschool antisuperstition courses, it's kind of an interesting shock to see how ordinary the whole thing is.

The preacher got up for announcements before getting into the sermon. "As everyone knows, I guess, there's going to be a baseball game on Adler Field this afternoon, so our fellowship dinner will be a picnic out there. We'll be playing the Catholics, who are currently in first place, with us a game back.

"I see that the Mullers and the Bakers are not here today. The Bakers, for those of you who can't see their ramtower, are flying quarantine flag, so there's no need for concern there, but there's nothing on the Muller ramtower, so some friend of theirs might want to phone to make sure everything's all right." He grinned a little. "Don't expect them to flip on the visual, by the way—Isaac Muller just took a new wife, and his oldest boy just got married too, for those of you that missed it.

"We've got another leak in the church roof; if the weather's good next Sunday we'll need a couple of you to go up and deal with it. I know that that's not strictly keeping Sabbath, but if we can repair our own homes in an emergency, I think we can safely fix God's house on His day.

"I'm going to mention the Perry family again; I got this from Abe Lester, their minister over there at the Methodist church. Charlie Perry and his people are real close to the line, trying to avoid a short-term. Charlie's boy Wesley was supposed to enlist in the Native Forces to help pay off the family debt, but he's been turned down, and now it looks real bad. They can use whatever help you can give them, especially salable trade goods. It's better to help them now while it's legal, folks; I know a lot of you already have, but I want you to know the crisis isn't over. So please, do whatever you can."

That made me prick up my ears. If the Perry family was in such bad shape that they might be forced to a short-term loan, they might be interested in what I had to say. After the big uprisings in 2076, rules had been made to insure that a reasonably solvent farmer wouldn't be forced off his land by fiat of the local GXS—and from what I understand, most of the public up in the ORs thought that that had solved the problem (although they probably considered it "socialistic" to meddle in the privately-owned GXS Corporation's foreclosure policies).

The catch was that if a farmer fell far enough behind, the Protectorate Administration required him to take a short-term loan out from the local GXS to pay his bills. To get the loan, in turn, he had to sign away all those rights. Where the local officials were honest and decent, conditions were merely brutal, and sometimes the farmer would work his way out of it.

But career Protectorate service did not attract many honest or talented people; there were much better jobs in the ORs. For the petty, greedy, or callous bureaucrat, a short-term was a license to squeeze a farmer and his family for everything they had, while their neighbors stood by helplessly. As the preacher had said, assisting a debtor, as a direct violation of the Economic Rationality and Anti-Collectivist Act, was a capital offense.

And if Protectorate officers enforced anything at all, they enforced ERACA.

HE WAS WELL INTO the sermon by the time I finished my mental review; most of my experience had been far away from anywhere I might come to the attention of the Protectorate—that was to protect my way home. An Earthsider with reasonable papers and some substantial gifts for the right clerks can get himself up to the Republics and even onto a liner to the Confederation and no one cares, but if he's been living near the local office and suddenly turns up with a big pile of money, they're going to ask where he got it.

The sermon was a lot of Biblical commentary, quotes and interpretations enough to make your head spin. I quietly looked around and discovered the usual split—one third listening and interested, one third fidgeting and thinking about something else, and one third asleep with their eyes open. It was the same ratio I had always noticed in my classes.

I slipped quickly into category three myself; I'm not sure whether it's the early training intended to prevent superstition, or plain lack of interest, but I've never really been able to follow a prayer or sermon all the way through. The songs are great, though—a lot of the lyrics are real, powerful poetry, and some of those old tunes are the most moving, majestic music

I've ever heard. If God ever comes to me, he'll have to do it singing.

After the sermon wound down—I was getting perilously close to being just plain asleep—we did some more singing and then everyone filed out to stand around and talk to each other. Manuel and Mary took it on themselves to introduce me all around; the preacher, I learned, was Sam Klein.

Except for the heat, it was just about the most perfect day I had ever seen on Earth—one reason everyone should visit there is that you find out how different days can be. The air was sweet-smelling, the plants—growing everywhere with no particular plan—were green as synthemerald.

The women were in their white dresses—it was more than a month past Easter, and *don't* ask me to explain the significance of that. Each of the men had put on his dress shirt but no one had new clothes and thus the favorite topic of spaceside discussion was ruled out. Instead, they talked about the weather, the upcoming game, and the state of trade around the lakes—fortunately Esterhazy had given me a good briefing, and since Rogers City didn't see many Sea Gypsies, I didn't have to worry much about getting contradicted.

Manuel and Mary—I noticed the two of them were hardly ever apart—swung back around to me again. "You're coming out to the picnic and the ball game, aren't you?" he asked.

I felt a little embarrassed. "I just got in. I don't have any food I can bring."

"Then you're in with us on it," Mary said firmly. "Manuel never eats much before he plays, and I always end up taking half the food home anyway. Besides, you wouldn't have time to run back to Jesse Snyder's dock and make it to Adler Field anyway—you'll need a ride."

Well, I was supposed to be meeting people, and these were the easiest people to meet—and besides, I like baseball. We climbed into their surrey truck and set off.

On the way, and at the picnic, we mostly talked about what it was like to be a Sea Gypsy, which was fortunately the Earthly subject that I was best versed in—the Sea Gypsies were the best friends the HHRF had, and almost all research expeditions were smuggled to the observation site in Sea Gypsy ships. For some reason, unlike most farmers, Manuel didn't want news from the Lakes basin, but stories about all the other places in the world—so, mostly, I told him about things that had really happened during my previous voyages with the Sea Gypsies.

After we ate, we all sat around talking lazily and waiting for the rest of the crowd to show up. Even though only the Catholics and the Baptists were playing, all of Rogers City apparently was coming out to the game—in fact every Sunday that the weather was nice, from Easter to the fall solstice, they did this. "Beats sitting home Sabbath and watching the turnips die," Manuel explained. "My cousin Noah doesn't usually come out—he's a real bookworm—but all the rest of my people do."

Mary grinned. "Aside from the food and the company, these things are always a good place to catch up on the gossip."

"You know what they say about Sea Gypsies," I said. "If you can't say anything nice, say it to me."

They smiled at each other, as if they were telepathic and I'd accidentally picked up a stray signal. He stretched his short, brawny arm out, running his hand down her long, thin one, and laughed. "Well," he said, "there's always us. At the moment we're one of the leading scandals in the community, I guess."

I tried to look politely puzzled.

Mary winked at me. "We might as well tell him before someone else does. Manuel was a big disappointment to a lot of the young ladies around her. After sowing his wild oats far and wide, instead of marrying some young eligible, he married an old widow lady. And furthermore, one that hadn't quite had a year since her husband died."

Manuel nodded. "On top of all the other things, she was from over on the other side of Rogers City. You know. That area where the Martians live.

"But it'll blow over in a bit. These things always do. That tall redhead over there had two babies before she got around to getting married—when the congregation sent Sam to talk to her, he asked her who the father was, not to be nosy, you know, but because the fellow should be supporting her, and she said 'I can't tell you.' He said it was okay, he was a minister and the secret could be kept, and she said she was afraid that with so many of them possible, they'd find out about each other and get into fights.

"About six months later she married one of Sam's sons, and now she teaches Wednesday night Bible school. The only reason people've kept up on us for so long is there hasn't been a good scandal to take its place. The redhead has a kid sister, though, Saul, so if you'd like to have everyone in Rogers City know your name by sundown..."

"Thanks," I said, "I'll keep that in mind."

"Here we are," Mary said. I looked up; the Catholics were coming across the field. Everyone was waving and laughing like they hadn't seen each other in a thousand years; the children were breaking loose to go talk to each other.

Manuel nodded with satisfaction. "Biggest game of the season so far. I gotta go and get warmed up with the rest of the team. Mary, why don't you give some guidance on the local talent to Saul? You do know the game?" he asked.

"Known it for a long time," I said, smiling. "Let's see, you're built for—hmm, catcher?"

"Everyone says that," Mary said. "But he's so quick they usually put him in at third."

"See?" he said, "she knows everything of any importance about baseball. She'll keep you informed okay."

"Especially about the errors you make," she added.

"Hush, woman, there's enough scandal without your imagining things. See you after the game, Saul." He sauntered off to join his teammates, stripping off his good shirt to reveal a heavy wool uniform shirt beneath.

It took them a while to get the game underway, but after it began I was really impressed. Despite all the self-deprecation, Manuel was a fine third baseman, really smart and fast.

By the fourth inning I had pretty much stopped thinking about the mission and was just enjoying the game; it was at least as good as anything we saw on vid back home—better, really, because the Coriolis does some funny things to high flies in orbital stadiums, and on the Jovian moons they have to use that silly "superheavy" wristbreaking ball, count it as a fly on the first bounce, and stretch the basepaths by a factor of three.

On the other hand, the players back home aren't old at thirty. That thought came to me when I noticed the long, grim row of the dying behind the bullpen—emaciated wrecks that had been human, perhaps had played on this field not even a year ago.

The ghastliest of all, the ones they never show you on the vid, were the tiny, hairless, withered children; in one corner there was a whole family, a father, mother, and daughter, all shrivelled like dry fruit.

These were the ones who were dying the way Earthsiders usually do—their skin cancers had metastasized. I searched for Sam Klein, to see what a vigorous old Earthsider looked like, and saw him sitting, incongruously, facing the person next to him on a folding chair, rather than looking at the game. Then I realized that his friend or relative there was narrating the game to him.

"He's an incredible old man," Mary said, looking where I was looking.

"I hadn't realized he was blind."

"He fools most of the travellers we get because he has so much of the Bible memorized. Still, I'm sure it's terrible for him. It happens when you get that old because of the UV over time. That's what the skyboy doctor at the GXS says—he says that we ought to all wear dark glasses, but most of us die before we're old enough to go blind. Sam could see 'til he was almost fifty. Now he's sixty-two, if you can imagine anyone being that old. He can remember things that happened way back in history, stuff that isn't even in the books at the GXS school."

I nodded, thinking suddenly of Mendenhall, who had to be well past seventy and was still hell on wheels at six-wall handball—and probably would be for another couple of decades. For that matter, Mary's hands and face were brown, freckled, and wrinkled—that and the permanent sagginess from high acceleration made her look older than either of my xmothr's xsistrs do—and I was eight or ten years older than Mary.

"Who's that?" I asked, startled to see a cosmorine uniform over at the edge of the field.

"Voorbeck," she said, the way people say "shit" after they've stepped in it. "He comes out and watches sometimes. No one knows why, except maybe to keep us from forgetting about him."

"I've heard of him." Esterhazy had told me a little—mostly just to stay clear of him.

"Everything you heard is true." She shook her head. "Incidentally, Jesse Snyder is one of his bigger informants. You might want to move to another dock. Voorbeck ran off the last four Sea Gypsies, and the one before that, too, if you count a hanging as running him off."

I whistled. "What was the charge?"

She shrugged. "Trading in goods he wasn't licensed for. Electronics mostly, I think. Of course, half the Sea Gypsies on the lake are carrying all kinds of stuff, and that law probably isn't enforced anywhere else, but Voorbeck said 'the law's the law' and strung him up right out on the landing field."

Her eyes were flat and dead; her mouth was set in a tight slit. After a minute, I reached out to touch her hand. "I'm all right," she said. "It's just…supposedly my first husband tried to kill him. I like to think so; it would be the best thing James ever did. But whatever did happen, Voorbeck beat my husband to death."

I didn't know what to say. "He must be a real animal," I finally said.

She shook her head. "James was a lot bigger and stronger. Voorbeck had him tied up first."

We were quiet for a long time after that, lost in our own thoughts. I think Mary watched the game. I watched Voorbeck standing by the edge of the field.

As far as I could tell he was standing at perfect parade rest without moving a muscle; or is that just my memory playing tricks with me, filling in details I only knew later? At the distance, I couldn't have seen his face, serene and tight halfway between a smile and a sneer. And there was no way I could have known that his uniform was in perfect order.

But not only has the memory colored all that in—from what I knew of him later, I am convinced of it.

After a while, the crowd pulled my attention back to the game. It was the bottom of the ninth, and the Catholics had the tying run on third, when the batter popped up to Manuel. He caught it cleanly, then suddenly bounded forward, catching the runner by surprise a step from the bag and tagging him for an unassisted play. The strikeout that followed ended the game neatly; both sides of the crowd stood up and applauded.

"It'll be a while before Manuel catches up with us," Mary said. "He has to get congratulated by a lot of girls first."

I looked at her sideways; she was smiling. "He cut a real swath through the local morals before getting hitched. I can't complain that I got someone else's leavings. In fact, since I'm twenty-seven, six years older than he is, you could say that's what *he* did. But he's not going to take off with some young honey—or at least he hasn't yet. He just enjoys the attention."

"Looks like he's getting a lot of it from that blond girl he's talking to," I said, "but neither of them looks very happy."

She looked up; her face tensed. "Such a shame," she said. "Come on, we might have a customer for you if you can give some credit."

"Sure." I followed her, but Manuel and the girl had stopped talking and he was headed toward us. As we came up to him I was startled to see tears in his eyes.

"That poor kid . . ." he said.

"It's the usual up there? At least it hasn't gotten worse?" Mary asked.

"They've come up with a new game. They're offering her a job at the General Office. If she doesn't accept, it proves the household isn't making the maximum effort to pay its bills. If she does—" he shrugged and looked away.

"There's no hope that Linsmann will get transferred?" he asked. "I tried to talk with Voorbeck and he brushed me off; Charlie's too distraught to handle it for himself."

Mary shook her head. "Linsmann's career. And he's Voorbeck's lapdog from way back."

"She said she wanted to talk to you."

"I'll go up and see her tonight. But poor Charlie. Priss is his oldest daughter, and he's always doted on her."

"What are you going to tell her?" Manuel asked as we walked back to the surrey truck. A couple of people said hello but Manuel just nodded and kept walking.

"It depends on her. Some women can stand it. And if she's clever she might get the rest of the family off the hook. Better just her than all of them, I guess." She shook her head. "But she's only thirteen. It's a pity she's so big in the chest, and blonde besides—that's just what Linsmann likes."

We walked the rest of the way back to the truck in silence. It seemed to me that the cosmorines were everywhere—the warm sunlight now felt as sinister as a prison spotlight.

Manuel wiped his eyes. "It's no use," he said finally. "If the Perrys were shitting solid gold the GXS would come up with a lien against their assholes."

None of us said anything as we drove back. They let me off at Jesse's place with a friendly wave and handshake. "Can I send Charlie Perry around to you tomorrow? Will you give him credit?" Manuel was obviously embarrassed. "I know it's hard to do that when you're first starting out in a new place," he added, apologetically.

"Like your preacher says, better to do it now before it's illegal. Of course, I'll help any way I can. Send him around first thing."

"Thanks." We shook hands again.

As I walked back through the Snyder farm to my boat, I realized that that was absolutely untypical of a Sea Gypsy—and that I didn't care. Mendenhall had said, during the little bit of training we'd had, don't be afraid to improvise. And it was the decent thing to do, anyway.

I caught myself imagining the grateful, rescued Perry family becoming my devoted bodyguards and snorted in self-derision; but that image stayed with me, off and on, for a long time. Even now, it sometimes comes to me late at night, and even if I'm all by myself, it embarrasses me.

4

I was up before dawn the next morning, getting the snapper going and tuning the lasers, but all the same there were seven people lined up by the time I was ready to see them. I walked up the gangplank, beaming in my most salesmanlike way, and hung out my shingle:

SAUL FOX, GENERAL SMITH AND MERCHANT
Spare Parts—Wells Drilled—Books
Cyberware—Livestock Semen
Smelter/Foundry
!!!! Easy Credit and a Fair Deal !!!!

"I'm afraid it's another narrow specialist," Sam Klein said, after his son Isaiah had read it to him. "I was hoping you did OrbiTransit overhauls and put the evil eye on possums."

"Make me an offer and I'll give it a shot," I said. "What can I do for a first-rate preacher? And will this be cash, charge, or do we barter for a miracle?"

"Cash this time," Sam said. "You got a proven-out GCU-138? If you just have the chip and a program copy that'll be enough."

I turned to the little podium terminal by the gangplank. "Got a complete one, if you'd like. I'm asking four credits, but it's opening day so I'd really say three."

"Well..." Sam said, stepping aboard, "I'd have to see the sheet."

I hit the faxer and ran it out for Isaiah. "No downtime to speak of in its past, and only twelve megaseconds of use," I said. "Stripped off a burned out homestead down on the

Southeast coast—in fact I remember the place, right on the tip of Tampa Island—in the Florida Archipelago, where steady operation is absolutely critical and maintenance is the best I've ever seen. This was inside the mill shed, which didn't burn. Clean as if it ran in a lab all that time.''

"Five sporadic misbehaviors," Isaiah read loudly.

The old preacher jumped on the point. "If it does that when we get a sudden backwash, like off an OrbiTransit landing wrong, and it misses the blades, I could be out one whole windmill. Two if I twin this one, and I was thinking of that..."

"No serious risk—you can catch that with a simple time-lapsed reset. Those problems might even have been a little bit of plain old static from a thunderstorm. That happens, you know, anywhere in the islands down there. Now, I can't say I'd twin this if I had an alternative, and it seems to me that since I have two more in stock—''

"Two more," Sam said, "sounds like one for each mill and a spare. That would be kind of nice, I have to say, but if they're in this kind of shape—''

"This kind of shape! These are first-rate—''

"Five decicredits each. I don't want to be unfair to you," Sam said. "And look, I even offered without you running out the sheets. For all I know they're dead as congress. Now, you can't beat that—''

"These are first-rate. You want the skyboys to have me up for dumping? Unfair trade is good for twenty stripes, you know, and that's a lot of skin to lose. Call it two, at cost, that ought to bring in business and you're walking off—''

"At cost! You just said you stripped them yourself—''

"Yeah, this one. But these two are dupe handmades out of New Macao, best workmen on Earth. I'm only asking two because I got this one to average in, otherwise it would be—''

"Let's call it seven-fifty centicredits. I won't be greedy. You have to get yourself established, I know—''

"One and five, maybe. I can see you're a sharp dealer, and I'll be lucky to get out of this with anything."

The catalog price, which we both knew, was one. Since I had to file paperwork for going over or under that by more than ten percent, and I was right under the noses of the cosmorines here, it was no big surprise that what we settled on was one. Real haggling goes into services; it's entertainment on goods.

The next couple were parts orders, too—no big surprise. Buying a part from a Sea Gypsy is about the safest way to twit the skyboys known. This would go on for a couple of days, and then the GXS would drop its prices through the floor, hoping to get me out of the area, and the local farmers would stampede in to the GXS to stock up. It was no surprise that they were glad to see us around the stations . . .

Of course, when I didn't move on, things were going to get tense. The GXS notion of fair business competition tends to get more elastic when Earthsiders win or don't quit. Esterhazy had a half-dozen spectacular scars from a beating he'd gotten near South Ontario District Office—something about giving paying jobs to two about-to-be debtors. But I should be able to hang on for a few months, and by that time, one way or another, I wouldn't be worrying about what the local officers thought about me.

The next two customers were contracts for services later in the week, replumbing a hydraulic ram and cutting some custom angle iron for a dome barn. Nothing special there, either. The sun was nearly halfway up the sky, there was a fine layer of sweat under my shirt, and UV or not I had taken my hat off.

There was some kind of scuffle at the back of the line, so I flipped the screen cover over and locked it, grabbed a pin, and went on back. Usually this kind of stuff started toward evening—these folks just didn't drink much 'til late in the day—but every community has its earlybirds.

I wasn't expecting it at all. It was the blonde girl Manuel had been talking to; her mouth was open and her face was red with pain. The cosmorine major was pulling her in close by the hair; his other hand gripped her breast. Without any thought, I started to slip around behind him.

I was vaguely aware that two men were holding a big, beefy man back, but my attention was on the back of the cosmorine's head.

I was closing in, figuring if I sacked him I could always run away and sneak back later with good credentials—not to mention a lot of satisfaction—when I heard a loud voice from the crowd.

"Linsmann, you're under arrest."

He looked around, his lip curling. "This is no affair of yours, Lieutenant. And there's no crime in messing with dirtsider gash unless you marry it. In fact, with stuff like this it's a crime not to mess with it. If Daddy over there gets loose and takes a swing at me, we'll have them for a short term for sure." He twisted her hair, pulling her in closer and forcing his hand between her thighs; she fought to get away, but she was half his size at best.

The other cosmorine came up from behind me. He was as tall as Linsmann, but gangly, without much on his frame, and he had one of the biggest noses and one of the worst cases of acne I've ever seen. There were dark stains around his armpits, and his legs moved as if they were being jerked forward by something outside him.

"I'm arresting you under the RMD issued 1/1/2098 and amended lawfully since. You're charged with disturbing the peace, molestation of Protectorate citizen, sexual abuse of a free citizen, and resisting arrest. My transmitter is on and a copy of this statement of arrest is being recorded at headquarters. Will you come along peacefully?"

"As soon as she does," Linsmann grunted. "Come on, Daddy." Old Perry tore loose from the man holding him.

The young lieutenant was quicker than I would have guessed—stronger, too. Before Charlie Perry could get to the major, the young officer had stepped between them, blocking Perry's path, then turned in a spinning kick.

There was a loud crack and Linsmann fell to the ground backward. The lieutenant finished his spin facing Perry. The girl ran to her father, huddling against him.

"You should have let me—" Perry sounded dazed.

The lieutenant shook his head and said, so softly that only I and the Perrys heard him, "You don't need a stretch in the brig just now. Get going—I'll get your statements later." The Perrys turned and went quickly, the man's arm around his daughter.

"You're an idiot, McHenry. I'll have you hanged for striking a superior. We'll stretch your neck down here in front of the dirtsiders, and we'll bury you here to rot, and the disgrace ought to just about put your father and the Progs right out the shitport." Linsmann was getting up slowly. "And don't expect to see me tried. The colonel and I—"

"Good work, McHenry." The crowd parted abruptly.

"Colonel Voorbeck! This man just—"

"Legitimately arrested you for a felony. You've been a good officer, Linsmann, or you'd be in real trouble. I'd heard your behavior had gotten out of hand, but frankly I hadn't wanted to believe it. This will go down on your evaluation. Get back to quarters and stay there until I get back." The voice was calm and almost soft, the tone was cryogenic.

The wind went out of Linsmann; he slunk away, head down, face and neck burning red against the mud-smeared blue of his uniform. Everyone watched him go in silence. Voorbeck turned around to speak to the crowd.

"Those of you who don't have business here, go home after Lieutenant McHenry takes your names. You won't have to attend the trial but we will need your depositions. Please confine your story to what happened here today; as you know, we can't try him for anything not witnessed by an officer of the Protectorate Administration. I do apologize for his misbehavior. Thank you."

He turned and scanned through the crowd. I had dropped my rolling pin into the wrench pocket of my apron; he didn't seem to notice it when his gaze fixed on me. "I don't recognize you. You must be Saul Fox."

I nodded, once, slowly.

"Is there some place where we can speak privately?" he asked.

"The cabin on my boat?"

"Certainly. It will just be a few moments, and then you can get back to business. After you, captain." There was something sarcastic in his use of the title, but nothing you could put your finger on.

He boarded like he was afraid of the gangplank; I suppose that the way he had his boots polished and his uniform pressed, a spill in the river would be a real waste. I could tell that he was annoyed with himself for showing the awkwardness, and when he stepped into the boat he straightened abruptly, rocking the boat but pretending to ignore it.

"I'll assume you don't drink on duty," I said, "but I do have a little coffee around if you'd like that."

"It won't be necessary," he said. "I'll just be a few minutes." He looked carefully around the cabin, at the plaques and paintings on the walls and the books on the shelves. The computer was blessed with three seconds of hard stare; the stove got a sweep of the eyes, as if there were something wrong with it—though I keep my kitchen clean.

"There are a couple of things we need to have clear," he said. "As you know," and he began quoting. "'It is the policy of the Protectorate Administration that although Sea Gypsies are legitimately entitled to exercise the right of free trade, they are disruptive speculators in the planned free market, they are inherently a collectivist force, and they should be discouraged as much as possible.'" He smiled but his eyes remained fixed and staring. "What that regulation drycake works out to is—you can trade if you want but you make a mess of the system, and we intend to make life as hard as possible for you.

"Let me get down to cases. I'm going to use every fair and honest method available to put you out of business and get you away from my station. You're an administrative headache, the easy credit you give is inflationary, the parts you sell aren't warranted, and you promote superstition with those books you carry—even if you're well-behaved. And to judge from your handiness with that club, I don't think you are."

I didn't say anything; there wasn't much to be said. He seemed to approve of the silence, and went on.

"This isn't a station like Central China or Eastern Baltic. I won't send someone around to hole your boat, you don't have to worry about fires being set, and no one is going to rough you up. But we're going to compete as two businessmen—and it's my opinion that if any dirtsider had any business talent, he wouldn't be a dirtsider.

"Let's face it, the individualist spirit is practically dead down here. We catch farmers trying to set up all kinds of socialist drycake all the time; equipment sharing, common pastures, withholding surpluses from the market, everything that goes against liberty and efficiency. Even businessmen like you hold things in common without the most elementary property arrangements. When I think of what this planet could be if people would just *use* the market instead of fighting it . . .

"But of course they won't. The best brains on Earth went into building the stations, and that's where they moved. Partly to get away from the genetic leavings down here. To see that you only need to compare our spaceside draftees with the dirtsider volunteers in the Native Forces. So in our little competition, Fox, the advantages are all on my side. I don't need to cheat, and I won't. Whatever they tell these new kids at the Academy."

Suddenly that frozen face cracked and he grinned at me. It was the kind of winning smile that I usually associated with candidates for Assembly and the students who worked on their campaigns, and he was good at it.

I worked up a little smile back at him, trying to look crafty but a little dumb, the way they expect. "All right, a free field and no favors, may the best man win," he said, and stuck out his hand.

I shook it. I think he bought my act; I know I didn't buy his, so I guess that round went to me.

"Honest competition," I said.

"I'll have you skinned." There was a strange pleasure in his voice, not as if he were threatening me but as if I had somehow touched him, offered him friendship. Years later it occurred to me that that was exactly it—he wanted Earthsiders to like him, and whenever they agreed with him, he thought they did.

"One other thing," he said quietly. "Just another little piece of drycake. This isn't a friendly place for your people, and there's a GXS to compete with you—how did you turn up here?"

I shrugged. "I hadn't heard—the past few years I've been in the back stretches of Huron. My home ship's the *Queen of Long Point*."

"Then there's no special reason you're here?"

"Just anxious to see somewhere new. Lost my wife a couple of years ago—that big wreck in the Women's Fleet; haven't felt good since. And I thought I might find a place that hadn't seen much of us for a while, and maybe open up a new avenue of trade. That kind of thing."

He nodded slowly, accepting it. "Well, I doubt you'll stay long. I'll see to that. But I'll wish you an honest profit."

"And a fair wind home...?" I asked, finishing the traditional blessing.

He laughed heartily, and for a moment I guess I really did like him; then I saw him watching me, peeping out through his laughter to see what effect he was having.

I kept my smile on for a moment more, and then said, "If that's all, sir, I do need to get back to business."

He wished me luck again, and we shook hands, and he went up the gangplank to collect Lieutenant McHenry. The line of customers, of course, had faded away at the prospect of trouble, and wouldn't be back until it was obvious that I hadn't been run off—which would be a few days. That was okay with me—I could fulfill the couple of contracts I already had in hand, get the word of mouth from that, and pick up some more local gossip.

I demounted the terminal and carried it back into the cabin, figuring business was as good as over for the day. At least there wasn't much locking up to be done, and I knew the lasers were all functioning—it would have been just my luck to have had to spend my startup capital on new crystals at the GXS.

The snapper was all right, too, but I did regret starting it up for nothing—although they can run for years once they're up (as long as there's no vibration or motion), fifty or sixty starts is about all the coils can take before replacement. I recharged the starting electret while I considered, and finally decided to just leave the snapper running—probably safer than doing a down-and-up with old coils.

Nobody would bother it here on the bank, anyway—farm people tend to be pretty honest, and what would anyone want with it anyway? As for the skyboys, they'd have to be ordered to go near it, and apparently that wasn't Voorbeck's game for the moment; he might send the Native Forces after me, but even that sounded unlikely just yet. So if I didn't mind being moored next to a running fusion reactor, I might as well let it run; I could always shunt some power to the e-rig and fill the hydrogen tanks.

The problem was I did mind. I have the spacesider's basic phobia about nuclear power—fusion is a good idea but it should be done *in the sun*, not someplace where a shielding leak could give you a neutron bath. Realistically, though, the greater danger is that when a coil goes bad, the next time it gets hooked to an electret you have a nasty little explosion, not enough to blow you up but hotter than a welding arc and more than enough to get a fire going on board. No matter how uneasy it made me, I was better off with the snapper running.

Those of you reading this in space probably are shuddering—I did myself; then realized, and laughed. It wasn't safety that biased spacesiders against nukes. I thought of Mendenhall—

The old man's eyes were down on the podium, fixed on his notes, his bald head was reflecting into my eyes. Kari squeezed my hand; I squeezed back. "When the cosmorines went down to collect the debts, the first thing they seized, and shut down, was the nuclear plants, because by the 2020s those were the only things effectively in competition with beamdown solar power. When the Earthsiders tried to renege, the first thing they did was to try to start up the plants—and since the trained crews tended to get killed during cosmorine raids, and the deuterium/tritium cycle is tricky anyway, there were some bad little accidents."

He looked up suddenly. "Pareto, Saul. Leave your xsistr's charming attentions for a moment and stand up. We have a Significance to determine."

The class went dead quiet with a little rustle that probably wasn't much different from the one that had accompanied the entry of the Christians into the Coliseum.

"All right. Of nine such accidents, eight were cleaned up by the cosmorines. Why?"

Much to my relief I at least knew how to start the answer. "Because, gospa, otherwise cleanup cost would have caused the Earthsiders to default, cosmorines or no, and the Bank of Bothasburg would have caved in," I said smugly.

"Explain the connection to your team's occupation."

I gaped. None of us had been powerriggers, ever—we were strictly a monovocational team, not pioneers like the Boones or the al-Ghirads. "I—" I said, and stopped.

He smiled. "Perhaps you'd better find out before you consider breeding any more. All right, simple question. What made modern social science possible? Quote my Gymschool textbook if you like."

"The computer, of course—"

"Which requires?"

"Electricity, gospa."

"Bravo. Where do you get your electricity from, now?"

"The grid, gospa. Outside, the solar panels—"

"Why?"

"Because—" and dawn came. "Because all space stations are powered that way, even where it would make sense for them to be nuclear, gospa. They're even using them for the new Titan Orbital station. The aftermath of those accidents—"

Those blue eyes were drilling holes in me. "Go on."

I took a breath. "A lot of cosmorines got cancer from exposure to secondary contamination, even with all the precautions, gospa. That was right about the time when they were finding out about the life-extension effects of weightlessness—so a lot of them died a couple of years after being told they could have lived to be three hundred. People couldn't react against the government or the banks responsible—"

"Why not?"

By now I was exasperated enough that I didn't bother with the gospa. "One, they didn't know the whole story until decades later—in fact some of the documents are still classified. Two, the organized political parties weren't about to launch an attack on the Bank of Bothasburg when it was the main financing institution for electoral campaigns. Three, they'd just won a war with Earth and they weren't about to topple their Republics on its behalf, and, finally, if they had talked about why the troops were down there they'd have had to talk about what they were doing to Earth's economy—and most people stop thinking if there's any danger of learning they're on the wrong side."

"Incomplete, but not bad." He smiled thinly.

"So the anti-nuclear idea, which had been dead ever since fusion came in, was resurrected among the spacesiders. And got built right into our culture. I'd be nervous around a reactor myself, gospa."

I came out of my reverie realizing I was leaning on the snapper housing. So much for primal phobia. There wasn't any more wrapup to do, so I decided to set a couple of lines and catch a nap.

When I saw the shadow in the trees, I had just settled myself under the canopy, so I waited for whoever was coming up the trail to get into plain sight on the off chance that they didn't have anything to do with me. It turned out to be Manuel Proxman after a minute; he headed straight for the gangplank, so I opened my eyes again and gave him an idle half-wave. "Come on board."

"They run you off?" he asked, coming to the point right away.

"Not yet. Your boy Voorbeck has a pretty scary way with words, if I'm reading between the lines right...but I think I can turn an honest profit out of all this just the same. You heard about the Linsmann business?"

"Yeah." He sat down on the deck and thought for a moment. "Listen, I don't have any particular right to ask you to do anything special, but I hope that gave you an idea of how bad the situation is for Charlie Perry. I think that's the first time she's actually been attacked, but she might be hiding other things out of shame. And Charlie's really against the financial wall."

"How'd he get there?"

"He sort of inherited it. His farm is upland, so power is a lot more expensive for him; no running water to drive a ram-and-tower, and that means no cheap power storage either. He's on all battery, and that's expensive. Plus, of course, he has to replace windmills every six months or so."

I raised an eyebrow. "They should be good for years."

Manuel shrugged. "He's on a landing path. Every so often backwash gets his mill. Not much you can do about that."

"Well, get him down here and we'll fix him up with a deal or two. I'm not profit-crazy; I like to make money but this is priority. The worst Linsmann will get will be a few days in the brig, and after that he'll be after the girl again. And if her father's a debtor—"

Manuel nodded. "Yeah. She winds up as Linsmann's chambermaid or worse. You have it."

"I can work some good deals out," I said. "And then, if he doesn't mind receiving stolen goods—"

"What are you running?" he asked, eyes getting wider. "We don't want anything from a vike. Even Charlie wouldn't—"

"Vikes are mostly legend, spread around by the skyboys to make it easier to recruit Native Forces. I *heard* about one, once, from the Sea Gypsy crew that sunk him.

"No, the stuff in here isn't stolen—yet. But if you have a list of what Charlie needs to get him through next month, it might get left on deck the night I don't wake up when the burglar comes aboard. Of course, nobody really thinks a Sea Gypsy would ever file a complaint with the authorities. I'll just mark the stuff stolen in both sets of books, in case anyone gets nosy. Then after a few weeks, when he's back on his feet a little more, we can work out a more conventional deal . . ."

Manuel stuck his hand out, and we shook. "I'll get you the list. Charlie probably shouldn't be seen around here."

"Try not to have anything like a complete new windmill on it."

"Mostly it's micro stuff, and some precision machine parts, I'm sure. Are you still open?"

"Anytime anyone has cash they want to part with."

"Well, while I'm down here, I'd like to get a book."

"Did you have anything in mind? Family Bible, mechanic's handbook, software guide—"

"Well—" he blushed. "Mary and I don't like what's on the vid much. Too much skyboy stuff. We were wondering if maybe you had a book of stories we could read to each other. We kind of like, uh, fairy tales."

So he went home with *The Jungle Book*. I figured a couple like that would have kids to read to soon enough.

I GOT UP EARLY the next morning, but since neither customer had brought by the money for his forge work yet and no one else was showing up—apparently they still weren't sure I was sticking—I didn't have much to do except fidget, eat a slow breakfast, and work out a list of what I needed to buy or trade for. I had reached the conclusion that I was about tired of eggs but not gotten much farther than deciding not to get any; that was far enough, I decided, so I threw a couple of fish lines over the side and opened up Pratt's *Criteria for Revolutionary Theory*.

With the consequent demand for the informatically skilled, much of the traditional source of the revolutionary elite dried up. Even the most severe status displacement can be overcome swiftly if the critical preadolescent training was appropriate to the original status. Add to this the enormously wider dispersion of institutional-manipulative competence through the proliferation of interest associations—the same phenomenon seen by de Tocqueville in a different context—and the prospects of an explicitly vanguardist social formation became dim indeed.

I thought about making a marginal note, then decided that, if the cosmorines went looking for academics, that might be hanging evidence. Besides, it was the same thought that that chapter always brought to my mind, and I didn't really need to write it down.

The *Criteria* was one of Pratt's earliest books; he was still in despair over the ease with which the world's regimes had reconsolidated after the Plague of '92. The plague had both revealed and solved the twentieth century's major problem: overproduction. A quite small number of workers, with the full exploitation of technology, could produce much more than a much larger number of people could even attempt to consume. Every national economy, from most communist to most laissez faire, was built around the proposition that individual productivity and consumption should somehow correspond; with no one to consume the goods, how could people be kept working?

If Pratt had stopped at pointing out that, by creating a severe labor shortage and a critical need for reconstruction, the plague had rescued the global economy, he would probably have found a place as a mildly honored eccentric. The problem was that he followed matters through to their logical conclusion—which Mendenhall, who sometimes talked as if he had known Pratt personally, said was Pratt's only other bad habit besides coffee.

The chapter I was reading was the result of that (and, if Pratt was anything like most academics, probably the coffee, too). Pratt pointed out that, historically, revolutionists had always come from previously well-off families that had taken a long slide for some reason; that created well-educated, articulate people with whatever society considered "leadership qualities"—in the lower class. From these people would come the revolution that, in Pratt's opinion, would achieve the necessary "decoupling of work and reward."

But the temporary global labor shortage had changed all that; everyone was now needed, working at the maximum of which he or she was capable. The legendary Ph.D. driving a taxicab suddenly found that there were several Ph.D jobs looking for him; for ten years, just to meet the plague-induced boom's needs, the policy of every organization in the world was promote, promote, promote. And the easiest people to promote were the downwardly displaced, who suddenly acquired a stake in the system.

Even then, Pratt might have found shelter as an apologist, except for that "next step" he was so fond of. He predicted that, when the long boom ended and the next inevitable production crisis set in, the new upper class, suddenly threatened with return whence they came, would turn savagely against the lower class—would use their enormous economic leverage to bar the status ladder against more climbers, and "bring down the full force of the state in an orgy of repression."

In context, of course, it wasn't really a prediction of the revolt, independence, and success of the Orbital Republics, but both sides of the struggle read it that way. And that put Pratt very much on the losing side. Children in the Republics' schools—I should know!—were actually taught that the Prattists had advocated enslaving the Orbital population and exploiting them to support the Earth's population in luxury.

From what we knew of his sense of humor, that probably would have delighted him.

I looked up from the book to see the figure coming down the road. I quietly slid Pratt into a not-too-visible spot behind the chair, and picked up Tolkien. It was someone I hadn't seen before; surely I'd remember any farmer who was that tall and thin. I thought about setting up the outside terminal for a moment, but this was probably not the first of a rush.

When he got closer, I saw that I did know him. It was Lieutenant McHenry. I placed a couple of mental bets that he would just come aboard uninvited, but in fact he stopped at the edge of the gangplank and said quietly, "I'm requesting permission to come aboard."

I was so surprised it took me a second to grant it.

Seen up close, he was if anything less prepossessing. He was clean and his uniform was neat, but he'd had a growth spurt after it was issued—his cuffs were fighting their way up toward his elbows and his pants were showing an extra three centimeters of his socks. A bad patch of acne covered his right cheek, his straw-colored hair seemed to have beaten the comb despite a valiant effort, and he stood stiffly, like he was afraid of falling over. "I need your deposition," he said, "and I need to talk to you."

"All right," I said. "Like to come in the cabin for a little coffee?"

He didn't turn me down. He may just have wanted the coffee, but since it's an insult not to accept something from a Sea Gypsy when you're invited into his cabin—coffee or wine or water or *something*—I gave him two extra points for that. When we were sitting, I said, "Okay, if your recorder's running, let's get the deposition."

"It's not running yet," he said. "And after your deposition I'll turn it off. What I need to talk to you about I'd rather not have recorded." I gave him a nod and a handwave; he cut the recorder on and got my version of what had happened the day before. Somehow I forgot that I had intended to brain Linsmann; the lieutenant was polite enough not to bring it up.

When we finished with that, he flipped the switch to "off" with a loud click and smiled at me hesitantly. "If we were in orbit," he said, "I'd ask you if the name William McHenry means anything to you, and you'd gasp and ask if that's my father."

"That's why you look familiar—news broadcasts on the vid," I said. "That *is* your father—leader of the Progs?"

"He wouldn't claim to be the leader. But, yeah, that's him."

I thought about what I could remember. The Progs were the smallest party in the lower house of the OR legislature; they got in on proportional representation, not being a majority in any Republic or kraal, and their percentage never went over ten anyplace.

To most of the Orbital population, they were dangerous lunatics and possibly closet Prattists—supporters of all kinds of free social services, a more generous policy toward the Protectorate, and so forth. One of them had even been discovered to be a practicing Jew, and having no living family to sign him up for compulsory rerationalization, had successfully resisted efforts to deprog him.

Most of us in the Confederation rooted for them in every election, even after that.

"If people around here knew—" I said.

He nodded. "Yeah. This relates only indirectly, but I wanted to make sure you understood. I need absolute discretion." He twitched nervously, then shrugged. "I guess I can't just run out now. Okay. I would like to buy a copy of *The Life of St. Francis*. Please."

I went and got one, quietly, and to sweeten the deal I threw in a catechism. He accepted that, too, and I could see him holding back his enthusiasm. "Family secret?" I asked, finally. "Are you all Catholic?"

"No. I was converted at my last station, by a Native Forces sergeant. My father is more anti-religious than most people—this would kill him. Especially since the whole idea of me coming down here was to have a distinguished service record to run for office on."

He slipped the books into the inside pocket of his tunic. "I'll be back," he said. "And one more thing about Voorbeck. He is...an honorable man, I guess you'd call him. But I've noticed his sense of honor has a lot to do with what he really wants to do. So—watch yourself. Don't provoke him. There are things he can justify..."

I said I'd be careful; we shook hands, and he went up the gangplank.

I waited until I was sure he was gone, then set the intrusion detectors for max range—anything big enough to be a person wouldn't be able to come within a hundred meters without my knowing. Then I brought up the inside terminal, entered a series of improbable phrases—"The elephant rides his stool only when the stone weeps for felicity" is the only one I remember now—strapped on the headphones, and got the transmitter going. I was due to report anyway, and even though I hadn't accomplished anything as yet, I certainly had enough to justify talking to Mendenhall.

Much to my surprise, he was near enough the comm room to be able to come over and talk directly. There's no point in putting a vid signal on a TBN, but I could hear the smile in his voice. "That's our Voorbeck," he said. "We've had our eye on him for a long time, and I don't think he'll disappoint us.

"I have two items for you, Saul. First, did you get the name of that woman who was executed for being married to a runaway cosmorine?"

"Yeah," I said. "Sorry, I forgot to report it 'til now. It was Rachel Shannelon."

"Good. We've been working on public sentiment here with horror stories from Earth; that's a good one." I don't know if I imagined the pause later; I couldn't see his face, of course. "The other news is about your old xsistr, Kari Levi-Strauss."

I felt my stomach sink. "She's dead," I said. "Did they catch her? Where was she?"

"Zanzibar. She got more going than she planned on, I think. Things took off too fast. An uprising was crushed, and they caught her with some suspect electronics in the search afterward. Her cover association with the HHRF held, and we protested the whole thing to the Republics. But it turned out the local commander executed her an hour after he caught her. I'm terribly sorry, Saul. If it's any consolation, everyone in the Confederation is fighting mad about it."

"Yeah." I knew who had seen to that.

He didn't have anything more to say, so I put things back in normal mode and sat down to read more of Pratt. I'd always thought the *Criteria* was his best work, but this time I kept remembering all the times Kari and I had argued about it. That helped me remember her, so I kept reading, even though it hurt.

5

The terrible thing about memory is that so often you recall what you wanted things to be, or what you imagined them to be. So though I would much rather write this whole account about it, I'm going to skip over the next period, the several weeks when, as my orders put it, I "established myself as a trusted figure in the community of assignment."

Even though I definitely remember it as a happy time.

It was a lot like academic research had been, of course—watching what was going on around me while I worked as a more-or-less legitimate Sea Gypsy—but since I didn't have to write a report at the end of it, I could concentrate on what interested me; I didn't have to spend my evenings recording data. So the days slid by without much of anything accomplished officially, except that I knew my way around better; things fell into a steady rhythm of up early, hard work 'til late afternoon, and then a swim in the river and into the bed with a book. Sundays, I went to church and then to eat dinner with someone, usually Manuel and Mary Proxman or Sam Klein.

This particular evening was a little different; it was the middle of the week, but Sam had had one of his sons bring him over for a visit. We were sitting in the cabin, sipping wine, half-watching the vid and not doing much of anything. He was in the main chair; I was in the fold-down.

The program was "The Loves of Larisa," a strange little spinoff of the last remake of *Dr. Zhivago.* In it, a blonde woman, supposedly a refugee from the 1917 Revolution, wandered from one picturesque Old Earth location to another, always as the lover of some shortly-to-die defender of freedom or other—one week Camus, one week Gandhi, one week Giap. Generally, to make the defender of freedom sound acceptable to the Orbital audience, they had to modify him a lot, and consequently except for the costumes it was sometimes a bit difficult to tell Martin Luther King from, say, John Scopes. I don't suppose it mattered much to the audience; they seemed to take it all in happy stride.

"Who's this guy she's kissing supposed to be?"

"I don't know—his Esperanto has a British accent, though." I flipped the subtitler on—"do you read English?"

"Yeah, and a little Russian. No Afrikaans or Japanese."

"English then. The lines are being said by—gee, this is a long stretch of fact even for VidCorp. George Orwell. He was a socialist."

"I can't wait till they do 'Larisa meets Lemuel Pratt.'"

I snorted. "Let's see, when he was twelve she'd have been—uh, okay, say she was seventeen in 1912 or so—when he was twelve she'd have been ninety-eight."

"Well, of course, the audience wouldn't accept him unless he was a pervert."

That sort of conversation went on for a couple of hours, through "True News" and well into "Captain Ito Jakov, ORN."

We had worked our way off of the vid programs and through baseball, the dryness of the summer, and whether it might break in July, and now we were on who might marry who. "Your friends the Proxmans used to be the big topic for this," Sam was saying. "Poor Mary just gets followed by scandal wherever she goes; James used to beat her, or so I hear from over on the other side of the base where they lived. That was the big gossip there anyway, and she sure had the bruises to show for it. Can't say I blame her for moving and getting married right away. Especially when it was Manuel."

"I like him a lot."

"So do most people. I sure was relieved when he got married. He'd about doubled my baptismal business 'til he settled in with Mary. Strange she hasn't had any kids yet; must be something medical, I guess; she sure seems happier now that she's married to Manuel."

"Yeah. He's, well, sweet—the way he breaks into tears—"

Sam laughed. It was a standing joke in the area that Manuel cried over everything. I had seen him crying his eyes out over

Bobtail, the six-month-old kitten who had just earned his name by losing his tail in the compost shredder.

However, before bursting into tears over it, Manuel had done a perfectly calm, competent job of patching the cat up. He wasn't weak, he just cried easily.

Sam trotted out a couple of Manuel stories to top the Bobtail one, and I followed on with one or two. We both skirted around the big one—what Mary did at the District Office. Supposedly that was why James used to beat her; Sam's view on it was that James just treated Mary like he did everyone else.

"There was something eating that man from inside; no one liked him much. Still, it was terrible what happened to him. Anyway, he was nothing like Manuel. I've always wished I could use Manuel as an example in a sermon. Of course, that would never go over. Two-thirds of the congregation wouldn't be happy unless he was beating her, too, but it seems to me that if the Lord could hang around with who he did..." He shrugged.

I reached over into the cabinet. "More wine?"

"Yeah. Saul, I've been wanting to get around to asking you something."

I poured the wine and kept listening.

He sat quietly as the glass filled up; as I topped it off, he said, "Saul, are you with the Underground?"

I didn't jump; partly that was because I had been nerving myself for this moment for so long, but mostly it was because the Underground hadn't existed in twenty years—he might as well have asked if I was in the IWW or the Girl Scouts. Still, the second before I spoke was a long one. "How did you get that idea?"

He ticked it off on his fingers. "One, you have to be losing money between all you've given Charlie Perry and that "local improvements" surtax Voorbeck has levied on your business, and the GXS prices being dropped down so low. Two, you don't talk about the skyboys much, but you sure listen hard when other people do, especially when they've got a complaint. Three, you aren't a skyboy spy, or if you are you're a real smart one, because you've moved so slow that by now people want to ask you into the church. Since there's nothing around here to spy on, you've gone to too much effort to be one of them. So, to be blunt, I think you're one of us."

At that I almost did drop my glass. "You're in the Underground?"

"I was. It's been twenty-two years since a contact came my way, and it was dying then. But I knew it was bound to be revived. The issues didn't go away. So I've been looking for you for a long time.

"But I can't say I'm happy to see it back. I'm old and blind now, and I'd just as soon shuffle off quietly when my time is up. Any new resistance surely will mean tough times for a lot of people.

"Well, I suppose we've got to do it, anyway. There's such a thing as living with yourself. I guess you know that. And I'm glad to see the Sea Gypsies are with us this time; last time they just did cash-and-carry stuff for us."

He turned his face to me, exactly as if he could see me; it was eerie. "So do you want to get a meeting together? I've got a pretty good idea of who we can get."

"Sure," I said. And then, because there wasn't much to say until the meeting, we had a long talk about the cross-the-lake trade, but I don't think either of us paid any attention to it. Eventually his son Thad came by to pick him up.

THERE WAS no moon—it was dark, in the way that spacesiders can't imagine—think of a big room with one very dim light. I slid quietly over into the inflatable dinghy, felt around for the paddle, and cast off.

Even on a river that sluggish, going upstream was hard work, but it was only about a kilometer to where I was coming in, so I put my back into the paddling. The water was black as space; everything on shore was blue. I shivered a little; it was cold and dank, but the physical work warmed me a little.

I came around the point and cut sharply, paddling as hard as I could to get in to the little beach there. After a few seconds I was out of the current and breathing easier, and as I slid up onto the beach I jumped out and dragged the dinghy up across the beach and under a bush I'd selected by daylight.

The back trail up to the church was narrow—according to Sam, it was seldom used by anyone over twelve years old—and

I went slowly in the dark, slipping every now and then on the wet grass but staying fairly quiet for someone as out of practice as I was. By the time I got there I was cold again, and my trousers were grass-stained.

I hadn't really thought about what I was doing before, but when I got to the church, there was a clear space of about thirty meters to cross, and as I started into the open I suddenly felt watched. In the back of my mind the thought came that someone could be watching from a tree with a rifle, the crosshairs centered on the back of my head, or that perhaps Sam was actually in their pay and they were just waiting for me to get to point blank range....

I went in the back door without anything happening.

It was even darker in the church, but I followed Sam's directions carefully. There was a concealed trapdoor under the pulpit, flush-fitted with the floor and covered by a rug. I pressed hard on the left interior cornice and felt the small handle pop up; I put a hand into it, grasped the door, and lifted it up, pivoting around to go down the ladder.

There were four little bulbs running off a battery down there, controlled by a switch that turned them off whenever the door was open (for some reason I never did get, Sam called it a "reverse frijj switch"). As I closed the door, the lights came on, and I came down, blinking for a moment.

"To judge by the sound of those boat shoes, the guest of honor would seem to be here," Sam said.

Charlie Perry was there, sitting dour and silent against the rough stone of the wall; it made perfect sense, though the first thought that crossed my mind was that the poor guy had enough trouble. Next to him was his son Wesley, a little stoop-shouldered guy I had never liked much. Levi Baker and his daughter, Judy, were sitting on the old rugging under one bulb. Next to them were the Underhills, Theo and Clark, big dark, heavyset men who lived further upriver on the fringes of the Black Swamp and ran a little trapping-and-furrier business there. Across the room from the Underhills, and looking at them a little apprehensively, was Mrs. Gothenberg, an older lady that I knew vaguely from church.

The real surprise, I guess, was Father Bob, from Our Lady of Plenty. He was sitting cross-legged in one corner, the light shining off his baldness and showing up dozens of melanoma scars.

Completing the circle was Sam, of course, and his sons Thaddeus and Paul—Isaiah was a little young to be there, I guess. The place was stifling hot from too many bodies in too little space, but the stone was cool to the touch when I sat down.

Sam cleared his throat. "Well, let's get this bridge party going. Saul, I think you know everyone, at least by sight. Some of our old folks were in the Underground like me; the rest had kin in it, or have good reason to be here. I'll vouch for all of them."

I nodded. This was the part I had been dreading—I didn't really have anything to say to them. Workers of the world, unite? Give me liberty or give me death? It might have been different if I had been here from some deep conviction that Earthsiders could share, but I wasn't. Long ago I had decided that when this time came I would just encourage things, let the rebellion go any old way it wanted to.

"The first thing, I think, is to talk about why we're here," I said. "I have a pretty good idea in some cases—" I nodded to Charlie "—but I think we need to know what we've all been thinking." I looked around, hoping that would be enough.

Sam cleared his throat. "I guess since I dragged my kids into this I should give them some explanation—especially since Thad was only twelve last time there was anything like this. Okay, to be blunt about it, we get treated like shit in our own home. The God-damned—and I mean that literally—skyboys are big on talking about freedom and all the rights they guarantee us, but the basic right to settle our troubles among ourselves, and to arrange things the way we like them—that's the one we don't have. I don't like two of them sitting on every one of our juries, as if we can't be trusted to keep our own justice. I don't like every candidate for the council being screened before he can run, I don't like not being able to form a standing political party, I don't like fax machines being licensed and regulated. And this is small, and maybe only a preacher would care, but it galls me—I don't see why in God or anyone else's name, if everyone in the courtroom believes in God, one way or another, we can't open with a little prayer for justice!"

"Amen," Clark Underhill added, startling everyone.

"It'd take more than prayers," Charlie Perry said. He coughed a little, blushing. He didn't usually talk much, and especially not in front of so many people. "I guess that stuff would bother me more, Sam, but I'm too busy with the other things, the money things. They talk all the time about the right of free trade, but they just mean that the GXS does what works out for them. Every year we make a half-decent profit the prices there go through the ceiling, and always on stuff they've got a monopoly on. No offense, Saul, but you and your people just can't make the electronic parts and the precision machine things we need—so we buy from the GXS, or from the GXS through you if we don't live close enough, and what we might have laid by isn't there when the bad years come.

"And the things they call bad luck! That backwash has killed nine windmills since it's been my place, and they never paid a millicredit on any of them—because OrbiTransit Company has already paid the Protectorate for unlimited air rights! The last time the guy told me that my windmill was probably creating interference on the radar and if I kept making a point of it OrbiTransit would countersue me—and probably win. I'm growing more than my family can eat, even in bad years, and nine-tenths of my overhead is repairing damage the skyboys do, but they kick me around like a dry dog turd because I can't make any money at their prices. I'm producing, I work hard, I take care of my own—and they want my blood. Yeah, and my flesh and blood, too," he said, glaring around him. "I don't really care about whose planet this is, or all those rights people talk about, or any of that pisswater. I just want a fair shake from somebody, or if I don't get that I want to get some licks in on him."

The room was very quiet for a moment.

Theo Underhill spoke abruptly, without looking up. "I don't like the way they say 'dirtsider.' That's all. All the rest is just shit like the guy on top always does. But I don't like the way they say that, and I don't like the way they push you around on the street when you come into town."

And then all of a sudden the place was in pandemonium, and I was glad that as yet the cosmorines had no idea of what we were up to, because I was sure you could have heard it three kilometers off. Everyone was talking at once, angry and loud and hard, gesturing to each other. It went on for several minutes; only Sam and I seemed to stay out of it.

Eventually they wound down; Mrs. Gothenberg's soft voice cut through the remaining babble. "One more thing galls me. They closed our schools."

A lot of the younger people in the room looked baffled, and I have to confess I didn't know what she was talking about myself for a minute. "Schools used to be local controlled," she said, "like constables and fire brigades. Used to be you could teach what you wanted—I did, I was a teacher.

"We didn't have to teach history the way the skyboys wrote it, and we could read from any book we had a copy of. My kids always got some Marx, some Tom Paine, even a little of Pratt— though even then I had to have them copy *that* from the board to memorize. I guess it wasn't much, but at least we had some voice in our kids' minds, and I don't think we do any more, now that the ORs run the schools directly. All of history is disappearing—they're already teaching that the people down here joined the Orbital side during the Revolution, and in another generation they'll have erased 2076 from the books. And it's so easy because we're so short-lived. Just to hear the truth told about how things got this way, once again, would be such a treat."

I cleared my throat. How many teachers, I wonder, ever get an entire class that is actually interested? "I think," I said, "that one thing I could provide here, especially for younger people, would be sort of a free school, a place to come and learn the real story. Would people be interested?"

Everyone looked around and nodded. "I'm one of those kids Bea is talking about. I'd love it. And we could bring people to your class," said Judy Baker, "to get them more interested."

"I never did much school," Theo Underhill added, "but this sounds a little more interesting than GXS School—and I might like learning stuff if it was true. There wouldn't be exams, would there?"

Everyone laughed a little. "Nope," I said. "In my classes, there's always been freedom to remain ignorant."

"You've taught school before?" Levi Baker asked, suddenly.

Fortunately, I had an Earthside answer that happened to be true. "Yeah. At the University of the South Pacific, when I was loaned to the Women's Fleet there. History, in fact.

"So we want to do that? There's a consensus?" There was. "Well, that's our first decision. Before we make another one, though, let's consider how we want to run this thing. Unanimous decisions, majority rule, consensus, what? And who's the chair?"

It had been a part of my plan from the first to bring that up. The Protectorate Administration, as part of its "Encourage Liberty" program, requires Earthsiders to do everything with elections, meetings, and procedures, and though most of "self-government" is carefully hamstrung into collaboration, at least every Earthsider is familiar with some kind of orderly democratic procedure. Now that they had psychologically begun their rebellion, it was important that they begin to think of it as a natural, normal thing, and nothing would make it seem more ordinary than a conventional discussion of rules and procedures.

To my surprise, there was a quick decision for consensus and one almost as quick for Father Bob as the chair for this meeting, with some kind of rotation to be worked out later. Everyone, it seemed, had some pet project that they wanted to get the group into, so procedural matters got settled in a hurry. I suppose that I should have paid attention to Gandhi: "If you are not certain where your people are, they are probably ahead of you."

Father Bob offered a fast prayer for wisdom; if it was any indication of how quick he usually was, perhaps I had picked the wrong congregation to join. Then he looked around the little room and said, "Why don't we just see what everyone has in mind? Then we can talk about what priority we ought to be giving the different things, and maybe come up with a program that way."

That seemed to sit well. Judy Baker spoke first, almost immediately. "I'd like to have somebody come up with a way of protecting women from them. A few of them are decent enough, but most of them act like we're here for grabbing—or worse. And they seem to spread that attitude to the Native

Forces, too—if anything, they're worse. If somehow we could just make it a little safer for decent women—''

"One thing we could use," Sam put in, "is a real newspaper. I know we can't use Saul's faxer, but it just happens we have an unlicensed one left over from the old days. And by now they might find it pretty tough to trace it from the manufacturer's records."

"Black market," Clark Underhill put in. "Undersell them, use the money to finance the Underground."

Half a dozen more things surfaced in quick order before Charlie Perry said, "No good ignoring this question. When do we kill our first skyboy?"

There was a stunned silence.

"Soon!" Wesley Perry put in, the first thing he'd said all evening.

I looked slowly from face to face in the yellow glow, trying to see in which way the wind would blow. Most of them were doing the same. Although all of us were sweating in the damp heat and stale air, it was as if a cold draft had blown in, but no one wanted to be the one who got up and closed the window. Clark Underhill and Bea Gothenberg went to say something at the same time, then each deferred to the other; then neither said anything. There was coughing, scratching, and whispering that somehow added up to a deafening roar without containing one meaningful sound.

For me, the situation was hard to figure out. The first of the three planetary alignments that would make the attack on the Republics possible was coming up in less than two months, so from a pure standpoint of carrying out my mission I should have been glad to hear them talking about big, dramatic things that were likely to bring the cosmorines into it—but I was resolved that it was going to be their movement, even if the Confederation did supply the agitation and money. I wanted them to go Perry's way—but I didn't want to have anything to do with leading them there.

Finally, very quietly and gently, the way I'd imagine he was with the mourners at a funeral, Sam spoke. "Why do you think we have to kill one of them, Charlie?" He raised a finger to hold off the angry reply he had sensed coming. "Seriously. I want to know your reasons, because I want to make sure I understand what you want to tell us. Please.''

Perry nodded, drew a deep breath and held it for a moment; he forced his fists to unclench. "Lots of reasons," he said, "give me a second to get 'em straight. I'm not used to talking this much in a meeting."

There was a silence of several breaths, during which the only noise was Wesley fidgeting. Charlie dropped a heavy, affectionate hand on his knee, and even that sound went away, leaving just the still heat and the occasional scrape of someone shifting position. I looked up at the wooden trapdoor and thought, if someone were to heave a grenade down here, right now, there goes the revolution for this district, maybe this continent, and we're talking about taking on the only military power worth talking about in the solar system . . .

Finally Perry spoke. "Okay, here goes. One, because it's the only thing that will work for a lot of purposes—like protecting women from them. They won't care what your newspaper says about them, but they will care if they might get killed for it." Judy nodded; I mentally raised the count to three for my side.

"Two," Charlie went on, "it costs them right away. They can't just ignore it or pretend it's not there, so they have to start putting men and money into it, and that brings it closer to the day when they give up from their losses. Three, it weeds out our own organization. It raises the stakes of joining, so that our members will only be the tough core. If you have to put your neck in the noose to join, and you join, then you can be depended on as far as I can see. And four, it means we get things going right away. If we set up an organization, work for some months or years, and then try to move into a real war, the organization itself will resist it—no standing organization likes change. If the organization plays for keeps from the first, then you never have to persuade people who've gotten comfortable with the way things are to move on to the next step when the time for it comes."

Sam nodded, again. "From that, I take it, you think we will have to use violence before they'll go home."

"Right," said Charlie, "I do. But there's one more thing, and that's the really big one.

"Dignity! Why do we take this shit from them? Why can they walk into a crowd of fifty of us, do something so insulting that no jury would convict the man that murdered them, and then walk back out untouched, calling us names the whole time? Because we have no dignity. Because to them we're a joke.

"And we are. One of them without a gun can stand down a hundred of us with, because we're afraid. You know their old saying, 'one cosmorine, one riot.' We know they could take our farms, take the little we have. We know they have thousands more cosmorines they can drop in any time they want. And *we give up*, before they even have to think about fighting. They look at us and see we're already beaten. The most stupid, weak, useless, inept cadet can push any of us around any way he wants.

"But the day we kill one—they might go crazy and slaughter a whole town somewhere, and they might get more insulting, even—but they'll do it in packs. They'll have to think before they do anything to any of us, and ask themselves what might happen back to them. When they walk around on our land, they'll know it's ours, whatever their claims are.

"They won't respect us until they fear us." He bowed his head, twisting his hands in his lap.

The Underhills were nodding slowly; five, I thought. Not enough yet. When he was done speaking, Sam nodded and scratched his head. "First, I have a question for Saul. In the old days, right after the 2076 Rebellion, it was the policy of Central that the time wasn't ripe yet for another violent revolt, or for violence of any kind. They wanted to get a structure of coordination in place, get the wherewithal to fight with built up first. They also didn't want local outfits breaking that policy without their approval. What are the rules this time around?"

Right then, I suppose, I could have given them any direction I wanted—but I didn't want to. I just wanted them to take mine, of their own volition. So I hesitated a moment, again looking up at the heavy planks of the trapdoor. Charlie was leaning the way Mendenhall and his government buddies would have wanted him to—but was that the best thing for these people, in their own sober judgement?

I didn't know either, so I slipped out from under. "There's no Central as such," I said. "One is supposed to be constituted about two years from now, from elected representatives of all the locals. I don't represent any central authority—I'm just supposed to help you start a local, and see that your representative gets to the meeting place. But locals are supposed to get as far as they can along whatever lines seem wisest to them. In other words, do the maximum that your own judgement will support." It wasn't a bad little lie for on the spot; I might have believed it myself.

"So if we judge that Charlie's right, and we're at a point where we can kill them, we should?" Father Bob asked. Sam was leaning forward, listening hard.

In all duty, I could not tell them to avoid armed rebellion if that was what they wanted. I said yes, that was right.

Sam seemed to stifle a sigh, and then again spoke quietly. "Charlie, your arguments aren't bad, any of them. But somehow, something in my heart tells me they aren't right. I couldn't really tell you what. Do we have to decide tonight? Can we just set a date for Saul's first history class and figure we'll meet after that, and talk about this again? I want time to think and pray."

To everyone's relief, I think, Charlie agreed, and since it was late and we were going to be short on sleep anyway already, we set the first class for a week from then and adjourned. Judy Baker and Sam sat with me for a while, working out the details of getting a class together out at Stadium Pond, wherever that was. I was glad the return trip was downstream. I felt tired and oddly ill.

6

"Where is this place?" I asked Sam, as I stumbled in the dark.

"Stadium Pond? It's a little clearing in the woods. Careful, Paul, you'll put your old father into the mud. I don't move that quick. One of those places from back when there was oil around here—a little tar pit with a pond lying on it; it poisons the deep soil, so the trees won't grow close to it. Kind of a natural auditorium."

We came around another bend in the trail. I had long ago lost any sense of direction; the trail deliberately seemed to wind through the thickest underbrush, and I constantly expected the pain of a stinging nettle on my hand or ankle. Above, the canopy of leaves cut out almost all of the half-moon's light. The sand was rough and gritty in my shoes; the air was a rich, damp fragrant salad.

"Who usually uses this trail? Why does anyone go out there?"

"Well," Sam said, as he sat down on a log to catch his breath, "The grass is soft and thick, there's a lot of privacy...and despite my status as a man of God, my human frailty of suspicion has given me the idea that some of my grandchildren got started out here."

"Dad!" Paul said, sounding a little shocked.

"For heaven's sake, you're forty-two; I've already buried two of your older brothers. You can stand to hear your old man talking nasty."

"Well, it's just that—"

"You didn't think I knew? Well, I didn't for sure 'til just now, but I don't think it hurt Sarah any to be conceived out here. She turned out just fine; in fact her daughter's just the age to be sneaking out here herself."

Paul laughed. "Dad, sometimes I think you sit up nights thinking of ways to shock me. Faith's thirteen."

"At my age, shocking you is one of the few pleasures left to me. And you ought to see about getting Faith engaged to that Bourne boy she hangs around with before she does get out here."

"What makes you sure she will?"

"Family tradition. Your brother Thad came along when I was between wives and not yet saved. Where do you think he originated?"

Paul snorted. "Maybe I should just keep her chained up."

"If you do, make sure it's inside, not in the yard. I got my breath again. Let's get going."

After a few more minutes of stumbling along that cold, slippery trail, we suddenly burst into the clearing. It was as Sam had said—a soft, warm little place, maybe a hundred meters across, surrounded by scrub pines, with a little pool less than twenty meters in diameter in the middle.

There must have been a hundred of them, all sitting on the ground on blankets, whispering to each other or just sitting.

"What the—" I whispered.

"Word of mouth builds up business in a hurry," Sam said. "Relax, they're all friends of one sort or another. And we've set up the cover story that this is a secret revival meeting for all the churches around. With what the skyboys tend to believe about churches, they probably think we're coming out here to dance around naked and shake rattles, even if they are aware of it—which I doubt, since so few of them stir off the base."

Paul led him forward; I hung back in the shadows for a moment.

"I guess we all know why we're here," the old preacher began. "And we all know enough not to talk about it away from here. You'll notice you can't see my face here where I'm standing, because of the shadows. I would suggest that even if you recognize our teacher's voice, you ought to avoid talking about who you think he is.

"At my suggestion, our teacher is going to make our first few classes kind of a view of the whole, true story. Then future classes will go into more detail. We thought it was important to get the basic truth out first, before going into the fine points, because some of our younger people have lived with the sky-boy version of things for so long that we don't want to hold the truth back from them for a minute longer. So, teacher, if you're ready—"

I stepped forward, not sure what to say, and stood there silently for a moment. I thought of something my mother used to say—when you don't know how to begin, begin and find out how from that.

"To start off," I began, "for the first sixty-and-more years of the Space Age, Earth was not 'under the thumb of the tyrannical United Nations,' as the standard textbook puts it. The UN was a weak, fragmented, generally ineffectual organization—guaranteed to be that way by its charter—and by the time the nations of Earth voted it any real power, collapse was imminent anyway. The real powers on Earth were the United States and the Soviet Union, in general, plus Japan later in the period. One sign of that, anyway, is that of the twelve Orbital Republics, five have American names, four are Russian, two are Japanese."

"That only adds up to eleven," Judy Baker said.

"Bothasburg is South African. The South Africans weren't a big power, but they were technologically capable, and they were driven by an obsessive idea that they might be able to preserve their way of life in orbit. And in a way, they have—there's certainly a lot of the Afrikaaner mentality to the present-day Orbitals.

"At any rate, the colonies were built in an atmosphere of intense international competition in the late 90s and early Ohs—a formal economist would have referred to it as a point of inflection on the Kondratiev curve, the particular point that is associated with explosive growth." I hurried on before Judy could ask about Kondratiev—she'd probably drop by the boat, anyway, tomorrow, and I could explain it then.

"The purpose, at first, was energy. The Great Plague of 1992 had reduced global population by considerably more than half, but mostly in the poor nations, which didn't use much energy, and it had also created permanent social chaos in many of the world's major energy-producing regions. So the big economic powers turned to space-based beamdown solar power, which was an existing, easy-to-use technology that didn't threaten the wobbling ecology. The first colonies were really just barracks for maintenance and construction workers on the solar power satellites.

"But once the stations were up there, it became obvious that there were lots of other uses for the things. For one thing, you could move most of heavy industry up to orbit—which was a big relief to the ecosystem right there. And with the use of robots and practically unlimited solar power, after the colony got big enough it could expand virtually without limit. And of course, the richer and bigger your space colonies got, the more powerful your nation was—or so they figured.

"And with every increase in the size of a space colony, it pays to make more things in the colony, rather than ship them up a gravity well."

"What's a gravity well?" Charlie Perry called out.

"Pretty much what a regular well is. Suppose you knew somebody who lived at the bottom of a well, say two hundred feet down."

"Around here, he'd be a hundred-and-ninety feet underwater," Charlie snorted.

"Suppose anyway. Okay, now you want to trade things between you, right? So you use a rope to lower things, and he uses a pulley and rope to lift them. Now, who has to do more work to engage in trade?"

"He does, obviously," Charlie said. "I can just put a drag of some kind on the rope. He has to haul everything all the way to the top. I think I see what you mean. But Earth-to-orbit is always more expensive than orbit-to-Earth. Everyone knows that."

"Yeah. Even our ancestors did, when it was happening. But still, they couldn't really stop it. It made sense to keep the stations growing, because that was increasingly the measure of national strength. Of course, you could only move a small fraction of the population up there, and you only needed a limited number of people down on Earth to do the receiving, but they got around that basically by expanding the military forces to sizes no one had ever dreamed of before. The American Army alone got up to twenty-five million people."

"Couldn't they have built—oh, roads or bridges or something? That sounds so useless—" Levi Baker put in.

"To a small extent, that's what they did. But the basic infrastructure—roads and so forth—had been complete for sixty or seventy years in the USA and thirty in Japan and Russia. You can only repair a thing so many times in a year, even as busy work, before you start to interfere with its function.

"And, too, none of those cultures had any use for idleness or for rentierism. Even though few of those twenty-five million were trained very much and most of them spent their time marching around in circles, sometimes literally, at least all those soldiers appeared to be doing something."

"What's rentierism?" Judy asked.

"It's a little off the subject, actually—I'm sorry. Rentierism is a system where people get money from the government without having to work for it," I said.

"I don't know that any of us here would like that, much," Matt Gomes put in, from the back. There seemed to be general agreement.

"It wasn't a question of liking it," I said. "Somehow they had to feed, clothe, and house a lot of people whom there wasn't work for."

"Couldn't they just cut the work up into smaller amounts and pay everyone more?" someone asked.

"Well, one problem with that is that some labor is hard to cut up that way. Farming for example, which requires constant attention, or some kinds of highly skilled work because you have to do so much of it just to stay competent. And more than that, the real market wage on Earth would have been very low—because the product had to sell as cheaply as something made better by robots in orbit. The problem was that the workers were on Earth and the money to pay for their work was in space. Somehow you had to get them together—and even with three million workers going up per year around 2010, it wasn't enough to ship workers. You had to move the money back down—charge the space colonies more in taxes than they got back in services."

"All that might have been no more than a headache, to be solved by gradually raising taxes on the colonies, if it weren't for the rescue issue."

"That was one they covered in school," Judy Baker put in.

"What they said was probably pretty accurate," I said. I found my mind racing back to being a kid, eight or nine years old, hearing the story for the millionth time even then, blood boiling as usual. The Terran countries had prohibited rescues of "non-national citizens"—and in the old days, when all the traffic out to geosynchronous orbit went through low-orbit switching stations and Earth-to-orbit ships didn't carry much spare fuel, there were a lot of rescues needed.

But space had developed its own ethic, like any basically hostile environment—the sea, the desert, Antarctica. The rules were ignored—flouted, really—at every occasion; and in the way of all empires faced with unruly colonies, the Earth nations sent troops to enforce the rules.

In an environment under martial law, all sorts of things that the population might have put up with became intolerable.

The Revolution, as such, was over in four days. We spent longer than that on it in school—I can still visualize the old ex-cosmorine, actually a veteran of the Revolution rather than an aftersettler like most of us in the Outer cities, clumping along on his artificial leg and drilling the story into us—the desperate fights in the corridors, the little round blobs of blood floating everywhere, the twitching of the drifting bodies, the melee without any recognizable direction where people just spun around killing and killing in all directions until someone killed them. I knew there were parts that had been swallowed in that official version—the victorious rebels chucking prisoners out the airlock at Port Armstrong, for one thing. But, somehow, it was the myth that stayed with me.

I have often thought that any kids of mine will be raised on stories composed of equal parts of Gandhi and Auschwitz.

All this was going through my mind as I stood there in the damp darkness, straining to see, quickly sketching in a few corrections to the official version. I also had time to think about the number of mosquitos eating their way through my trousers and to decide I couldn't scratch my inner thighs without being seen. That's one thing you learn from teaching college—how to talk to a class and think about something else at the same time.

"So, anyway," I said, "although their own hands are not free of blood, they certainly had some case against Earth at the time of the Home Rule Declaration. Of course, that was just over ninety years ago, and some things have happened in between.

"The main thing, of course, was that with the colonies independent there was no restraint or control on their economic activities—even the high-tax solution, inadequate as that had been, was unavailable. The situation got far, far worse...the last year that there was a UN to keep figures, unemployment was around 88%, which may have been low."

Mary Proxman politely raised her hand, and I called on her. "Didn't the Earth nations try to stop the trade?"

"Sure. You might have noticed that some of your older tools have 'Complies with NIA' stamped on them? That was the Non-Intercourse Act of 2021. Supposedly it prohibited any trade with the Orbital Republics. There was a law like that in every country.

"But any nation that cheated could have an unlimited supply of anything. Any bureaucrat could be bribed any amount to tolerate smuggling. And besides, the cosmorines—and later the Native Forces—could be sent to protect the 'right of free trade', especially as governments became unable to pay their own armies.

"In the late 2020s, famine broke out almost everywhere. As a lingering aftereffect of the plague, most governments had a lot of surplus land, and in general efforts were made to get as much of the population out of the cities and into the fields to grow its own food. That, incidentally, is how most of your ancestors wound up as farmers. It probably did help more people survive, but it also embittered the conflict—the Republics wouldn't ship an ounce of food down without payment, on one hand, and on the other the increased food production down here cut into AgriCorp's profits and led to the first real depression the Republics had ever seen.

"The last straw was piled on in 2034. A bunch of nations in the Mideast—it's never been untangled who did what—had all been accusing each other of violation of their various nonintercourse treaties. Somehow nuclear weapons got unleashed; there must have been about seventy-five megatons expended in Arabia, Palestine, and Mesopotamia...it wiped out maybe two thirds of the ozone layer.

"It also gave the skyboys the pretext they'd been looking for. Cosmorines dropped out of orbit onto all the surviving military bases and facilities on Earth and seized them. Ships at sea were given a few days to get to port—then bombed if they didn't. In about three weeks, the governments of Earth had all signed the Protectorate Treaty.

"And since then, you've been under the Protectorate. What that means, what it's done to Earth, things like that, we'll talk about in future sessions. Meanwhile, are there any questions?"

The cool, dank breeze refreshed me; there was a meeting later that night, but for the moment I was done. There were a couple of stirs in the crowd.

"Yes?" I asked.

"Why didn't the ozone ever come back?" a voice I thought I should know asked.

"It did, to some extent. It's well over half of prewar levels. The research has never really been done," I said. "Almost certainly, though, it's because of OrbiTransit exhaust. There are probably three or four hundred flights up and down in any given day—OrbiTransit company doesn't release figures—and there's good reason to believe that the fuel they use is methane and fluorine, though that's secret, too. That seems to be the explanation—especially since OrbiTransit has filed an interference-with-trade-secrets injunction against research into the ozone question."

"Is the ozone why the weather changed?" someone else wanted to know.

"No, that's the extra carbon dioxide. Some of the great oil pools in the Mideast were ignited and burned in the war; and the ozone depletion led to partial suppression of ocean algae. So the atmosphere stabilized with a bit more carbon dioxide than before. That made it a little warmer, but it also increased snowfall in some places, so the winds and currents changed quite a lot."

There were other questions, mostly minor; everyone seemed really interested. After a while, people began to get up, shaking hands with neighbors and getting into parties to walk home together. It might have been the revolutionary classroom to me, I thought, but for them it was kind of a social, the way church league baseball was. The wind sighed softly again, the pines moving a little; there were clouds hiding some of the stars now, and there might be rain by morning. I followed the trail back through the pines and into the hardwoods, then on for a half-kilometer until I got to the road, figured out where I was, and headed toward the Baptist church.

On the way I was planning out the next lecture. It was such a pleasure to teach the willing, to teach things that mattered to the student, to teach without having to constantly satisfy a bureaucracy. I thought to myself, as I swung along the dim road, that I would certainly enjoy the next few weeks.

I CLOSED THE TRAPDOOR and the lights came on; as I climbed down, I saw that we had some new people. We'd need a new meeting place soon; the stones were already dripping with condensation from too many people in too small a space.

I might have expected Mary and Manuel to be there; they were outsiders in the community, and smart enough to be interested besides.

What I didn't expect was Lieutenant Billy McHenry.

He gave me a little smile. I nodded at him, stepping off the ladder and picking my way to a seat between Theo Underhill and Father Bob. "Levi's chairing tonight," Sam said. "You're the last here, so we're pretty well ready now."

"Sorry I'm late," I said. "But if I could ask—" I gestured at McHenry, not sure how to put the question.

"He's here at my request," Father Bob said. "He'll explain."

McHenry was so obviously uncomfortable that I immediately decided that whatever he was doing here, it wasn't spying, so I nodded again.

Levi Baker began. "We were at the point, last time, of discussing projects we might want to take on. I'd like to start off by seeing if anyone has any thoughts on anyone else's ideas, as proposed last week—let's see if there's anything with fairly broad support."

"Something we need to know first," Sam said. "I guess I don't object to our having a guest, this particular guest I mean. But I'm not sure we want to speak freely around him until we know how far in he is."

There was a low rumble of assent. Father Bob put up a hand. "I'm responsible for bringing him, I'll vouch for him."

"That's not enough. That can't be enough," Sam said. "Some of the things that have been proposed are good for a lot more than a flogging or a stretch in prison. And under the skyboy law they could have us for conspiracy, which makes us all equally guilty. With all our necks in the noose, nobody's word is good enough."

"Goddam right." Charlie Perry grunted, an ugly, abrupt sound that it hurt my throat to hear.

Despite the heat, I felt a little chill run over my skin. I looked at the prominent lump of Billy's larynx, scarred by acne and clumsy shaving, and thought what it would be like to push a knife into there.

"Maybe I should explain," he said. "Then you can decide on whether I belong here. And if you say to go, I'll slip back to base and say nothing, regardless of whatever happens in the future. Fair enough?"

Everyone looked around, hoping someone else would speak.

Charlie shrugged. "You're here. I don't think the group is ready to kill you to shut you up. We might as well listen, and then trust you. We can't do anything else." He turned pointedly to Father Bob. "But I don't think this was the right way to do this."

The old priest looked back calmly. "I heard ideas, in this room, last time, which I think are utterly wrong. I think that Billy here can offer us another way, a way that makes the other course less appealing, and help us avoid adding one more sin to a history already too rich with it. I for one am willing to take this young man's word. If you must examine him, then do so. But I think you'll find what I did, and I believe you'll see what our right course is, as I believe I have."

There was a split second's silence. "Some of us," Charlie said, "are not used to having decisions made for us. Some of us, for that matter, are here because we don't *like* having decisions made for us."

Billy coughed, after what seemed a hot, sweat-smelling eternity. "Should I go ahead?"

"Might as well," Clark Underhill said. "Not much else for you to do. Like Charlie says, we have to trust you anyway, unless we want to kill you."

Billy gulped a little, took a deep breath, and straightened his uniform shirt. "Okay. For those of you that don't know, I'm a Catholic. I've been sneaking over to Father Bob for secret Mass, and I've been reading everything Saul can get for me. If I got caught, I wouldn't be killed, just deprogged—the kind of thing they used to do during the Great Rationalization. But I do have some stake in this.

"What I told Father Bob is this. There are lots of cosmorines who don't like what we do here. The defection rate is almost one percent. A lot of these guys are just putting in time, hoping to go home; many of them sympathize with you."

"You couldn't tell it by me," Charlie said.

"Enlisted men and lower officers go out under the supervision of a senior officer. It's like a game—you compete to see who can be most brutal."

"Most of you play pretty well."

"Yeah. But some of us think we ought to go home and leave you to run your own affairs.

"I know who they are. They could be talked to, organized—and some of them go home every two weeks. Word of conditions down here could be all over the Republics in just a month or two. That would bring reporters, the vid, lots of attention. And from there you could see some political pressure for real change." He took a deep breath and let it out slowly, obviously forcing himself to relax. The sweat stains under his arms seemed huge, even in the heat. "Look, I haven't lived through it all my life like you have, but I can see injustice. When I think about what people are like back home, and what they do down here, the difference is just unbelievable. With the right public relations, with the right approach, we can make people feel that 'til it hurts—and when it hurts, things will change.

"I know I'm an outsider here. But I want to be your friend. If it comes to war between our peoples, I know you'll have most of the justice on your side.

"But you might lose. And even if you win, there will be a lot of suffering and innocent blood spilled, and that will happen here, not there. They're out of your reach. It seems to me that we have to try peace, first. I know you've already given us a lot, more than we had any right to... but I'm going to ask for one more thing. Help us to make it right.''

I watched a mosquito slowly hover over my arm, gently bringing my other hand down to crush it. Wesley Perry pointedly looked at the wall. Bea Gothenburg opened her mouth and closed it twice.

I don't know what anyone else was thinking, but I was realizing that no matter what I did or said next, I was going to regret it.

McHenry's proposal was stupid, of course. There were reporters down here already; because ''History stopped on Earth'' this was where VidCorp broke in their new reporters. Plenty of the new reporters were shocked enough to send up stories; those were always spiked, usually with a nod to the law about ''abuse of free speech to impugn legitimate exercise of property rights.''

Even if honest reporting were to get onto the vid somehow, my faith in the Orbital Republics' innate sense of justice was minimal; and conditions Earthside were *not* unknown to the population up there—a universal male draft saw to that. True, some cosmorines went home disillusioned, even shocked by what they had seen—but for most of them it was simply a boring stretch of time spent where the air and humidity controls didn't work very well and the gravity was too high. And the shocked ones, the best of the lot, generally confined their activities to joining the Concerned Orbital Citizens or voting Prog.

On the other hand, he was dead right that another rebellion was not going to be easy on the Earthsiders.

I would have bet on Charlie Perry to be first to speak, but instead it was Sam. ''One question, Billy. What could we do here that would help or hinder you doing that? I agree that sympathy wouldn't hurt our cause, I guess—but I don't see how what we do would have an effect one way or the other on what you do.''

Billy looked down at the rough concrete floor and mumbled something.

Judy Baker spoke sharply. ''We didn't hear you.''

"Time," he said. "What I do need is time. If the battle lines get drawn too soon, the hardliners will get more support."

"Would you try, even if there was no time? Even if war broke out tomorrow?" Sam asked, coolly eyeing the boy.

"Yes. I mean, if you were right. Uh, I mean...I don't know what I would do. Like I said, I'm already in line to be de-progged, if I get caught. I guess I'd do whatever I could. It might not be much. I don't know how much courage I have for that kind of thing."

"Neither does any of us," Charlie said, with a warmth that startled me. As I looked up, though, it was not Charlie but Wesley that caught my eye. He was glaring at Billy McHenry with unmistakable jealousy.

McHenry looked up, as if there were some hope, but Charlie shook his head. "It wouldn't be a good idea for you to know what we decide about this. You ought to just do what you think is right. We can't tie our freedom to your salesmanship with your own people. If you can do something, well, God give you the courage to do it. Just the same, there is one thing you could tell us. But it's a personal question."

Billy nodded. "Ask anyway."

"Why are *you* down here?"

"You all know about my father?"

We all nodded. It was a common enough story around the farms, and the main reason that civil cases were generally brought into court only in the weeks that McHenry presided.

"Well, most of the cosmorine officers just plain wouldn't have a thing to do with anyone named McHenry. Voorbeck actually asked for me. I'm his little project. He likes to think he can turn any of us into what he calls a 'good officer,' which roughly equates to someone who does just what Voorbeck would do in any situation. He's just about exactly the model officer as far as the top brass is concerned and he knows it. So he took on the ugly job of turning Billy McHenry into a real cosmorine officer. So far I think he believes he's succeeding."

We all laughed a little; Billy shrugged.

Levi Baker looked once around the room. "Okay, I think it's a consensus. Billy, we appreciate your coming, but there's not a lot we can do for each other. You go your way, we'll go ours, and it's good to know that some of you are decent at heart. We'll need that when this is over. 'Til then, however, go.''

Billy nodded, got up quietly, and climbed up the ladder without a word. The lights were out for a moment as the young lieutenant went through the trapdoor. We heard his footsteps go away quickly.

''I think,'' Father Bob said, ''that we have made a tragic mistake.''

We let him speak; I guess it seemed the least we could do. ''What we need, more than anything else, is some sort of change in the human heart, the sort that comes only with—and I'm sorry if I offend anyone with this—with Christ. Young McHenry, for one, is Christianized, and you can see the miracle of courage and decency it's worked in him. The spread of that spirit—to love our enemies, and loving them to love us— that is our one real hope. All other paths lead to bloodshed, to misunderstanding, to fear and hatred in a never-ending cycle. Let us renounce such a possibility.

''We must make the world over again, into the perfect justice of God. I don't say that that is the easy path. I say it's the right one.''

I scanned the room frantically. Bea Gothenburg, the Proxmans, the Bakers, were all impassive. The Underhills and Perrys were angry. Sam Klein looked torn and wretched, and his sons looked at him, obviously hoping he would tell them what to do.

''I say,'' Charlie said, ''what I said before. Before they can love us, they'll have to respect us; before they respect us, they'll have to fear us. I hope McHenry gets somewhere. I hope he can make them feel how wrong they are, so they stop doing it. But I know that, whatever they feel, they have to stop, and soon...and for that, I trust fear more than love. It's a hard thing to say, I know. Maybe not Christian. But if we want to hold our heads up on our own world, we have to teach them that their blood flows as easily as ours. If ten of them died next week, we'd be that much closer to freedom.''

''You'd only bring down more troops,'' Sam said, softly.

''Which would raise their goddam taxes.''

''On us.''

"On them. As long as they can't collect them from us, they'll have to tax their people. And with boys going home in boxes, they'll get a different view of us."

"They'll want to kill us!"

"They want to now. Only right now it's because we're smelly dumb dirtsiders. You can't surrender to that kind of critter. If we're killing them, we might be monsters or ogres or baby-eaters, but we're something to be feared, not cleaned away like a mess! They might want to hunt us down like mad dogs, but that's better than being managed like cockroaches."

"And at the end you can admit that you lost to a mad dog easier than to a cockroach!" Clark Underhill added.

Bea Gothenburg nodded. "In the old Underground, we lost members to hangings every year. Oh, they hated us. But there was no fear of us...and perhaps if there had been, there'd have been a little less contempt."

Sam sighed, long and hard. "I've been having my boys read to me from Dr. King's books for this past week. I'm not entirely sympathetic with Bob...I think there has to be action. But you don't have to kill a man to have him respect you. All you have to do is not let him treat you like a dirtsider. That's tough, but it doesn't require murder. Strikes, boycotts, sit-ins, there are all kinds of things that can apply pressure—"

"And get the ringleaders arrested and hanged," Charlie Perry said. "What you're talking about happened in a country with a free press. Despite what that kid says, we'd never make the news, except as evidence of a subversive plot. And they could wipe out a whole town of us without raising an eyebrow back home. There's only one VidCorp—and the same people run that that run OrbiTransit and the cosmorines and the GXS."

"And if we turn to bloodshed—" Levi Baker began, softly.

"They can at least be afraid of retaliation!" Clark Underhill snapped back at him.

And after that, there was an hour of pandemonium and anger with no outcome at all. Eventually we agreed only that it was too damned late to keep going, and adjourned by exhaustion.

On my way out of the church, I felt a tap on my shoulder. It was Thad Klein; he pulled me over next to his father.

"Saul," Sam said, impassively.

"You want to talk?" I asked, feeling stupid.

"Yeah." He sniffed the night air. I looked out across the dim lawn; the moon had set hours ago. "This new underground doesn't have a thing to do with the old one, does it? We used to weed out guys like Perry. Now they get their say... there's no Central to keep things in line or reasonable. I find myself wondering why."

A cold chill came over me. I wished that I could see Thad's face in the gloom, because I was sure he was studying my expression to fill his father in later.

"I think the truth is this," Sam added. "The new underground wants a war. They want it now. They know that if fighting breaks out, it will spread. And they've decided to have it break out here, now, this summer. Which means we'll take the brunt, we and our families.

"And you sit in the back and don't say much, but you make sure that the hotheads get to talk, and they talk about action and we talk about reason, and we're going to lose. And it will look like it was all our decision, locally. You won't have a drop of blood on you."

He was halfway across the lawn before Thad caught up with him.

Then Sam spun around, bellowing "Pontius Pilate!" at the top of his lungs, setting echoes going up and down the river so that I cringed, sure that platoons of cosmorines would sweep down on us at any moment.

But at the same time I felt like giggling. Blind as he was, he'd gotten turned around and bellowed it at an inoffensive grove of walnut trees.

WHEN I GOT BACK to the boat, I decided it was time for a TBN message. I opened the concealed door and took out the headset, then typed in the activating commands.

The stray thought occurred to me that in the days before tight beam neutrino transmission, a spy's job must have been really nerve-wracking, never knowing when a radio message might be intercepted. And before radio, the sheer isolation... I shuddered, turned up the heat, and settled back to talk. My report was short and to the point; I didn't want to talk a lot, just to talk.

The blip took me by surprise. It indicated specific orders were about to be sent. I settled back to listen carefully.

The voice was Dr. Mendenhall's. "Saul, I'll be direct. We need a full-scale war in progress, on Earth, in no more than eight weeks. Your sector appears to be the furthest advanced in North America. I know you really need more time, but we can't spare it. We're all counting on you to get something going right away. Good luck. I have faith in you."

The blip of message-over jolted me. I carefully put the headset back in its hiding place and changed the computer back out of TBN mode. I checked my calendar and found nothing on the schedule till noon the next day.

As I got into bed with my bottle of wine, I remembered that there had been a time when I'd have killed to hear Mendenhall say he had faith in me.

7

I guess I could claim it was a premonition, but actually, having drunk myself to sleep, I just needed to piss, so I was standing there, peeing off the stern in the gray light just before dawn, when it went by.

It was blue-black and gooey, at least 30 centimeters across, and it was bobbing down the river, just barely on the surface. Then I saw four, five, ten more of them floating by.

I was on top of the cabin almost before I knew it, fumbling for rockets and flags. I dropped three orange rockets into the launch tubes and slammed the trigger bar; they went whizzing up, bursting overhead as I hooked up the blue flag with the black smear and hoisted it. I fired off another triple.

A minute or two later, other rockets and flags were going up from every ramtower in sight. There wasn't going to be much leisure this morning; I took a look at my parts inventory and wished I had a hundred times as many pop valves and filters.

I DON'T REALLY KNOW everything that happened. I know that the legends are mostly wrong and the vid not much better. I knew Manuel and Mary—so this is my guess, and at worst it won't be as far off as most others.

I remember seeing Manuel's rockets go up almost immediately after mine; so it must have been about quarter to six in the morning that it all began.

He lurched through the kitchen door, sat down in his chair, and began to weep quietly. Mary watched him for a few minutes as she got breakfast; he cried easily, of course, but even Manuel rarely started the day in tears.

"What's up?" she asked quietly, as he subsided into honking and blowing.

"Jet fuel in the river. The lower valve on the ram is completely gunked."

"How much water's in the tank?"

"Eight or nine hours of power if we cut nonessentials right away. The separator, heat pump, vid, and lights will have to stay off till I get it fixed.

She nodded. With the corrugated iron roof, the house would be like an oven before the ram was fixed, but there was nothing they could do about that. "Will it cost us anything to fix it?"

"Yeah." He winced. "That's the trouble. It'll be several days to recondition it, even if Saul doesn't have anything else to do. And with the mess in the river, he has plenty. He won't have more than a dozen valves to sell, at best, and I'd bet it's too late to get in line for them even now. I guess I'd better go try, though." He was up and out the door immediately, drying his eyes as he went.

MANUEL'S LUCK seemed to be with him at first; there were only five people in front of him, and I hadn't yet put up the "NO MORE" sign. If it hadn't been for the disaster in the river, it might have been a nice day; the morning was mild and pleasant.

Three farmers behind Manuel, I set up the "NO MORE." After that I concentrated on the men in the line; I didn't want to see the faces of those who would have to go to the GXS.

Manuel had just come down the gangplank and I was filling out a purchase agreement form when I looked up and saw the uniforms coming.

There were about twenty of them, but most of them were just Native Forces, carrying only nightsticks. The five that counted, though, were the cosmorines; they were all armed, and the ensign with them was still space-pale and looked young. All of them, except one older sergeant, looked scared to death.

The sergeant drew his men up, facing the line of customers, cosmorines in front with riot guns leveled, NFs behind them. The ensign read from a card, "Under the Trade Regulation Authority created by section 4, Protectorate Administration Regulations, General Orders, we have been issued a warrant of class five, requirement to sell. The person named below, Saul

Fox of the Free and Associated Company of the *Queen of Long Point*, currently master of the johnboat *Spirit of Monroe*, is hereby ordered to sell all parts of description hydraulic ram lower valve GXS-PS-H-98766-4-2093 and description water inlet filter GXS-WS-24422-1-2102 to the local officers at prices not to exceed catalog, in preference to all other customers, the instant this shall be received. All unconcluded transactions in progress are hereby declared null and void for these items.''

It was a buy-out; the oldest trick in their book. The crowd muttered angrily, but there weren't many of them—the "NO MORE" sign had seen to that. At the sergeant's command, the Native Forces walked slowly forward, past the cosmorines, raising their riot sticks. The farmers turned and walked away, except Manuel.

The sergeant holstered his riot gun and walked slowly up to Manuel, tapping his baton in his hand.

"I claim my right as a free citizen to observe any legal transaction," Manuel said, looking straight into the sergeant's eyes.

The baton came up. "He's within his rights, sergeant," the ensign added.

Manuel stood absolutely still.

"You one of McHenry's boys?" the sergeant asked. He kept the baton raised.

"I *will* report it." There was a quaver in the ensign's voice, but his jaw was set. "You'll answer to Voorbeck."

"So will you," the sergeant said. "The Old Man knows the difference between treating dirtsiders decent and letting them run loose. You don't." The baton lashed out and down, catching Manuel across the jaw; he fell to the ground, clutching at his face. "Report that if you want, ensign. See how far you get."

"I will. Now let's get on with this. Pursuant to the warrant, we're coming aboard," he added, to me.

They came on board and tracked mud everywhere, turning the whole inventory upside down to make sure I didn't have any more valves or filters hidden. They ran a bunch of decrypts against the computer without finding any more than a perfectly normal second set of books—that was just a misdemeanor citation. Mentally I counted my blessings as they passed up the evidence of the TBN transmitter and completely missed all three weapons caches, since either of those would have gotten me shot right there, but it was a poor consolation watching them rip through months of careful sorting, arrangement, and preparation. The sergeant deliberately purged part of my business records, just for spite.

At the end of it they had everything they had come for, and some things they hadn't, all bundled up on the deck. "Your warrant didn't call for you to grab all the religious books," I pointed out.

"They'll be returned after Superstition Control looks them over," the ensign said. "They're still your property. Here's the payment for the valves and filters."

It was a check on the Bank of Bothasburg. "I'm afraid FundGram Terra has suspended operations 'til further notice," he added, not looking at me.

The sergeant looked me straight in the eye as he added, "So with surface mail and turn around time in the OrbiTransits, you should have your money in about a month-and-a-half; be sure you stick around to collect it. Of course, with brig time, that shouldn't be hard." He smiled; I kept my face relaxed and perfectly still.

"Careful, you'll drop those," he added to the NF trooper picking up the Bibles and tracts, and threw the whole pile over the side, making a loud splash and spraying water on everybody.

The ensign opened his mouth and closed it once. I didn't even do that; I didn't want to be charged with water pollution as well.

They left without another word. Manuel was still sitting on the bank. "How's your jaw?" I asked him.

"It stings. Nothing serious. Did you have anything hidden?" he asked.

"No valves or filters. Things happened too fast. God, I'm sorry, Manuel. They got the works. If you want them you'll have to buy at the GXS now. I might be able to lend you a few decicredits if you're hard up—no interest, of course, this is between friends."

He shook his head. "Other people will need that worse than I will. And you shouldn't risk getting busted. They're out to get you now, Saul. See you next meeting."

I nodded. "Good luck."

He turned abruptly; a thought struck him. "You know, they usually don't know that jet fuel's gotten into the river 'til their intakes downstream catch it."

"They've caught it by now." I couldn't see why he was so interested.

"But they couldn't have at the time they sent out the cosmorines to get your valves and filters."

He was right. "They knew it was going to happen. They dumped the fuel on purpose," I said.

Manuel nodded. "I think word of that should spread." I noticed that his cheek was turning angry red where the baton had clipped it.

"You're absolutely right," I said; then I made him come in and use some ice on that bruise. He left in a hurry, anyway—he wanted to see Mary off when she went to work.

HE PROBABLY didn't have time to do much more than tell her about what had happened and kiss her goodbye before the hoverbus picked her up to take her to the base. He looked the situation over and did some figuring; baby carrots were currently in demand at the Officer's Mess. Six bushels should give him what he needed; taking that much now would cost a third of the crop come fall, but there wasn't much else to be done.

It was nine o'clock by the time he finished pulling them, and because of the drought the carrots were small. It was really more than half of the crop. He got them into the six 35-liter canisters and loaded the canisters into the surrey. Fortunately the windmill that drove his e-rig had been running unseasonably steady, and there was a fresh, full hydrogen cylinder to strap in—he wouldn't need to buy a refill to get back. With a last glance around the farm, he started for town.

As he came down the road, he saw old Sam Klein standing there at the hoverbus stop and pulled over. "Need a ride into town?"

"That's what I'm out here for. The boys are all busy trying to tame the ram, and I got deputized to go for parts."

"Well, jump in, the front seat's empty."

"It is Manuel, right?" he said as he got in.

"Naw, it's Voorbeck. I'm learning to do voices."

They were off with a little whirr and popping noise; "I'm gonna have to adjust the timing again," Manuel said. "You'd think with only two cylinders this thing could keep them straight."

There was a thump as they hit a pothole. "I might pump up the shocks a little too," he added.

Sam nodded. "Did you hear the bad news yet?"

"You mean, besides the jet fuel in the river? I don't think so. What's up?"

"Charlie Perry just took out a short term. They got him."

"What happened?"

"Same as always. OrbiTransit wiped out his windmill—backwash took the whole derrick down. Complete loss, and the insurance people at the GXS won't pay because it was an 'unforseeable accident involving proprietary rights to airspace.'"

Manuel spat over the side of the truck. "Have they been after Prissy yet?"

"Yeah. She's hiding out somewhere. They took Wes and gave him a beating, trying to find her, but if he knew he didn't tell. They gave him a scar on his face he'll carry to his grave—he's crazier and madder than ever."

"I'll bet. A lot of us are getting madder."

Sam shrugged. "I've been afraid of that for a long time...but I guess if it comes, it comes. I just hope I can live through it with my family, I guess."

"You think we're going to fight?" Manuel asked. "I thought you were against it, trying to hold it down."

"I am. But I can read the handwriting on the wall. This last dumping has to have been on purpose. Mostly I think to run Saul out of the area, but there's a couple of downstream farms that'll get forced onto short-terms, also. Maybe we'd just have taken it a couple of years ago; but Saul's class last night got some people thinking, and even if he cuts and runs, he's already revived the idea of resistance where a lot of people had lost it. Maybe a Gandhi or a King could keep this on the level of nonviolent protest, but I don't think we have anyone like that...so I'd say there's ugly times ahead."

"It's ugly enough right now." Manuel swerved to miss a pothole. "All the time. The best farmer in this district doesn't make enough to keep his head an inch out of the water. And every time the crops come in good, the GXS drops their buying price through the floor and jacks their selling price through the ceiling. I even get sick of the posters in town.''

"'Work Hard and Get Ahead?'"

"Yeah, that one and all the others. It's true, is what bothers me. If any skyboy worked as many hours as hard as we do, he'd be rich. But we have to do that just to break even. They're crazy, Sam, and I'm getting tired of humoring them.''

"I know what you mean," Sam said. "I just wish I had a good answer for you. Anyway, town's coming up; we should talk about something else. How do you feel about the game next Sunday?''

"If Jesus will take care of the weather, I'll take care of third base. You want a ride back?''

"Don't wait for me."

"The day's shot already. It's no trouble. I'll wait with the surrey if you're not there when I'm through with business.''

There were forty or fifty surreys pulled up outside the GXS compound. As Manuel went in, he noticed that someone had scribbled on the familiar "Work Hard and Get Ahead" poster. Under the picture of the joyous farmer leaping up from Earth into the open arms of the skyboys at Gagaringrad Immigration Center, there was a scrawled "Perfect Solution to the Servant Problem." He looked up from it, glancing at the fenced compound that was the local brig, and went on in.

There were nine desks open in the trade office, and farmers were lined up at every one of them. Manuel noticed the ensign who had done the buy-out that morning sitting at one of them, joking and trying to make a grim-faced Israel Curran laugh—with no success. On an impulse, Manuel got into that line.

As he moved up the line, he studied the ensign. His tunic was pulling out of his pants; the boots under the table were unpolished and scuffed. The ensign himself didn't look to be over twenty.

Maybe it would be worth trying something. "I brought six bushels because I wanted to get some windmill parts and some cash, too," Manuel said, as the ensign went over the papers. Oh, yes, definitely very young.

"How much were you thinking of for the valve?"

"Call it half a bushel," Manuel offered magnanimously.

"Maybe for two bushels..." the young man said, trying to look shrewd.

"One," Manuel said. "And the other five for a windmill generator."

"I don't want to cheat you, but that's silly. Let's stick at two, and for the other four you can have a blade control cyber unit—"

Manuel looked stubborn.

"With, say, two credits thrown in?" the ensign added hastily.

Manuel spread his hands and looked mournful. "You guys are too damn smart. Okay, it's a deal. The carrots are out in the surrey."

The skyboy turned around to get the valve and cyber unit for him; Manuel helped himself to two pens and a stapler from the desk. Then they went out to the surrey and got the canisters.

As they lifted the canisters onto the dolly, the skyboy asked, "What's your name? You look familiar."

"Manuel Proxman."

"I'm Jefferson Smith. Do you live near here?"

"Up river toward the landing field..." He was beginning to wonder what this cosmorine was up to—this wasn't the usual prying; it was more like childish curiosity.

"Have they been dumping jet fuel again?"

"I don't know. It looked like jet fuel." Just what was going on here? Officially the landing field people never dumped anything. There were occasional "accidents," paid at ten percent of value, and "spills from undetected former dumps," on which nothing was paid. But no one officially ever "dumped" anything.

The skyboy put the last canister onto the dolly. "I don't have anything to do with the dumping. I filed a protest about it spaceside. They told me to mind my own business." With a grunt, Manuel pushed the dolly up the ramp into the galley; the ensign followed. "There are a lot of things that just aren't fair down here. Not that I can do much about it. Every time I mention it to my father, he starts asking about subversion rates and how full we keep the brig. He doesn't understand a thing about other cultures—none of the oldtimers do. Even if they do have private centrifuged gardens in their rooms and folk art on their walls.''

They got the carrots stowed in the galley without too much further conversation expended. As they came out, they almost collided with Voorbeck.

Manuel grinned with all the delight he could manage—quite a bit considering what he'd just gotten for his six bushels. He often said his favorite sign of the many in the GXS was the one over each desk that said "All deals final unless merchandise defective."

"Free Citizen Proxman," Voorbeck said. The commander was in good form that day—his boots practically glowed, not a hair out of place, blue eyes as keen as ever. "What brings you into town?"

Manuel had taken off his cap and was holding it in front of him. Though he had put one over on the GXS, and Voorbeck's honor would let him keep it, if the jet fuel in the river signalled anything coming up it would be a good idea to be on Voorbeck's good side. "Something gunked up the hydraulic ram," Manuel said. "And the backup cyber for my windmill got left out in the rain."

He had long ago learned that Voorbeck would always believe any stupid story of neglect.

"And what did you skin Ensign Smith here for?"

"All deals final," Manuel said, grinning so hard that his face hurt.

Voorbeck nodded. "Quite right. Let me throw in a decicredit for the wine to celebrate." He flipped Manuel a coin, and dismissed him with a wave of his hand.

When Manuel told me about it later, he said he was startled to realize, just then, that Voorbeck was fond of him—that that was why the commander always stopped to talk and sometimes gave him money. Behind him, he could hear the ensign getting a blistering chewing-out. He went across the square to the small goods store, whistling and thinking idly that it was a pretty strange world.

Sam was also headed for the store, guided by a small girl very intent on the responsibility.

"It's okay, Susie, I'll take him from here," Manuel said.

"I guess I can trust this one. Thank you, Susie," Sam said. She went skipping away to rejoin her parents.

"How'd you do?" Sam asked casually.

"That new ensign, Smith, he's easy to trade with. Got my valve and a windmill cyber for Charlie, plus two credits in change. And Voorbeck just flipped me a decicredit for his conscience."

"Sharp trading. How'd you do in free trade?"

"Some pens and a stapler Saul might take in trade. They're starting to chain down the expensive stuff, and I didn't bring my wire cutters."

"Serious oversight. As your spiritual advisor, I remind you that the Lord favors the prepared. Any other business in town?"

"I thought maybe I'd get spices and coffee for Mary at the general store. We haven't had anything but salt, pepper, and garden herbs these past few weeks, and we've been drinking dandelion root since June. You have time to stick around?"

"The boys are working on that ram faster and better than I can. The longer we take, the less there'll be for me to do when I get home."

Billy McHenry was on counter at the store. "What can I do for you?"

"What will eight decicredits buy in chili powder, cloves, cinnamon, oregano, and—let me think—uh, nutmeg—if it also covers five pounds of coffee?"

"Hmm . . . call it three ounces of each. Spices are cheap this month."

"Big surplus? I thought that couldn't happen with the Planned Free Market," Sam said.

"Part of the Plan is dropping any mistakes on you," Billy said, carefully dialing up the order. "They had a lot of trouble in Zanzibar this year. All kinds of rioting all spring. They ended up confiscating most of the crop, which ordinarily they'd have burned, but a bunch of tourists from spaceside had come up with the idea of doing a real old-fashioned voyage, clipper ship and all, so they hired a Sea Gypsy crew, loaded up with cloves, and sailed all the way to New York Harbor. Unloaded right on a couple of the highest old piers, at low tide, of course. But instead of just letting it wash away, they insisted it had to have something 'authentic' done with it. The brass didn't want too much of anything valuable getting into the Sea Gypsy trade, so they scooped it up and shipped it out space-a to every GXS in North America. We're supposed to unload it as fast as we can."

"Isn't that classified?" Sam asked.

"Yeah. But go ahead and put it in Saul's newspaper, as far as I'm concerned."

Manuel looked down at the counter. There was a *Life of St. Francis* lying there. "You need to hide that," he said. "What's happened?"

"'After due investigation' they've figured out that I'm 'going native' and 'getting dirt under my fingernails,' as they put it. Linsmann's got me."

"But I thought that—" Sam was startled.

"Besides being Steward, he's also Chief of Subversion Control. A fact I didn't know either until he and Voorbeck took me aside and informed me I'm going spaceside in a week—to be deprogged."

"Brain surgery? Shock?" Sam was pale.

"Not quite that bad. They just put me in a box with a multiencephalocorder—the 'MEC Machine' that your mother probably threatened you with—and keep me awake and spaced out on drugs while they yell at me. When the MEC says I really mean what they tell me to say, they let me out. I'll probably be out in time to see my father humiliated on the Convocation floor over this."

"I'm sorry," Manuel said.

"Yeah." Billy took the sealed spice jars out of the hopper and set them down on the counter. He glanced around once. "They don't ask questions under the MEC, you know—they just give you answers—so whatever I know will stay with me."

Sam coughed. "I hadn't thought of that, but it's nice to know."

There was a little patter as someone came up on the porch. "Do you want that coffee sealed?"

"Yes, please, in separate packs."

"Right." The gangly young man spun around and dialed it up; twenty packs of coffee dropped into the bin. "You did want that for a four-cup pot, didn't you? And by the way, you ought to return the screwdriver you just free traded off the rack."

Manuel put it back. "I learned a lot," McHenry said, with a smile. "That's why they have to wash it out of me. And at least this Sunday I can go to Mass and then to the ball game openly. They claim they're going to let me play a couple of innings, which probably is Christian charity."

Manuel nodded. "It's a shame they can't keep you longer. You're built for first base. Good luck." He turned to go, and Mary was standing there.

There was really no question at all. She wasn't wearing the gray cleaning-and-maintenance or the pink house-servant's uniform. The short dress unbuttoned nearly to the waist and the heavily powdered face told the whole story.

He stood dead still for a moment; finally he looked back to where Billy was trying to find some dirt to wipe up. "You might as well give me her order, Billy. Mary, I guess we're going home. You'll have to go back across the street and tell them you're leaving early today. Be back in a few minutes." She turned and left, still without saying a word.

Billy set a small box on the counter. "That goes on the company account, not your family account."

He nodded, picked it up, and dropped it in the bag with his other things. "See you Sunday. Send a line drive my way." He tried to smile, but it didn't work, so he just went out and sat down on the concrete stoop.

Sam came out behind him. "Come on, Manuel, they'll get you for loitering. You can't afford three days in the brig."

The younger man got up and shuffled along toward the truck, Sam hanging on his elbow. "Manuel, sure as sin I thought you knew."

"I did. Sort of. I'd just never seen her in uniform before, and we never talked about it." He rattled the bag. "Birth control pills. She couldn't work if she got pregnant. That's why we don't have any kids and we've been married a year."

"She'd have gotten pregnancy leave and job security. That wasn't the reason." Sam said. "You should ask her about that. You're in shock right now—don't do anything while you're upset. You—"

"Don't worry," Manuel said. He swallowed hard. "I know all that. And I love her." He cried a little there, leaning against the surrey, Sam's hand resting on his shoulder.

An hour later, driving back with Mary beside him and Sam perched in the back, he pulled up at Sam's place. "Would you mind guiding me up to the door, Manuel?" Sam asked.

As they went up the path, Sam said in a low voice, "Are you going to Saul tonight?"

"Maybe."

"I guess it had to come." The old man's voice had a flat, dead sound to it. "You know there won't be much choice. They're after him as it is. He can't just hide you. You'll have to—"

"We'll have a talk," Manuel said firmly. "What we decide, we decide."

"Can you stand a little scripture?"

"I've turned the other cheek enough."

"And besides, he came not to bring peace but a sword. No, I meant Matthew 26: 'The Son of Man goeth as it is written of him: but woe unto that man by whom the Son of Man is betrayed! It had been good for that man if he had not been born.' In other words, it's a bad idea to get caught in history."

Manuel shrugged and turned away, leaving Sam at his door.

OF COURSE, I knew about what happened in town from what Sam and Manuel told me later. For the next part, I only have my own guess, but I knew them both well, saw as much of their marriage as any outsider can see of anybody's, and this is what I've always imagined happening as they bumped home down the crumbling old highway in the blistering summer afternoon.

After a long while, Manuel said, "Why didn't we ever have any children?"

Mary turned to him. Her voice was very soft, as it always was when he was upset. "I took the pills because I want our child to be your child. I know I might get cancer any day, at my age, but I didn't want to bear you a skyboy bastard. I'm sorry."

"They have a pill to keep them sterile. They don't waste their precious sperm on us. You didn't have to—"

"Officers don't have to take the pill, and Voorbeck doesn't. He says he values his manhood, and a few of his bastards would improve our breeding stock."

"You did right, then." He let a breath out. "Did he give you the bruises?"

"I didn't know you'd seen those! I dress in the dark—"

"I saw once, by accident. You're marked up a lot."

"I was sixteen when Voorbeck bought my family's contract. I'd only been married to James a few months. You have to be married a year before you don't count as a worker in your parents' household. That was a long time ago...and there've been a lot of scars since then." She sat straight up. "And you didn't know! You didn't want to know! You thought James put them all there!"

"No, I didn't. I'm sorry."

"He can't manage unless he's the master and I'm dirty, so once a day I put on the dog collar and—"

"Shut up. You're mad. You have every right to be. But you probably don't want me to know those things, even now. Later, when you're calmer, if you want, you can tell me."

The fight went out of her; she sagged dully into the seat. "I have to go back tomorrow. How can we live without the benefits package? And there aren't any jobs for men."

"I don't know. We'll have to think."

The rest of daylight would have gone into getting the ram working, making sure the tank was clean, and checking over the turbine and generator. There was enough of a breeze to run the house without using water power as well, so he just let the tank fill and got some power reserve back.

It would have been dark before the last time he climbed down the tower from the tank. When he came into the house, Mary was roasting a piglet. "I know it's wasting food, and we can't afford to do it, but it *is* your favorite, and you got the cloves and some stuff in the herb garden came in—"

"It's all right, Mary. We both need something nice." He kissed her on the cheek.

He went out to the cool house to get some of the good wine, and by then the wind had picked up a little and they could turn on the air conditioner. I like to imagine they spent a long time over dinner, sitting with arms around each other's waists, sipping wine and not saying anything. Finally, Manuel got up.

"I'm going to go talk to Saul," he said. "About what we can do."

Mary got up beside him. "Do you want me to come?"

"I can't stop you if you want to."

"It looks like it's either this or back to Voorbeck. I'm coming with you."

As he closed the door, Manuel said, "I'm glad." They went down the path to the rowboat hand in hand.

IN THOSE DAYS I slept lightly; it came with both my occupations. By the time they were two dark shadows moving toward the gangplank, I was wide awake, sitting in front of my cabin with a shotgun across my lap.

"What do you want?"

"We've got trouble. We need to talk to you."

"Manuel and Mary?"

"Yeah."

"Come on in then." I led them down the gangplank and into the cabin, pulling the inside blackout shutters over the windows before I flipped on the light. "What can I do for you?" I asked, setting on a pot of coffee.

They told me their story in bits and pieces, interrupting each other and adding points as they went. At first when they'd stop I'd ask questions, but after a while they got going and I just shut up and listened.

"Have a seat," I said, as they finished. "The cabin's too low to stand in and you'll give your necks a crick." They sat, and I poured the coffee for all of us. "I guess we could run you up to the lake and see what we can do about getting you hidden somewhere away from the skyboy stations, or maybe taking you on a bigger ship if I can find one on short notice. I know it's tough, but we'd have to leave tonight to do that."

I'm not sure why I offered that, even now—it was contrary to orders, to say the least—but I'm still glad I did, and I sometimes wonder what would have happened if they'd taken me up on it.

Anyway, they didn't. Manuel gave a little twitch of the shoulders, not even a real shrug; Mary flatly said, "No. You know what we're here for. You try to hide your views to be fair, but we know what you'd like to see happen around here. What we're saying is, we're ready, let's do it—whatever the others decide."

I stared up into the electric light, letting it blind me a little. I was thinking as hard as I could and still wasn't getting any place I wanted to get to. I knew my duty to the Confederation. I knew what a sober analysis of our odds would be if we launched an armed struggle. And I knew Mary and Manuel, as people and as friends.

What I didn't know was whether to be a loyal agent, a realistic analyst, or an honest friend.

"You don't like to push anyone into anything dangerous, do you, Saul?" Mary asked.

"No, I don't."

"But you aren't," Manuel said. "It's our fight. All you've done is make us think. We're grateful, I guess. But now...we're going to fight. You can join us if you want. That's what we came to tell you."

For a long time after that, I would tell myself that with that invitation I had lost my responsibility, and I only had to follow and help, which put me well within Mendenhall's orders without making me the guilty party. Still, I didn't say yes; I said, "All right, what's the thing we can do to them—say us plus the Perrys—that will hurt them the most?"

There was a long awkward silence. "We could blow a bunch of them up with a hydrogen cylinder," Manuel said, "and then run into the Black Swamp and hope some more people would come to join us."

I was suddenly beginning to realize just how meager my intellectual resources were for this. Mendenhall's little "subversion seminar" six months before hadn't been much help. We had all dutifully read the IRA and Tupa literature, and listened to two old coots who claimed to have gone through KGB school in the early 2000s, but in my case, the political stuff had stuck better than the military. And my combat experience was all at inside fighting in space cities—want to know how to run a back-and-bag on a J-turn corridor with a vertical lock? I'm your boy. Want to know how to fight a protracted guerrilla war in a swamp? You want Francis Marion, or better yet Osceola...

"It seems to me," Mary began, and in ten minutes she'd laid out pretty much the maps and timetable we ended up using, covering my desk with little scribbled notes and filling a lot of space in the computer.

That's probably the thing the newsmen and historians have asked me about the most. All I can say is, Mary had an instinctive feel for it that never steered us wrong; a keen sense of how long each thing would take, how far apart things were, and where the hitches would be. It was a knack, something I guess she was born with. I once was beaten nine games in a row by an eight-year-old I'd just taught chess to; some friends of mine over in Team Firth were astonished when their retarded son taught himself to play the piano.

There's a lot of talent of all sorts that never gets found. It was a big stroke of fortune for me to find Mary—most of the other agents had no such luck.

On the other hand, I'm not sure it was lucky for her.

8

"The biggest bitch was getting these cylinders filled," Charlie whispered. "The whole time we kept rubbing ice on it and it kept getting hotter. I was ready to swear the farm was going to get blown to bits any minute. Not that it matters, I guess, now."

"We're sixty percent over rated pressure on this one, with a two to one by volume hydrogen-oxygen mix," Wesley said, patting it gingerly. "Will that do it?"

"Oh, yeah," I said. "Let's get going." Millimeter by millimeter, we lowered the tank into an empty fuel drum. I packed a small, precious wad of plastic explosive into the nozzle connector, getting it as far in as I could; we were using up an alarming portion of things I had brought on this first raid, but I wanted to make sure that this one, when we'd be catching them flat-footed, did the maximum damage it could. "Okay, now we hook the radio fuse to the cap, and the cap to the charge. That takes care of the explosive part. Let's put in the jet fuel next to cushion things."

Manuel started pouring in the hundred liters or so of jet fuel blobs we had retrieved from the dump. "This stuff burns hot, but it make such a mess nobody ever uses it," Manuel said. "Is it supposed to explode or something?"

I shook my head; for a moment I wanted to avoid the subject, then I wanted to rub his nose in it. "It sticks to skin and clothing. It makes pretty good napalm."

He handed me a bucket; we poured more in. With the drum half full, we shoveled the nails and broken glass carefully down the sides, away from the cylinder, until the barrel was full. "Pull it up now?" Wesley asked.

"Might as well," Charlie said. "Less conspicuous, and it's already pretty dark." We threw the line over the tree limb, attached it, and hauled the barrel up into the tree, maybe six meters above the winding dirt road that led from the back of the GXS compound to the river. That part of things had been unexpectedly simple, probably because as yet the Resistance hadn't done anything more illegal than break curfew—not that the skyboy who found that gadget wouldn't hang us on the spot.

Just as I finished making the line fast—I never will be able to trust landlubbers to tie a knot—Mary, on lookout on the GXS side, gave a low whistle, and we all headed into the bushes. Mary and Prissy joined us a few minutes later. "Just Jesse Snyder going home," the girl said.

"Jesse's too tight with the skyboys," her father grunted. "We're going to have trouble with him."

Wes nodded. "Maybe we could raid his place, set a couple of fires, smash his windmill. If he cooperates with the skyboys, I mean."

Charlie shook his head. "That wasn't exactly what I had in mind. I don't really know how we can deal with it. I just know it's going to be trouble. What time is it, anyway?"

It was eight thirty, not even near time, so we all stretched out among the equipment and pretended to go to sleep. I guess I could have set out sentries, but I figured most of us wouldn't be able to sleep.

I certainly couldn't. I kept turning it over in my head, trying to make some kind of sense of the whole business. The agreement on Voorbeck as target number one had had a lot of good reasons behind it: he was a visible, unpopular symbol, and because the connection to Mary was well-known, people who didn't understand the politics would still feel some sympathy for Manuel.

But we had sat down and planned it calmly.

Fighting in space, if you're a common soldier like I was, isn't like that. You jump through the port as fast as you can, kill the people that are facing you, and help the ones going the same direction as you are. It's bloody and gruesome, and at distances of a meter or two anything but impersonal. But there's no real calculation to it. You just pick your door, go through it, and "kill until killed."

What we were planning felt more like murder than war. I knew, of course, that Voorbeck had committed any number of murders and called them justice or law enforcement or protecting the rights of citizens. Beating a tied-up James to death hadn't been exactly heroic. But somehow, warfare was supposed to be—

Glorious, that was the word, and Kwanza was dead right. I was thinking in terms of another kind of war in another kind of place. This was people's war, not the kind of war I'd been in—not gallant, personal, face-to-face combat fought a few minutes from hot showers and emergency rooms, but an ugly, drawn-out contest of savagery fought to exhaustion. Murder was basic to it. If one of my students had made that sentimental mistake, I'd have quite properly jumped all over him.

Okay, so Voorbeck had to die. I was just glad, way down in my guts, that I didn't have to do it myself, and ashamed, somewhere around there, that I felt that way.

And then I'd start to think that perhaps I felt that way because what we were planning *was* murder, and the whole cycle would start over again. I found myself passionately wishing for Kwanza to talk to, and then for a quiet evening at Roget's, and by the time it was finally midnight I think I had wished to be teaching a giant freshman section of Bureaucracy 101, Ethics and Epistemology of Filling Out Forms.

There was a faint beep from my watch and I almost jumped out of my skin. "Time," I said. Everyone was up and moving at once; I don't think anyone slept.

Mary and Prissy slipped around behind some bushes to get into their uniforms and makeup; the rest of us concentrated on the guns. Manuel and Charlie had flatly refused automatic weapons, even though they admitted we needed every bit of firepower we could get. They were comfortable with their big, awkward deer rifles, and that was all there was to it. Wes and I had little low-caliber high-rate-of-fire jobs, cooked up by the engineers on Juno (though I didn't tell Wes that). Basically they were an improvement on the old British Sten and Chinese "burp" guns—auto weapons that were easy to home-build copies of, and to hand-load for. All of us wore night-vision goggles, simple little amplifiers that had the added advantage of hiding most of our faces.

"Okay, by the numbers," I said. Even though it was Mary's plan, and I had told them that I had never done anything like this before either, the Sea Gypsy reputation had gotten me elected chief of operations. "Mary, I'm declaring it exactly midnight . . . now."

She set her watch. I went on. "We'll make our break-in at 12:25 or as shortly after as we can manage. Manuel starts exactly eight minutes after Wes and Charlie get through the door. By Mary's figures, that gives the group in the mess hall twelve minutes before you need to get going. We all rendezvous at the agreed point no later than 12:50—12:47 is the target. Right?"

"That's the way it works out," she agreed. "Prissy, you have your part down?"

The girl nodded. The uniform and makeup made her look even younger; back on Eros, girls her age were playing with toy sunsailers. "I hope so," she said. "What if there's more than one of them?"

Mary sighed. "Then it will have to be your judgment. Saul, how many can you handle?"

"Two is pushing it," I said. "But we might be able to do something else, depending on what we find. Try not to worry—this isn't really dangerous," I said, giving her a smile I didn't feel.

"Remember, Prissy," Mary added, "the hotter you get the man the less he'll be thinking and the easier it will be for Saul. If you can get him to take his pants down, he'll be almost helpless for a few seconds."

Charlie nodded. "Don't worry about what I might think. Just get back safe."

"I just want to get it right," she said. She was huddled against her father, who was not looking at her.

Mary looked up from her watch. "12:04. I'm going."

And she slipped away. "Okay, six minutes and then we move," I said. They all nodded, and then we sat there, alone with our thoughts. The wind in the trees was soft, with a strong hint of rain in it; there were no stars. It was warm and pleasant; the kind of night when I might have slept out on the deck.

I found myself wishing that that was exactly what I was doing.

The watch beeped again, and I jumped with it. "Let's move," I said. "Stay in order—careful with that second gas cylinder."

Prissy Perry and I led the little parade; Wes and Charlie were behind us, carrying the gas cylinder, with Manuel covering our rear. It was unlikely that anybody would be coming up this way from the river at this hour, but it was possible. After all, we were counting on Mary and Priscilla doing things that were far from uncommon.

Mary said later that she had no trouble at all; she just told the captain at the night desk that she was supposed to meet Voorbeck in the mess hall, and in she went. The only hitch was a brief second when she was afraid the captain was going to call Voorbeck and tell him that his "friend" was here.

It was different with us. The perimeter guard was at his post, all right, but he had company; they were talking and laughing, both of them. The second voice was unmistakable. "Linsmann," Priscilla said.

"We've got about three minutes to spare. We'll see if we can wait them out," I whispered. There was a good screen of brush up close to the perimeter there—that was why we had picked it—but it was still ten meters of open ground.

I noticed the girl's fingers had clamped on my arm, hard enough to hurt. I let her hang on, anyway. Finally she reached down and turned my wrist, checking my watch. It showed 12:24.

I thought "wait" but didn't say it; she got up and walked straight toward them. She was too far away for me to hear what she said, but the sentry turned around to watch the base instead of the perimeter, and Linsmann followed her straight back to the bushes, his arm around her shoulders with one hand clamped on her breast. I nudged Wes, who drew his knife and raced silently toward the sentry.

Linsmann was leading Prissy down the little trail that ran to the road from there, the same way we had come. I went down the trail as quickly as I could in the dark without making noise, but he was hurrying her along. She must have known they were going too fast for me to keep up; I heard her asking him to kiss her, and at the next bend in the trail I almost walked into them.

"Do you like this?" he demanded.

"I—it hurts. Please—I want you. Take off your pants, oh, please," she was gasping. "You're scaring me with the knife."

That was meant for me. I hadn't been able to see that he had a knife. There was a ripping noise as he slashed her dress open. Prissy's eyes were wide—she was staring at me.

I couldn't get in. With Linsmann's knife between them, there was no way to be sure of getting him before he got her. I kept circling, closing with his back, coming to within a step of him; he was too engrossed in what he was doing to Prissy to notice me. "It's supposed to hurt," he said. "You're supposed to be scared. You've got the nicest big tits. Now this is going to hurt more—"

I heard her gasp and sob, and suddenly they were fighting for the knife; she had pushed it out to the side, both her hands locked on his wrist. I slashed out, cutting across the back of his hand; he dropped the knife.

I stepped in, my free hand going under his Adam's apple and around to catch his collar. I had timed it right—at the bottom of his exhale, so that he couldn't yell even if he broke the grip—and he had just time enough to stiffen before I slammed the blade into his kidneys, once, twice, three times on the right, then on the left, never letting go of the neck, then around front and up in under the rib cage, as they'd taught us in the dojo. I held the strangle grip for a mental count of ten, them dumped him and jumped back; he was dead or dying. "Prissy," I whispered, "are you okay? Did he hurt you?"

She was on the ground, twisting grotesquely, her face distorted beyond recognition by pain. "What is it?" I started to ask.

Then I saw what was in his other hand. There was a dart in her belly; the stickergun lay by his hand. Standard issue for Subversion Control, I realized; of course he carried one.

When I looked back, she was dead.

Wesley was suddenly at my side. "He killed her," he said. "It's what he always meant to do..." He knelt by Linsmann's corpse.

Charlie and Manuel came running up. Charlie rushed to Prissy; Manuel stood and stared at the scene.

Wes found leverage and rolled Linsmann over. Before I could stop him, he crouched over the corpse and slashed the throat.

"What—!" Charlie hissed.

Paying no attention, Wes swung the knife wildly, gashing the cosmorine's corpse shallowly in a dozen places on the face, chest, and stomach. "He's dead," I said, stupidly.

"What are you doing?" Charlie gagged. "Stop it!"

Wes stood up, breathing hard. He bent down again, and gently laid his knife in Priscilla's hand. "No matter who finds them, Priss will get a decent burial and Linsmann's name is shit. What would you think if you found them like this?" He gestured. "We can't carry her, and this way she's taken care of. Besides, this should get the farms all roused up like nothing else. I'm sorry she's dead, but this way we don't have to take care of her and she can still do us some good. She'd have wanted it that way." He was beginning to whine, a little, and I was already too sick without that.

"Come on. We're behind schedule. Did you get the guard?" I pulled Charlie with me as we went.

Wesley sounded very satisfied. "Right across the throat. I dragged him over into the brush afterwards. The way's clear."

My watch showed 12:33 as I took my slicing wheel and cut a hole two meters square in the fence; there would be a sentry check in twelve minutes. Charlie and Wes staggered through the gap, carrying the second hydrogen cylinder, pushing themselves to get the heavy thing across the open compound quickly. A light flared for a moment as Mary opened the back door to the mess hall, then cut the light. The two men headed for the small dark square.

"That will kill Charlie when it sinks in," Manuel said.

The light flared again, as Mary turned it on to show us the cylinder going inside, then switched it off. "12:35," I said. "You go in at 12:43."

"Yeah." He patted the rifle affectionately. "Got a surprise for Voorbeck." I saw his lips twitch into a smile, but couldn't see his eyes behind the light amplifier; the effect was ghastly, like a wink from a hooded executioner.

Mary told me later that getting the cylinder wedged between the hydrogen tanks in the mess hall, and getting the timer set, was a frantic, desperate little operation, and that the clock seemed to spin out of control as they struggled to get it done. For us the wait seemed like forever.

At last I cued Manuel, and he went through the fence like a greased shadow, sprinting through the base toward Voorbeck's quarters. I sat there, watching my watch and thinking. I noticed a strange scent on my sleeve, a funny odor—and then realized that it was the cheap scent Priscilla had sprayed herself with as part of the outfit. Enlisted men were supposed to like them heavily perfumed. Somehow I imagined that I could smell Prissy as well, under the cheap scent, a bright, pleasant, healthy young kid . . .

It was a relief when I heard the shots. Manuel had smashed the window by Voorbeck's bed, whipped the rifle to his shoulder, and shot the commander full in the face as he sat up in bed. The next shot was fired at the aide who burst in; it didn't hit him, but it kept him on the floor while Manuel fired three more shots, hitting three widely-spaced barracks windows.

The three shots were the agreed-on signal; I looked up to see Mary and the Perrys running across the open ground toward me. Without the cylinder, it was less than a minute for them to get to me, but lights were flipping on all over, and as they ran to the hole in the fence the big spotlight on top of Headquarters came on, beginning to sweep the field. Charlie turned, leaning back against the fence, swung the rifle to his shoulder, and shot the man operating the spotlight; he fell down the headquarters roof, and the light pointed crazily up into the sky.

The lights came on in the barracks nearest us; Wes swung his gun, spraying the windows. Charlie turned and swatted him. "Stop that! We've got to let them get to the mess hall!"

Wes glared at his father; for a moment I was afraid I was about to see one of them shot dead, but the son nodded, barely. We all moved back from the fence into the brush to wait for Manuel.

He burst from between two buildings, scrambling wildly. All across the base we could see cosmorines, most of them half-dressed, pouring in toward the front door of the mess hall, the assembly point for emergencies. He was out of most of their paths, but as he came nearer we could hear shouting behind him. Four or five men were chasing him.

I got up and ran for the hole in the fence, wondering the whole time why none of them had fired. Maybe they wanted to take him alive. I slapped the button on the side of my light amplifier, jarring my face a little as I kicked it up to its highest setting, and turned the knob for magnification. I looked carefully at Manuel's pursuers, pointed the gun to miss Manuel, shut my eyes, and blazed away; the amplified light of the muzzle flash was like hot sunlight on my face, blinding even through my eyelids.

I opened my eyes, blinking, and saw that they had all flung themselves down, except for the one nearest Manuel. They were all, I suddenly realized, completely unarmed. In fact, most of them were Native Forces. They must have simply chased Manuel when they saw him, not thinking of any danger to themselves.

The one still chasing Manuel was wearing an ensign's uniform; I suddenly recognized him as Jefferson Smith, the one who had handled the buyout and who Manuel had cheated. Manuel was outdistancing him easily, but the young officer was gamely trying to keep up—I don't think he had realized that the men behind him weren't with him anymore, and that there was nothing more he could do. I could have shot him easily, but something about that desperate boy's face bent on a pointless errand stopped me. I lowered my gun and waved Manuel on.

There was a short burst from Wesley's gun, and Smith crumpled over, bits of him hitting the pavement behind. I stood staring at the body until Manuel leaped through the hole in the fence; a couple of wild shots went by us as other cosmorines came around the corner, and we raced back, diving into the brush and slipping around to the agreed meeting place.

The five of us lay there, breathing heavily, trying to gather our wits. There were shots all over the base, as panicky cosmorines fired at anything they saw moving and others shot back. "I yelled that there was mutiny in the Native Forces as I was running," Manuel said. "Maybe the cosmorines will do something useful for once."

Men boiled like ants around Headquarters, where someone had finally gotten the searchlight working, and into the mess hall, where officers shouted and bellowed, trying to get troops into their platoons and companies.

There was a deafening roar as the cylinder went off and took the storage tanks with it; the walls of the building blew outward and the roof rose, crumbling, a meter or so before crashing down onto the inferno beneath it. There were more men screaming than I had ever heard.

"Let's finish it," Manuel said, and we all rose and headed for the gate where the river road came into the base.

The explosion in the mess hall, besides killing almost a third of the garrison, had started fires all over and knocked out the main power. As we came up on the road ten minutes later, we saw by the fires that there were a few crews climbing into the hovercars. "There they are," Manuel said. He fired a shot at one of the hovercars; we heard the high shriek as it glanced off the armor.

Slapping fresh clips in, Wes and I opened up on the hovercars; at our range we weren't going to do any real damage, but we'd make them get their heads down, and more importantly we'd get their attention. We each squeezed off two whole clips in short bursts, brap, brap, brap, spraying around them; they all went flat to the ground, a few of them shooting back without looking up or aiming.

Then the searchlights on one hovercar lit up. Charlie shot one out; the heavy machine gun on another hovercar fired wildly in our direction, and we ducked and ran down the road, firing again to make sure they knew where we'd gone.

We seemed to run down that dirt road between the trees for hours, lungs aching and throats dry with dust, before we finally heard the whine of the hovercar starter engines behind us. We kept going, putting on whatever extra speed we could manage, until we got to the first bend Mary had picked. Wes ducked right and ran up the side of the ditch into the undergrowth at the bend.

Three more bends on the pale road in the dark, and Charlie and Manuel dropped off to take that post. By now we could hear the wound-up jets. They were on their way. Mary and I ran on; I had a nasty shin splint going, but I kept pounding it anyway. The woods smelled damp and dusty at the same time—it's amazing how much moisture there is in even a very dry forest. In the dark, the shadows on the road looked like holes, pits, rocks, but I did my best to remember that there wasn't much to trip over.

There was a sharp, high-pitched brapping noise in the distance; Wes had fired at them. We came around the curve and ran under the barrel; I had a stray thought that this would be a bad time to trip and fall on the button.

We ran up over the little ridge by the road and lay down; now we could hear rifle shots, along with the high scream of hovercar engines being pushed as hard as they'd go. By now, shot at from so many directions, they had convinced themselves they were pursuing a small army; they would try to cope with scattered fire by roaring past it to confront the "main body." At least, that was what Mary was betting on. I crawled forward to where I could see and took out the radio control, flipping the arming switch on, and resting a nervous finger on the firing button.

They came around the curves ahead of us, lights flashing wildly through the trees, engines howling, and suddenly they were charging through into our stretch of road—three of them, two gunboats and a troop-carrier, the carrier in the middle missing one of its two searchlights.

I flipped the trigger. The cylinder exploded—not as big a blast as the hydrogen tanks at HQ had made, but impressive, as close as we were. Nails, glass, and gobs of burning jet fuel sprayed everywhere; about two meters from Mary, a blob set dry leaves on fire.

The home-made bomb had burst between the lead two hovercars; their tops had been down, and the men on them took the full spray of shrapnel and napalm. The gunboat went spinning out of control and crashed among the trees; the troop carrier had been knocked down hard enough to take a hard bounce; bodies, some of them on fire, flew out of it.

The driver must have survived the explosion, because he set it down, but before it had even grounded the liquid-methane tank breached. There was a low, heavy crump and a jet of fire shot up into the trees.

The tail gunboat reared and flared her skirts getting stopped; I could see that one of the gunners was slumped over, but the other one was raking the woods and the driver seemed not to be hurt. They stopped short of the blazing troop carrier and whirled to head back to base; I stood up and shot half a clip at them, but they were higher than I was, as close as we were, and hovercar armor is heaviest on the sides and bottom. They went screaming back to base without even stopping to check for wounded—not that any wounded were likely, given what had happened to the other two craft.

"Are you all right?" I asked Mary.

"Yes," she said. "Better head back to the boat." We got up and got onto the road, walking down toward where I'd moored the *Spirit of Monroe*. "Charlie told me about Priscilla. That was terrible."

I nodded.

"Next time," Mary said, "I'll have things better planned."

"I thought it went pretty much the way your script did," I said.

"We ran way behind schedule. Prissy got killed."

"That's more or less average snafu for a military operation."

"Not for the ones I plan." She was adamant; I didn't see any reason to keep arguing with her, since sooner or later she'd learn. Besides, I knew perfectly well I couldn't have planned anything as well.

The others were waiting at the boat for us; no one seemed to have anything to say, so we all piled in and I started up the motor. Normally, of course, we'd have sailed, but I wanted to get some kilometers behind us, and hopefully get past the landing field before they figured out that they needed to guard the river. With a little luck, we would be deep in the Black Swamp before sunrise.

Mary took my hammock; Charlie, grumbling about beds that move, used the pull-down bunk. Wes stretched out and fell asleep in the bow. That left Manuel and me, sitting on the tiller bench.

We'd gone around two bends when Manuel pointed. "I left a light on on my ramtower. There it is."

I was going to ask him why he'd done that, but then I saw him shaking. He was crying, hard and ugly sobs that shook his whole body. He did that almost the whole way to the edge of the swamp; then he straightened up abruptly, sighed, and started giving me directions, as if nothing had happened.

As far as I know, after that, Manuel never cried again.

To tell the truth, I didn't plan it. I was in the right place at the right time. I was desperate to get something going after

Mendenhall's orders, and when Manuel and Mary had come to me I had hoped only to have one good raid and make the sky-boys spend a while hunting us in the swamps.

But the next afternoon, when we watched "True News," we began to realize what we'd done. I turned it on because it had become a habit with me—looking for news that might be leading up to the outbreak of Mendenhall's war. The rest were just around—temporarily there was not a lot for us to do—and came into the cabin after Manuel shouted.

"Hey, Matt Gomes is on 'True News'!"

He was, too, talking to a nervous-looking young reporter about the working-over the cosmorines had given him; apparently they had seized about twenty people and beaten them, trying to find out where we were. Then they showed pictures of all of us, taken from our citizen ID photos; mine was unaccountably missing from the files, so they showed a not-very-flattering sketch.

As always, the reporter stuck to the strict details, staying within the law by avoiding any mention of any private business that some viewer might "construe as having provoked the incident"; however, since cosmorines and the Protectorate Administration were government institutions, he was able to wrap it up with "And there we have it. Another outbreak of banditry in North America, threatening to make it another long, hot summer. The weary taxpayer settles in for another soaking in the name of civilizing Earth.

"Yet are these things truly inevitable? A habit of beating up the citizens that they are supposed to be guarding seems to possess the men of the Protectorate Administration. The brig here has been one of the fullest in North America, the flogging post one of the busiest. The old hands here will tell you that running a tight ship prevents trouble. But this latest incident can only make us all wonder; the late Nils Voorbeck ran a tight ship, and the trouble was certainly not prevented."

Then they turned over to some news about a new stellar probe that was apparently to be privately financed, and about a woman in Tereshkovagrad with thirty-one children in sixty years who was now pregnant again. "Well," Charlie said, "at least we made some news. People all over the Earth know about this now."

"It won't do much good if the next thing they hear is that we've all been caught and hanged," Mary said. "When was Clark Underhill supposed to be by?"

"Should be within an hour," Wes said. "Of course, he doesn't do much by the clock. He's hard to find, too."

Manuel nodded. "They tell me Theo's worse. Did he seem to think he could find us a good place for a base? Personally, I'd love to be able to get off the boat, and I bet Saul wouldn't mind us doing it."

"Amen," Wes said. "Yeah, in fact he has a place that he says should be a good camp for two or three hundred people to hide out in."

Mary laughed. "Even with being on the vid, I doubt we'll get more than ten recruits out of the whole district. But at least we won't be cramped."

In less than a week, we had almost a hundred people. Most of them had done something and then run—fired a shot at a hovercar or into a window on the base, set a fire somewhere in the GXS compound, beaten up a Native Forces trooper home on leave. Matt Gomes, goaded by revenge, had poisoned two pounds of ganjj and sold it to an officer that he knew was planning a party; that had filled the few remaining beds in the District Hospital.

Suddenly skyboys never went out in anything less than an armed party of ten; for trips of any distance, they took hovercars. We'd have figured ourselves for a raving success if we hadn't been so busy struggling to find ways to feed everyone; as it was, we weren't getting much more done than to patrol the swamp around our camp.

Manuel, to my surprise, seemed to be everyone's choice as leader. I'd have picked Mary myself, but I figured Earthsiders just had the typical attitudes of agricultural people about women.

After a day or two I gained a little respect for democracy, at least when practiced by people who all know everything about each other. Manuel was quiet, and not much of a speech-maker, but he listened carefully and had a good sense of priority. There was something spooky about how quiet he'd gotten to be in the past few days, but there was a feeling of strength and sureness about him, too.

About ten days after the attack on the GXS, we were holding a staff meeting. The Underhills had been added to the staff because they knew the swamps better than anyone else; Mary, Charlie, and I were the rest of it. Wes, I think, would have wanted to be in, but he wasn't obviously upset by his exclusion. If nothing else, he'd been cutting quite a swath through the young women in camp on the strength of his heroics in the first raid.

"Okay," Manuel said, "order of business for today; one, escape routes and evacuation; two, supplies; three, operations. Everyone agreed?" We all did. Manuel got things going. "Does everyone know what the escape routes business is about?"

Charlie Perry and the Underhills shook their heads. "Sort of," I said. "It's Mary's idea—"

"Then I'm in favor of it," Charlie said, triggering a laugh from everyone.

Manuel grinned; he liked it when people complimented Mary. "Okay. Let her tell it."

She nodded, tight-faced the way she always was when she was thinking about strategy. "Just seems to me that if I was in command over at the GXS or on the landing field, I'd be interested in finding out where this camp is—so I could hit it before it gets any bigger. The reason people are fighting back is that they can run to here. If this camp goes, so does the Resistance. So we can expect a big raid here as soon as they get better organized, which is as soon as Voorbeck's replacement gets down from orbit."

"And we need a back door to get out quick," Theo Underhill added, catching on.

"We were wondering when you'd ask about that," Clark said. "We have some ideas."

Manuel looked around. "It's a consensus, then. Mary and the Underhills work out the escape plans?" It was. "Okay, next step. Supplies. We need, according to Bea Gothenburg, something like forty-five times what we have of everything, just to feed and house people through the winter. Any ideas on where we get that?"

"Skyboys," Charlie said. "We take it."

Manuel nodded. "What and when?"

Charlie grinned. "I have this idea...the OrbiTransits are still coming in on a regular schedule; I guess they think that guard tower on the field is enough, along with the fences..."

"There's no problem with rushing one as soon as it lands," Mary said. "The problem is getting away with the loot. We could get pinned down inside the OrbiTransit, and they'd have lots of time to go for reinforcements. And even if we got away from the field all right, that's a long way to carry supplies across open country. Those hovercars could chase us right up to camp without any trouble. If we had the people to rush the control tower, guard tower, and barracks compound all at once—"

"What if we attacked the parked hovercars first, as a diversion?"

She sat quietly, thinking about it. "Maybe. Let's go over that later. This has some promise."

Manuel looked around; once again there was a consensus. "All right, operations. That's my proposal."

Everyone stuck out a downward-pointed thumb.

Blushing a little, and grinning sheepishly, he went on. "In a way, it's already something we're doing. The way people get to be good fighters is to fight. Some of our younger hotheads— Wes is an example that comes to mind—have been going out on night raids. A couple of nights ago they caught a party of sky-boys on foot and shot a couple of them, for example, and the night before that they got onto the base and cut a main power line.

"I think that kind of thing is good, especially if we can organize it. We might even be able to steal some supplies that way. What I want everyone to do is to look around for people who want to fight right away; I'll hold some kind of general meeting tomorrow night, if that's acceptable. I was thinking of appointing Wes as our Director of Harassment. Comments?"

"Good idea. And Wes needs something to keep him working," Clark said.

"Just so we limit their resources. We don't want any raiding parties bigger than five or ten people going out." Mary was brusque. "I don't want to piddle off resources on anything harebrained."

Charlie shrugged. "I'm hard on that boy. I don't know. He's sneaky and he fights dirty. You all know him. He's been a liar and a thief since before his mother died. But this job calls for a sneak, and he's got guts, and I probably don't give him a fair shake. You decide."

Manuel looked around. I thought about how fast and loose Wes could be with a gun—there had been little reason for some of things I had seen him do. On the other hand, he would certainly keep things hot for the skyboys, and that's what I was supposed to be doing. "Good with me," I said.

Everyone looked at Theo. "Give him a shot at it. He might grow."

Manuel nodded. "I make that three strong fors, one weak against, one neutral."

"I'm a for, too," Mary said. "I just don't want the operation getting bigger than its purpose."

"Okay, it's settled. Meeting will be at six tomorrow, here at the Council Tree. Any other business?"

There were a couple of little things, but the meeting broke up pretty quickly. On the way back to camp, Mary tapped my shoulder. "Hang back a minute," she said.

I waited.

"Who do you really work for?" she asked.

"The Under—"

"No. That stuff you had hidden in your boat is Orbital make—or beyond. You're from the Breakaways, aren't you? There's going to be another war." She looked straight into my eyes.

"Yes," I said.

"You'll help us against them?"

"That's what we're down here for."

"I thought so. That explains why the vid has blacked out most of Earth news, and there are all those callups being announced. The rebellion must be going on in a lot of places."

I nodded again.

"You're not doing this out of charity. If you were, you'd have been here long ago."

The hard swallow must have said it.

"Just don't expect to be loved and trusted afterward," she said. "If it's good for both of us, good. But you go your way, and we'll go ours afterward. Okay?"

I said I hoped it would be, but it wasn't in my hands. That seemed to satisfy her.

"One more thing," she said as we walked back to camp. "Manuel and the others don't suspect. Don't tell them you're from space. They think you're their friend."

9

About eight months after the war, there was a really dumb vid show, "Manuel of the Swamps," that depicted us as having a complex network of tunnels and electronic gadgets to make us nearly invisible. It was silly on the face of it, of course, though I suppose spaceside audiences might not be aware that you can't dig a tunnel in a swamp—not an earthwalled one, anyway. And while there's a lot of stray electronic stuff around on Earth, most of it is heavily hardwired—you can't just take a windmill blade controller and use it to run a network of personnel detectors.

There were really several reasons they left us alone in those critical first weeks. In the first place, they couldn't get men or supplies; there were uprisings all over Earth that month, and the logistical bureaucracy had atrophied quite a bit in the more than thirty years since 2076; the manpower situation was especially bad. The longer a "universal" draft runs without a war, the more loopholes it gets. Second, though there were enough men and weapons locally to mount an offensive against us, we'd bagged Voorbeck, and the higher-ranking officers under him had been handpicked for their ability to let other people do their thinking. Also, the first raid, and Charlie's OrbiTransit raid two weeks later, had destroyed enough hovercars so that an expedition against us would have needed to move on foot, which was unlikely. If you're reading this on a space station, think of wading through a gooey, body-temperature mass of all kinds of complex organics and trillions of microbes per cubic meter, in clothing that doesn't keep it from getting on your skin, down under your boots and between your toes ... it takes a while to get over the phobias all spacesiders have about mud and bacteria, and since the average cosmorine spent as much of his hitch as he could indoors, getting them to wade through the glop was next to impossible. I understand there was an actual mutiny in the Mekong Delta when some zealous officer tried to take cosmorines out overland.

They could have tried with Native Forces, I suppose, but the cosmorine officers didn't think much of them, and by and large, they were right. The best elements of the NF—the ones who had joined to get their families out of debt, or for the free schooling—were deserting at every opportunity, generally taking their weapons with them, and joining the Resistance. The ones who joined for the pretty uniform and the chance to carry a gun, or the chance to push their neighbors around, were the ones staying. The occasional competent ones who stayed loyal to the Republics were too few even to supply scouts for the cosmorines. So, even though later in the war some NF units gave us a lot of trouble, in these first few weeks we had little to fear from them.

We did do our best to hide from aerial observation; that wasn't much, unfortunately, but at least it helped us maintain discipline in camp. There again, it was more their difficulties than our success—for years everything had come down from space on OrbiTransits, which they'd then fuel up just enough to make a little suborbital hop to the launching catapults along the equator. As a result, there was no air transport to speak of even between main bases and the small stations that reported to them. It was cheaper to ship "through the triangle" than directly. And an OrbiTransit makes a lousy bomber, let alone spyplane—no windows.

I was explaining some of that to Wes one lazy Sunday afternoon as we hand-loaded for the "froggy guns," as the little automatics had been dubbed. The occasion was that a big OrbiTransit had taken off, roaring up in an arc across the sky to disappear south of us. "So he's not going straight up to orbit?"

"Nope," I said. "Probably to Senegal or the Galapagos. Then they fuel it up there, put some more cargo in, slap it onto the catapult, and fling it up."

"What more cargo do they put into it?"

"Military secret," I said, "but I guess the skyboys won't mind if I tell you."

"I won't tell them you did."

"It's a deal. Okay, the main thing they ship up is disassembled OrbiTransits."

"What?" He almost dropped his crimper into the cap jar at his feet. Judiciously, we moved it.

"It's true," I said. "The water, ammonia, and methane they ship up go in big unmanned things—the 'ice barges'. All that goes up in OrbiTransits is folk art, returning cosmorines, and disassembled OrbiTransits. Obviously, because they fly things like hovercars and prefab buildings down, they land more OrbiTransits down here than they have use for to fly stuff back, so they just tear apart about two thirds of them and ship them back space-a."

Wes laughed. "I think my father is right. They are all crazy."

"Just possibly." I looked at him sideways. He was more erect than I remembered him, tanned and getting muscled, generally in better form. He looked you in the eye, too, and he had a sense of humor. The war was certainly agreeing with him.

It might have been no more than that girls were finding him attractive; enough heroics will do that for anyone. Or maybe he'd just always wanted to kill some skyboys. Whatever the reason, he was calmer, less bitter, now. I had been on two raids with him, and his lapses of control hadn't repeated themselves; nowadays he led most small raids, and they generally succeeded. Less than a month had made all the difference in him.

Perhaps, I was thinking, there are just people who are better suited to war. Surely a psychopathic killer, for example—

"Saul, look!" He pointed abruptly.

The shambling, broken, half-human figures emerged from the swamp across the firm-bottomed pool at the "front gate" of the camp. At first I thought that the skyboys had managed to come overland after all—it looked like black uniforms—and then I thought that it was just shadows.

Then I realized they were facing the sun. They were dark because of soot and mud.

There were a lot of them. I had thought five at first, then a dozen, but there were now at least a hundred I could see and more seemed to be wading onto the island every minute. As they reached the island, many just lay down on the ground and stayed there; others wandered around in little circles. Parents carried children; husbands and wives leaned on each other. I could see two of our sentries splashing through the water, shouting for Manuel.

I was running down to the water before I had even sorted out what they were; Wes was right with me. As we got there, others from all over the camp were pouring in, too.

Somewhere in the middle of the crowd, I thought I saw something familiar; then I was sure. "Sam! Sam Klein!"

He was staggering, holding up a little girl, six or seven years old, who was guiding him, and his other arm hung at a strange angle. "That you, Saul? Ruthie needs help; some of her teeth got broken, and she's having trouble breathing."

I picked her up and carried her, carefully keeping her face pointed downward so she could spit out blood. "Doesn't feel like any broken ribs," I said. I looked around; Manuel was waving the council members over to where he was—a stretch of wide, flat ground. Judy Baker, muddy and bedraggled herself but apparently unhurt, ran up and took the girl from me. "We'll get her to her mother," she said.

"This way, Sam, this way. I think we're about to get organized," I said.

"Can you get on my left side?" he asked. "I think my right arm's dislocated."

The most amazing thing, to me, was the complete lack of any sound at all from the refugees. There were, when we got them counted later, just over three hundred that made it to camp— but they made less noise than a room full of undergrads taking a final. They shuffled along, blobs of mud falling off them, bent around their injuries, most of them with no expression at all. A few of them seemed to be locked in some inner conversation; one old one I hadn't seen before was twitching his jaw so hard that the muscles stood out like ropes on his neck.

I noticed that Sam was in his preaching suit, now completely ruined. As I looked around, I saw that almost everyone else was in Sunday clothes; a few were in nightclothes. It was about four; these people must have been walking since morning...

"Jesus, Sam, what happened?" Wes asked.

"About ten minutes 'til the end of the service, they tossed in tear gas bombs."

"The skyboys?" Wes asked; then he took off, having seen something.

"Yeah." Sam went on without knowing Wes was gone. "They beat us with riot sticks when we ran out. I think they killed the Rechler baby. They held people down and hit them in the face. Then they burned the church. They got the Methodists the same way, at the same time."

The smell of mud and smoke was overpowering as I pulled him gently through the crowd toward Manuel. "Did people get burned trying to save the church?"

He shook his head. "Their homes. And their animals. The skyboys fired every building on every farm belonging to a Baptist or Methodist."

Then we were there. Manuel had just succeeded in shouting some quiet into the crowd. "Okay, now, all of you standing around, get over there and help bring people up here onto dry ground. Ezra McLaren!"

"Yes, sir." The boy looked to be about fourteen.

"Get your raiding party out to our north. Make sure we get warning if the skyboys come in behind these people."

McLaren gave a high-pitched whistle, and five kids younger than he was came running up. They were moving out in less than thirty seconds. "Good kids," Wes said, coming up on my left. He was a mess from dragging an old woman bodily out of the pool where she'd fallen. "That's my diversion team."

I remembered that on the last raid I had gone on, there had been a burst of firing that had drawn off half the guard just before we had rushed through the gate into the warehouse. "They don't—"

"They don't fight unless they have to. But they make a lot of noise where we want it, and they don't make any getting there."

Manuel was still straightening out the confusion; his eyes lighted on us. "Good, you're here," he said. "Wes, get your kids out there bringing them in; Bea and Judy will handle them once they're in camp—over at the south end. Sam, let's get you over there—"

"I thought maybe Sam could tell us all what happened," I explained.

Then I saw that the old man's face was white with pain, and was about to go find someone else, but he said, "Sure." The Council was all there, and the rest of the camp was tending to the refugees now that they had some organization; we started without preliminaries.

Sam told it all in a few sentences; Baptists and Methodists had been beaten and burned out, Presbyterians and Apostolics were in a compound at the GXS under some kind of temporary arrest. Only the Catholics had been untouched. "A lot of us just got on the river road and started walking; that sort of snowballed. I'm not sure who got the idea of coming here. We just did. I guess it was the only place for us to go, really; no homes left. I think quite a few people sheltered with the Catholics, too, and there was a big group that went down Old Columbus Road—I imagine they'll find places to stop." Then he started to weave, and would have fallen if Charlie Perry hadn't caught him and half-carried him over to the long rows of the injured.

"Okay," Manuel said. He ran a hand through his matted hair, the fingers stumbling over the knots. "What's going on and what do we do, I guess is the question. What I think is this: they've driven these people out partly to be able to find us, and partly to slow us up. They're counting on us not being able to move with all these injured people, and it's a clear day so you can bet the satellites watched the whole bunch of them in the swamp all the way here. We could get hit with something any minute."

"They've put a big strain on our supplies, too," Wes said, returning again. "I've sent runners to the outposts, so if anything's coming we should know in a minute or two. And the raiding parties are out looking for stragglers now. Anything else you need before I go out myself?"

Manuel shook his head. "Not just yet. Good job, Wes. Let me know before you bring them in."

"Right." He was off into the swamp.

Manuel turned back to us. "Mary, will that evacuation plan work with this many people?"

She shrugged. "It'll have to."

The next few hours were insane. First, I would move the supplies by boat, to the scattered places that the Underhills had picked out, with enough people to set up some kind of receiving camp. As each one got set up, small parties of refugees would set out on foot from the old camp, guided by our experienced people.

The last was the worst—hauling the badly injured. It was the middle of the night, to begin with, and we were keeping a blackout, so Theo Underhill sat up in the bows calling out directions. We knew that some kind of attack had to be coming, and we didn't know how many more trips we might be able to make, so we were packing them into the *Monroe* 'til we had barely ten centimeters of freeboard, thick enough that it would have been hard to go forward without stepping on them, even across the cabin roof, and there were more in the cabin. They didn't cry or moan, usually, but whenever we bumped the bank or a low branch scraped us, there would be little swallowed groans and gasps.

And the whole time, of course, there was the fear that we could be coming back into a battalion of skyboys. Wesley Perry had a rearguard set up, but it was only a dozen people or so, counting a twelve-year-old girl.

I guess we should have realized that they weren't going to attack on the ground, but living on a planetary surface all the time, you get a certain narrowness of viewpoint. We had two loads, maybe twenty-five people, to go, and we were heading back for the first load of them, when there was a sudden blue-white flash far out in front of us. "Saul?"

"Right here. Are you okay, Theo?"

"I'm not sure. I may have been blinded...night vision's gone, anyway." I heard him feeling his way back, and then he was sitting next to me. "Sorry. That was—"

There was a sharp, short, deep boom, followed by a much louder one; a hard blast of air rocked the boat a little as the noise died away in rumbles. "What's happening, Saul? I still can't see."

"That was the clincher," I said. "That flash was from the direction of the camp. The first explosion was a sonic boom; the second one was the impact noise. They hit the old camp with a GOEP. We'd better see if there were any survivors. Are you in pain? Can you give me directions?"

"No pain. Just that light was awful bright and I was looking right at it. All I can see is a big purple blotch. What's a 'goat'?"

"GOEP, jee oh ee pee. Guided Orbital Energy Projectile. Ever hear of the Iron Ball?"

"Like in 2076?"

"Yeah. It's a shaped mass of iron covered with an ablative coating to keep it from eroding away during re-entry. They put it in a low orbit, then deflect it toward the target—it's moving at orbital velocity, maybe as much as eight kilometers a second. When it hits, all the kinetic energy—energy of motion—gets converted to heat. A good deal of the Iron Ball vaporizes instantly, and that gives you the explosion. Not as big or hot as a nuclear weapon, and no radiation, of course."

Theo sat quietly beside me for a while as we made our way up the creek. I knew the next two forks, but I confirmed them with him first.

Finally he said, "Saul, what are we fighting for?"

I wasn't quite sure what to say. "To chase the skyboys out, I guess," I said. "I haven't given it much thought." At least not any that I could share with him.

"I know." He spoke slowly, carefully, as he always did; his brother Clark used a lot more words, but Theo got the maximum value for each. "What I mean is, why are we fighting when we can't win? Any time they want, they can just kick the board over. Even if we chase them off this planet completely—and I don't know how we could keep them out of Antarctica or hidden bases somewhere in the deserts or on islands—they could bomb any city or town we set up, dump poison on any field we plow, sink every ship at sea, and then just wait a generation or two until our children are ready to crawl back into their hands. In fact they might even like it better if we all just lived like old-time Indians anyway. They wouldn't have to administer us at all after the steel tools wore out and the electronic stuff was all dead—just thin us out now and then."

That was the longest speech I ever heard Theo Underhill make. The next day, in fact, he apologized for "talking my ear off." I was a little astonished, and worried, too. If too many people figured that out, my mission was down the tubes.

"So, what do you suggest?" I asked, pulling the oldest and dirtiest trick for defending the indefensible.

"Maybe strikes, disobedience, stuff like Sam was doing." He shrugged. "At least that way you're still talking to each other, and you might win them over. This way, all we can do is kill 'em. And they're most of them out of reach."

"You saw what happened to Sam and his strike."

He pointed off in the direction of the old camp, still about four kilometers off. "And what did our way get us?"

The rest of the trip was dead silent except for directions. Toward the end of it, Theo's sight started to come back.

"Hey!" It was Wes, wading out to us. "I've got most of us here," he said, grabbing the gunwale, dripping much onto the deck. "We saw a satellite, real bright, go directly over about an hour-and-a-half before, and I started to think it might be a bomb or something. We moved all the injured we could move, and kept the ones we couldn't covered. Sarah Osburn stayed behind to tend them. I think we only lost her and the five worst injured. And we have some people who got flashblinded, but I don't think permanently."

"Good job, Wes," I said.

Theo nodded. "You saved what could be saved. Where do you have people holed up?"

"All around you. I guess we'd better get them aboard quick. Some of my people are holding up two of the wounded. If we can get them all into the *Spirit of Monroe*, and the rest of us walk behind it or beside it, we'll all be wet but not dead, and we can be under cover before dawn."

There wasn't much else to do, so that's what we did. Wesley's group pushed the boat most of the way—it saved precious hydrogen and it was less visible to infrared cameras that might be overhead. The night was cool, dank, and vile to the touch, and space-black dark besides; I couldn't imagine being out there wading in the sulfurous mud, and felt guilty for having the soft job at the tiller.

When we got to that last camp, I insisted on doing most of the off loading, finally leaving the two worst cases in my cabin and stretching out on the deck. I did not wake up until past noon the next day; by that time a little girl in the cabin had died, despite Bea's best efforts. We never did find out whose she was, and her face was too bruised and swollen for anyone to recognize.

THE COUNCIL MEETING, two days later, was a lot more somber than previous ones had been; we all knew how bad the situation was, and none of us really had any idea of what to do about it.

Charlie Perry finally said, "Well, I'll break the ice. Maybe I'm talking for my son Wes more than for myself, but it's a point of view I hold with anyway. We have to hit back and hit back hard. We can't let them do this to us."

Manuel nodded. "I think, as far into this as we are, that's all that's open."

"As far in as we are," Theo echoed. I watched him closely for a second, but that was all he said, to my relief.

"Does anyone know why they spared the Catholics?" Mary asked.

"The Bishop of the Great Lakes has excommunicated everyone who takes part in the rebellion. 'Render unto Caesar,'" I explained. "I got that from Sam Klein. I think the idea is to split them from the rest of us. Some of the farmers were given written notices that said their land had been confiscated and would be turned over to their Catholic neighbors. For some reason they've decided to try to win the Catholics to their side, against us."

"It won't work!" Mary said firmly. "We've all been neighbors for generations. There's a lot of inter-marriage. I've got cousins who are Catholic."

There was a dead silence. Charlie Perry scratched under his shirt; the Underhills whispered to each other. Everyone else looked away. "Most people are Christian enough to not take their neighbor's land, or to just hold it for him," Manuel said. "But some people aren't. It only takes a few to get the hatred going. And you know there've always been a few in every church that thought all the other churches were houses of blasphemy. Oh, they'll get it going…tear us all right down the middle if they can. Those pigrapists are smart. Did everyone hear about Jesse Snyder?"

There were headshakes all around.

"I just learned this morning. He was Methodist, you know. They shot him dead on his doorstep, then grabbed his wife and all six daughters. They've got them drugged up at the GXS, and they're using them for whores."

There was a lot of commotion among us then, everyone talking at once. Manuel thumped the side of the tree that his crude tent leaned against, and said, "Come on, let's have some order."

"Sorry, Manuel. It was all just so strange. The skyboys never had a better friend than Jesse Snyder," Charlie Perry said. "Why the hell did they do a thing like that?"

Manuel shrugged, shaking his head with the "they're all crazy" expression.

I remembered a little theory, and put in, "Several reasons. It makes them a lot more terrifying if they're unpredictable. It sharpens the religious distinction and helps them get hatred going among us. And the main thing is, it trains their own boys. The group that arrived right before the first attack was mostly raw recruits—some of them with less than a month's training. They have a lot of ideas about good guys and bad guys and so on, and a lot of the young ones have some Prog sympathies. This way they get blood on their hands, get them directly involved, make them—"

"Make them see us as dirtsiders. Like the old hands do," Clark said flatly.

"That's it exactly."

Manuel nodded again. "That makes some sense. Well, I guess we're down to figuring out how to hit them. If anyone has any idea—"

He looked up, slightly startled. Two men I didn't recognize were approaching—Wes was crashing through the brush after them.

"I'm sorry, council meetings are closed for reasons of secrecy," Manuel said mildly.

"We didn't vote for you."

"That's true. And neither did anyone else. Wes, take these people back and talk some sense into them." Manuel turned back to us; we could see that he was hoping it would work.

"We aren't going to take this," the taller one said. "You claim to represent all of us against the skyboys. We think you people are doing a damn bad job of it. We didn't come out to join you until we had to—and the only reason we had to is that you murdered all those cosmorines.''

Manuel turned around, his face impassive. "And you? Who do you represent?"

"Ourselves. Others who think like us."

"How about you?" Charlie Perry said, glaring at the short, fat one. "By the way, folks, this is Ted Clearny, old Five Percent Clearny, occasional farmer and mostly a commission dealer. Sort of a Methodist—we used to see him at Christmas, when he'd come around to take orders for the next year. How about you, Ted?"

"Don't start in on me that way, Perry. I don't care if you are in the self-appointed government now. You're still a marginal upland farmer as far as I'm concerned, and a bad credit risk. Sure, I was a commission dealer. You know the skyboy stuff is better than anything we can make. I was just helping people get their hands on it on easy terms. You people have ruined my business, and you've cost Nahum here his job. Of course we don't like that."

Something clicked. "You're that NF sergeant," I said. "Nahum Cantrell. The one old man Cantrell wouldn't admit to having fathered."

There was a dawn of recognition on everyone's face. Wes tapped the froggy gun that hung from his shoulder strap; Manuel nodded.

Even before, Wesley Perry had sometimes had kind of a frightening look to him. He seemed almost to switch it on now. "Okay, you two, you're taking up the council's valuable time." He had the gun leveled on Cantrell's chest. "Now, let's get you back to camp."

Cantrell was cool; I'll give him that. He looked over at Manuel. "I have a petition for you; a list of complaints."

"I've seen it," Wes said. "Bring it back when you get some names on it, besides the Clearny family's."

"The rest of them are afraid to sign, with Wesley Perry's goons watching them all the time," Clearny said.

I think I only imagined that Wes's finger tightened on the trigger for an instant. Manuel had turned away from them; the rest of us began to look pointedly away. The breeze, I noticed, was warm and smelled dusty, even here; the drought was certainly the worst in years, and we had been lucky to have so much dry land available.

When we looked up, they were gone.

The rest of the meeting was one long frustration. All of us were wondering how much trouble Clearny and Cantrell might stir up; none of us had any ideas on how to hit back at the skyboys. I spent most of my time half-listening, admiring the mud, the algae, and the mosquitos. At last, Manuel gave up. "Okay, there's nothing much we can do right now. Might as well get some sleep or something."

We were just leaving as Wes turned up. "I've got bad news, if anyone wants it," he said glumly.

Charlie sat back down, the rest of us followed suit. Manuel, with a sigh, joined us last. "Okay, Wesley, what's the story?"

"I had my diversion team shadow those two. They're going from camp to camp, looking for anyone with a complaint, getting them worked up about it."

"Complaints like what?"

"Like that some families got split between camps. And that people have to be sworn in before we let them carry guns. And the injured ones that got killed—"

Wes looked miserable on that last one; Mary hurried to say, "If it wasn't that, they'd complain about something else. You couldn't move those people and they couldn't stand up in the water. And you couldn't stop the Iron Ball from falling."

"I know," Wes said, looking at the ground. "But they're saying that, anyway. And of course the business about no elections, and they're only looking for the reasonable chance to negotiate an end to the war before there's any more killing, and remember that some of the skyboys are quite reasonable. McHenry's their favorite example—"

"Stop," Manuel said firmly. "Okay, what do we do about it? I tend to think we don't do anything."

"They're getting quite a few signatures. Not a majority, but enough to make trouble."

Manuel sat, staring into space. "Well, let me put it this way. We're used to running our own affairs. The skyboys left a lot of things in our hands. Get any three of us together and we elect some office or other.

"I don't know if we want to change that. We need to put out our own view, and we need to win any election they force on us, but that's all."

Charlie Perry shook his head. "We can't stop at that; and giving them an election won't help. The small wing never likes an election anyway. They'll call for them 'til we hold one; then they'll denounce the tyranny of the majority."

"They already are," Wes said. "I sent Lizabeth Kirst around to play with the Clearny girls. They're already talking about how people should have the right to go back and live under the skyboys' 'protection,' at least among themselves."

"The skyboys won't take them back without something in exchange. Like where we are," Clark added.

Manuel nodded. "All the same. We have to think about this. There isn't any easy way."

On the way out of the meeting, Wes dropped back beside me and Charlie. "Dad, Saul? There's something I could do—"

I didn't think at all. "Do it," I said. Charlie nodded. Wes disappeared into the brush without a sound. He really was getting good at this stuff.

"DAMN IT, Manuel, this is not a time for parliamentary niceties!"

He nodded. "I know, I know, I know. But answer me this. What are we fighting for? Who are we to do that kind of thing?"

Theo Underhill looked up at that, sharply, for a moment. The council had reconvened, like it or not, in Manuel's shelter less than an hour later; first Charlie and I had gone to talk to him and Mary, and then the Underhills had joined us.

Charlie Perry looked him straight in the eye. "What kind of thing?"

"Murder them," Manuel said.

"We've all spilled blood now," I said.

"Skyboy blood." Mary said it flatly. "Space people are different." I thought she looked at me.

And then Wes came in, with the blood still on his shirt, and they all knew. Charlie and I had to put up with a lot of getting shouted at, and Manuel threatened to resign three times in the middle of it all, but we told him that since he wasn't elected and didn't have a title, he couldn't quit. Eventually they settled on stripping Wes of his jobs as chief raid leader and council guard, and the meeting broke up with everyone mad.

It was late in the day, and I still had a little concealed liquor, so I invited Wes and Charlie to come back and share it with me. "I have to get up early. I'm doing a little raid of my own," Charlie said. "Thanks for the offer, though." He shambled off; Wes stuck with me.

"I wouldn't worry much about it all," I said. "One advantage of outfits like ours is you can go back up the promotion track real fast."

He laughed, and said, "That's not it. I hated doing that." He looked away, suddenly serious. "I waited 'til they were way out in the swamp, between camps; then I ran up and got Cantrell real fast from the back—both kidneys with two strokes. Clearny was in the lead, though, and he had time to turn around. He got down on his knees, wrapped his arms around my legs, started begging and pleading. At the angle it was hard to get a good cut, so I kept slashing and he kept screaming...finally I grabbed his hair, lifted his head, and cut his throat..."

He turned off the trail and vomited until he was dry. Back at the boat, we didn't do much but drink 'til he thought he could get to sleep. He stretched out the mosquito net and went to sleep in the bow, and I was dead to the world in my hammock as soon as I could get it strung.

When I woke up there was a thumping, scraping noise on the deck. I grabbed for my shotgun, made sure it was loaded and cocked, and was out the door in an instant, staying low.

Someone small was bending over Wes; it was Wes's foot banging on the deck that I had heard. "Hey," I said stupidly. The boy sat up, staring at me, the moonlight catching his face.

He had a long, curving knife in his hand; it was dripping with blood, and more was puddling on the deck around him.

Wes was dead, his throat slashed so deeply that he was almost decapitated; the banging and thrashing had been death throes.

The kid dropped the knife. I got a good look at his face in the moonlight. The resemblance to Ted Clearny was unmistakable.

I brought the shotgun up. The boy's lips were trembling, and tears were welling up. "Daddy..." he whispered, trying to explain. I lowered the gun, cursing myself the whole time.

I TRIED not to remember that I could have spared myself this as I snugged the noose around the boy's neck. It was unbearably hot and muggy, threatening a thunderstorm; it was impossible to tell which of the itchy spots on me were flies, and which were drops of sweat. His skin, too, was wet, but the soft down just coming in on his neck was standing straight out; he was cold to the touch. I had a strange urge to put an arm around his plump shoulders and tell him it would be all right.

I sprayed a little extra silicone on the rope, to make sure it would run free through the slipknot. I'm told there was once a special hangman's knot but I didn't know it, and Sea Gypsies carry out a death sentence by doping a man unconscious, weighting him down, and pitching him over the side, so I'd had no chance to learn it if anyone still did know it. I just put the loop of the slipknot around his neck, and carefully brushed his hair up over the rope so the noose wouldn't pull it, and then Abe Lester stepped in to pray with the boy.

"Jealousy!" It was Clearny's widow. "That's what it was. No one could stand my husband for being a success. He used to say you were all afraid of a free economy because you knew you'd fail. And he was right. You couldn't stand him for doing better than the rest of you. Oh, you were all jealous of us—and now you've killed my husband, and you're taking my son, too!"

One of Wes's lieutenants whacked her across the back of the head with the stock of his froggy gun; it made a sickening little thud, and she fell face-first to the ground. Everyone looked away.

I looked at the boy—he was in tears again, and I felt sick, so I thought of Wes, and of Charlie when I'd had to tell him, and raised my hand in the signal. The picked crew hauled on the rope, and the little body went shooting up into the tree, kicking and thrashing as the face turned purple and the tongue came out. Deliberately, I kept watching until he stopped twitching and the staring red eyes began to dry.

I looked down into the Methodist preacher's shocked face.
"I hadn't finished the prayer," he said.

"Better that it was a surprise." I looked away from the
shadow on the ground.

The crowd came apart quickly, silently. I turned and went to
the other side of camp, where we'd buried Wesley Perry. Charlie was there by the grave; I was afraid I'd have to hear him say
all the things Wes would have walked through hell to hear, but
he didn't say anything. Eventually Mary tapped my shoulder.

"There's something we should meet about tomorrow morning. Will you see that Charlie comes to council right after
breakfast?"

I nodded. "What's up?"

"I think we have a way to hit them hard. I just wish Wes
could be in on it. He'd have loved it."

"He was a brave kid," I said.

She nodded. "And a good killer." She turned and walked
away before I could think of anything to say; luckily, I think
Charlie didn't hear her.

10

"Watch that leg! Back up!" Charlie shouted an instant too late. The derrick abruptly tilted as the muck under one leg gave way; the crew on the rope tied to the opposite leg frantically backed into the swampy creek, pulling as hard as they could. The rickety structure swayed and then held; a bunch of us ran forward with rocks and buckets of gravel. As the crew strained on the rope, we pushed all the big, heavy stuff under the sinking leg that we could, dumping gravel in around it.

There was a long, anxious second while we got out of the way; all of us were soaked with sweat and looked like walking mud pies. "It figures, the one place we can do this is the only place left this summer that isn't dry," the man on my right said. I nodded, too tired to say anything. We had been at this since the middle of last night, and the sun was well on its way down.

The leg held, and the younger boys swarmed up the rig, nailing and tightening. I noticed Ezra McLaren on top, dropping a plumb line for Charlie to check.

"We're in bounds," he said, straightening up. The work seemed to agree with him; still, he didn't smile and except when he shouted he had no emotion in his voice at all. "Okay, get the bent length out, couple it up, let's try it again."

That was my crew's job; even though this wasn't much like a well, and I had certainly never drilled in a swamp, at least I had some experience with going deeper than ten meters. "How much further to go?" Charlie asked.

"Two more lengths," I said, "eight meters. We've got eleven in now."

He nodded. "Might as well try."

It took all eight of my crew to haul out the twisted wreck of the last length we had fed in; luckily, this one came cleanly out with its connector. When I looked down into the hole, there seemed to be nothing wrong with the pipe below. A clod of dirt slipped out from under me and I scrambled back; it pinged its way down until it broke up or hit bottom.

It took a little jockeying, and a couple of people had nervous slips toward the pipe opening, before we finally got the new length in. "We should all gain a little weight, for safety's sake, if we're going to do this," I said. "None of us is quite 75 centimeters across."

"Rations have been a little short for that," Matt Gomes said. "If we find anyone that big, we can use him for the wadding."

I nodded. "Or roast him and serve him to the rest of us. All right, let's let her run." Everyone backed away as I clamped the improvised drive wheel over the top of the pipe; it was pretty good for a piece of my home forging, which is to say it left a lot to be desired.

The "motor" was just two sets of coils, one on the drive wheel and one on the derrick, built from spare snapper coils; the whole power of the snapper was used to drive it. Inefficient, noisy, and ugly—but it provided only a brief flash of infrared, and we were far enough north that I was hoping they didn't yet have enough satellites deployed to give them continuous coverage. With luck, the trees would absorb most of the flash anyway.

I tightened the drive wheel clamps on the new length one more time, looked it all over, and headed back to the dugout. The setup could only stand the full power of the snapper for a few seconds, which was enough as long as nothing slipped or gave way. If it did, you didn't want to be near by; that was why we were all huddled in the dugout.

I had also been elected snapper jockey; when everyone was clear of both the derrick and the snapper, I closed all the switches, waited a few seconds and shunted the full power to the drilling rig, cautiously peeking over the edge.

The big coils, the size of a man's torso, jerked around slowly once, twice, three times and then ran up to speed, whining and then howling. The shaft thundered and shook; the whole derrick shuddered, bending inward where the field coils were mounted on the legs. The arcs around the brushes were blindingly bright, and the smells of ozone and burning grease filled the air.

Then I brought the power down to idle, and the drill spun to a halt. The length of pipe was sunk up to its top in the ground. My crew and I ran forward; ahead of us, the boys were going up the derrick again, but it looked like nothing more than minor tightening would be needed.

"This one's in clean," I shouted to Charlie, a moment later. "One to go."

We must have picked up some kind of momentum, because the next one went in easier if anything, and we were done, for the moment. My crew went off to rest; I had to supervise getting the coils and electrets rigged up right, lowering the whole assembly fifty meters down the shaft, and then charging it up. It was almost dusk before we were done; not until then did I realize I hadn't eaten all day.

Back at camp, I washed as much as I could in the sulfur water we had there, figuring I'd quietly fish out some dehydrate back at the *Monroe* and make a meal of it. I was heading for the boat when Judy Baker came running up. "Dinner, Saul. Plenty of it. You might as well get some."

"Did Martin's raid—"

"You wouldn't believe it. Come and see." She led me back to the kitchen; I noticed her hand on my arm, but decided I must be a father figure. She was about half my age, and even though by Earthside standards my thirty-six looked like twenty-three . . . then again, given what we were doing out here, Judy and I could expect to die at about the same time. I put an arm around her, and she leaned into me.

"Right here," she said. The fragrance of roasting meat filled the swamp; if the work site had been downwind of the camp, we'd have lost the whole crew the minute they smelled that.

"What happened?"

"The skyboys are having trouble getting stuff down to their troops, so they decided to requisition all the meat animals in the area. A lot of the local folks decided better us than the skyboys, and just drove their animals into the swamp, where we caught them. We don't have a lot of fodder, so we're slaughtering and smoking a lot of them, but tonight it's fresh. How about a great big steak?"

"I think I could see my way clear to it."

She insisted on plopping me down and bringing the food to me; the steak was rare, seared on the outside, pink and juicy on the inside, exactly the way I like them. It was several bites before I realized I hadn't specified it, and a couple more before I realized that Judy had sat down beside me.

I looked up, smiled, and kept chewing. She was a beauty, I realized; it was hard to believe she was only eighteen, not just because the ultraviolet had aged her skin, but because she had a maturity about her that the kids spaceside never do. Of course, half of her life was over, I reminded myself sternly; she was a grown-up, and entitled to be treated like one.

Looking at her brown hair, as she let it loose to fall down around her freckled face, I suddenly knew that wouldn't be difficult.

"You know why I wish this all hadn't happened?" she said. "I was really enjoying your class. It was so different from what they teach at skyboy school. And it sounded truer."

I swallowed and said, "I'm glad. It's hard for a teacher to know whether the students are getting anything under the best of circumstances, and in pitch darkness there isn't much feedback."

"Eat," she said, grinning at me. "We can talk after you're full. I've been cooking all day, so I'm off now, and so are you. I was hoping there might be some spare room in your cabin tonight." I started to open my mouth. "My father won't care much, and neither will anyone else," she said, heading me off. "Besides, Sam is busy tending wounded. He can't take time off to marry us just now."

I finished the last bite and realized that for the first time in two weeks I wasn't hungry. I had almost blurted out "Marry us?" but I was well-enough trained to avoid that gaffe. It was a serious, flattering offer.

Marriage on Earth is casually proposed, and divorce is rare, because being single is such an enormous economic and social handicap. In the Republics, of course, people agonize for literally decades before launching into marriages that last two months. But there, the advantages go the other way. And in the Confederation, we don't get married, but we're born into a

creche in a team, and people leave only to join another team—
unless, like Mendenhall, they want to be second-class citizens.

I remembered a quote from Pratt that applied: "It's amazing how people will do what it pays to do."

"SAUL." She rolled over, kissing me on the cheek. "One more
thing before you go to sleep."

"Just so it doesn't take any energy," I said, hugging her. Her
skin, from her knees and elbows inward, was soft and white, in
sharp contrast to the rough brown of her arms, legs, and face.
I ran my face gently along her belly; she giggled.

"It's not that kind of thing." There was a deep seriousness
to her voice; I checked to make sure the blackout shutters were
pulled, then rolled over and flipped on a light.

The *Spirit of Monroe* rocked in the rising breeze, and I
lurched a little as I got back onto the bunk beside her. "That
wind had better not keep up; it could really queer things."

She nodded. "Yeah. Is there anything you need to do?"

"Not unless I can re-aim the hole."

Her gray eyes had a funny, puzzled look to them, but there
was worry there, too. "Then we can talk? I don't want to upset you just before the big operation."

I didn't know what was going on, but I put an arm around
her, and said, "You're not going to. Okay, what's up?"

She bit her lip a little. "My proposal was serious, you know."

I squeezed her hand. "That's why I want to think a little."

"I know. But there was something else. I—I've been asking
about you, around camp, for a while now. Wesley Perry...he
really thought you were a god, you know, just admired you to
death; and Manuel said 'be a good wife for my friend.'"

There was a strange, warm, lonesome feeling in my stomach.

"Sam didn't say anything except that it was my life and yours
and we had our own ways to make. But Mary—"

It was hard not to tense up. I'm not sure I succeeded; Judy
was kind enough not to say anything.

"What did Mary say?" I asked.

"She said, before I proposed, that there was something you
should tell me, something I should know. She said you'd know
what it was."

That morning, I hadn't particularly thought one way or another about this woman; I had liked her, of course, and known she was beautiful in sort of an abstract way, as I knew who her father was and the color of her hair. Spaceside, a night like this would be a little bit of fun and excitement—even Earthside, in normal times, it might be, but now…with so little time left…

"Judy," I said, "I'll tell you, and then if you still will propose, I'll probably accept.

"I'm from space. From the Solar System Confederation."

She looked puzzled; I realized that though that was what we called ourselves, that term was never used on the Orbital Republics vid. They usually referred to us as the "breakaway colony of" whatever.

"I'm from the Breakaways," I explained, trying again.

Judy took my hands and stared into my face; she had no expression that I could understand. "What are you doing here?"

"The Confederation and the Orbital Republics are at war."

"You're here to draw Earth into the war?"

I nodded.

"What about you, personally?"

There was a big lump in my throat. Kwanza is right, I'm a sentimental fool; I really believe all that stuff, but it's hard for me to say two words of it without choking. "I'd been here before. In peacetime, I was a historian. At Confederation University, on Eros.

"I saw a lot on trips down here. I know what the skyboys are like; my mother died fighting them, and I fought in our Independence War. If we win…Earth can manage its own affairs."

She stared at me, her mouth tight and flat. "We get all kinds of freedom from the skyboys we have now. In fact, we're so free, they send thousands of them down to make sure we're free enough to please them."

There wasn't much I could say. Space people, after all, are space people; mice don't differentiate between calicos and tabbys. I sighed and lay back. "Judy, there's nothing I can do as a gesture of faith. I'm not the Facilitator and I don't sit in the Assembly. The Confederation might just set up their own occupation, though with our low population, it's going to be hard for us to hold the Orbital Republics in line, let alone Earth itself. We need allies—that's what I'm here for. I'm enough of a historian to know that allies often fall out after a war; but the Orbital Republics will be a threat to you, and to us, for at least a generation to come. That should count for something.''

She touched my arm lightly. "What are you fighting for?"

"Me? I—"

"The . . . Confederation. What do you Breakaways want?"

"Not to starve or freeze, and not to surrender," I said. "The issue is volatiles, when you come right down to it."

"How is it volatile?" Judy rolled over, resting her hands on my chest and her chin on her hands.

"Volatiles. Water, ammonia, methane, carbon dioxide. For stations as big as our cities, hundreds of thousands of people, it costs too much to control the leaks perfectly. You lose gas to space all the time, which means you lose nitrogen, oxygen, carbon, and hydrogen—the basic life-stuff."

"At GXS school they said Jupiter and Saturn had a lot of that stuff."

"They do. But it's down at the bottom of a deep gravity well—volatiles from Earth, or the comets, or some of the moons of Jupiter and Saturn are much cheaper."

"Aren't some of the Breakaways on those moons? Why can't you get volatiles from there?"

I put my hands on her back; she didn't try to shrug them off. "Well," I said, "the big cargos of volatiles—and the typical shipments are several cubic kilometers, frozen and then covered with reflectors—are moved using solar sails. South of here, around the equator, you can sometimes see sun sailers being assembled; most of them are just sailing from low orbit up to the Republics or their colonies on the Moon, but some of them are headed out to the Confederation cities."

She nodded. "Sometimes you can see them, just along the horizon, to the south."

"Right. Well, it's much slower, and thus more expensive, to tack inward, toward the sun, than it is to sail outward, away from it."

"Why does the speed matter?" she asked. "As long as it gets there eventually, and you keep launching them?"

"We have a saying: 'you can't outrun compound interest.' It takes enormous amounts of capital to fund one volatiles shipment. The return on that, over time, has to beat or equal the return on anything else you might do with the money—and that adds up to a lot. And to make matters worse, the nearest Confederated cities are on Apollo and Eros, asteroids that orbit between the Earth and Mars, and they're bone dry, and five times as far from Jupiter as from Earth. So the Republics can always drop their prices just low enough that it doesn't pay to use our domestic sources, then make demands and threaten to cut off the volatiles. That's what this war is about, basically. We want to buy our volatiles from Earth, for a fair price; the Republics control the Earth. So if we want to buy from you, we have to get you independent of them."

"What happens if you don't get the volatiles?" She was so serious, so intent—and so pretty—I took a chance and kissed her; she kissed me back. "I like you, too," she said. "Now, what happens?"

"We have to close all the stations sunside of Jupiter. That's about two-thirds of our population. That far from the sun, energy is a lot harder to gather. We'd have to put most of it into just staying alive."

She nodded. "They have you like they have us."

"Very much," I said. "What we want is the right to buy direct from Earth. We think you'd be willing to sell."

"And what if we set prices as high as the skyboys did?"

I shrugged. "Then we pull back to Jupiter, and the Orbital Republics come back. We think you'd rather deal with us—we're further away and we have fewer troops." At least, I thought, that was what Kwanza and I had been told when we'd asked that question. I hoped it was true.

"What happens to Earth?"

"We set up some kind of planetary government. We'll need to give you some help, to get you set up so you can keep the ORs out, and so forth, but the plans I've seen say it's your show."

"Would it be legal for us to be married?"

"Well, in the Confederation, we don't exactly have marriage. That's what the Independence War was about."

"Not have *marriage*?" She pushed herself up on her hands and looked down at me; I admired the view. "Obviously, I missed a lot of history at GXS school. How did you get into a war over that?"

"Well, it wasn't just over that. Basically, the Republics set up regular mining colonies out in the asteroid belt, because they needed iron and it was easier to get from there than from the moon. That goes way back, maybe eighty years ago—in fact, one of Pratt's last books was about the long-run effects of colonizing the outer Solar System. It wasn't one of his best—he was getting old and he babbled on a lot about 'spiritual renewal.'

"Anyway, the Republics started with a chain of bases to make the trip to Mars easier, because they had a big research effort going on there—they still do, in fact, though now they pay tolls to us for the privilege. And then there were the mining bases in the asteroids, and then on Jupiter's moons—more raw material close to the surface than on Luna. So by about twenty years ago they had a lot of cities out there, but they didn't allocate much in the way of resources to them. So, to survive, people got used to using minimum resources, which meant sharing everything."

"You were all violating ERACA!" She giggled.

"Exactly. And for the same reason you do. It's cheaper. And we ended up fighting the Republics for the same reason—they won't tolerate 'collectivism.' "

"You mean the way you were doing things—"

"Yeah. It struck them as 'collectivist.' And they were right, too. See, it's hard to live six to a room for years and years unless you're all very comfortable with each other, basically know all of each other's quirks. So what we do is arrange for groups of four to eight people to all be born at the same time—we freeze embryos and then implant them in several women at the same time—and all those people are brought up together, and hold all their possessions in common. They're sort of all married to each other at the same time. We call the group a creche."

"You mean . . . all the men with all the women . . . ?"

"Yep. And the women with the women, and the men with the men." She looked a little shocked but she didn't actually get up and run screaming out of the cabin; it occurred to me, belatedly, that I was asking a lot of broadmindedness of an Earthsider, let alone a Baptist. "Two to four creches make up a team—that's a group that shares work together, that all work on the same big project together. My team, for example, does formal mathematical history based on fieldwork. Then anywhere from thirty to four hundred teams, whose projects all support the same purpose, will all live together in one tower. We call that a kraal. The University, plus some things that support it, is all one kraal. And there might be one to forty kraals in a city. But, anyway, if you want to be married to me here, that's fine; if we move back up to Eros, what you would do is join my creche. There. Now I've proposed to you."

She looked apprehensive. "What would I have to—"

"Well, Team Pareto would have to accept you as a student member. That would just mean you'd study and work with us until you were doing your own creative work on par with the rest of us."

"That sounds like fun. I've always liked history."

"And, of course, Kwanza would have to like you."

"Who?"

"My xbrothr."

"Your what?"

"He's the other member of my creche. We lost the other four members in the war." I knew that was a slight lie, but I didn't want to talk about Kari just then.

"Would he expect me to . . . you know, with him?"

"Not unless you want to. But of course, we'd all be sharing one room, and nobody in space wears clothes at home. You might find that, after a while, you wanted to."

"But you and I can be together, either way, married or—?"

"Xbonded."

"Married or xbonded? There's no Native Relations Act?"

"Not in the Confederation. And if we win the war, not on Earth or in the Republics, either."

She held my face in her hands for a long minute, then smiled. "I bet you hate being called a skyboy," she said.

"Yeah."

"We'll need a new word for you guys after the war. I'm not going to let anyone call my husband a skyboy."

I realized, in the back of my mind, that I had gone past the point of no return; the next thought that ran through my mind was, well, why the hell not? If we both survived the war—and the rest of Team Pareto did—and the Confederation won—time enough to worry then.

Then her hand slid down my belly; my skin was almost painfully sensitive. "No telling when we'll get time with the preacher," she said. "We'd better get this consummated, and then get some sleep." She stroked and pulled lightly, and in moments I rolled over onto her; I have the odd little memory that her feet felt tiny and cold on the backs of my thighs.

"Just so we get it down there within the hour," I said to Charlie. "We have a date at 2:16, you know."

He nodded, soberly. "We can't just throw them down on top of the electrets. The sling system is fast enough. Three minutes down and up is all. Those cylinders weigh an awful lot, you know. The crew just can't lower them any faster and keep control."

"I know. Just looking for something to push on, Charlie. Sorry." I sighed.

He gave me a clap on the back. "You're a little short on sleep this morning. If these were normal times, you'd just be getting up and going for a talk with Levi Baker and Sam to get the wedding set up. You *shouldn't* have to work your ass off this morning. You're allowed to be a grouch."

The burn I could feel spreading up from my neck probably wasn't as visible as I imagined that it was.

Charlie's snort didn't help, either. "You know we love gossip, Saul. And out here where everyone can see what everyone else does . . ."

I nodded, still feeling sort of sheepish. Judy had moved her few things, mostly spare clothing, onto the *Spirit of Monroe* early that morning; Levi had made a point of having breakfast with us, and he was plainly pleased. Somehow, I had always thought getting married would be more complicated—and I hadn't thought I'd have any direct interest in the subject, anyway.

"Anyway," Charlie went on, "we have four more hours or so. And half the tanks are down there now. You wanted one red, four blue, per group, three groups, right?"

"Right. The red is methane, the blue is fluorine. And together, they're the best damned evidence we'll ever have against OrbiTransit. This use is a little more urgent, though."

"You say this proves that they destroy the ozone and cause the cancers?"

"Pretty near proves it. This is the fuel for the main driver on the OrbiTransits. Methane plus fluorine gives you carbon tetrafluoride and hydrofluoric acid as fallout. That forms a lot of organic fluorides, quite a lot of which are cancer-causing, in the environment. And the see-eff-four definitely triggers a reaction in the upper atmosphere that destroys ozone." Of course, on Eros we had known about all that from the exhaust spectra for a long time—in fact, there were some former OrbiTransit employees in the Confederation to give direct testimony. But as far as I knew, this was the first time any Earth people had gotten their hands on the evidence.

"I thought they used that gloppy stuff."

"For the maneuvering jets, yes. And *officially* they use it in the main driver, but since it's a protected trade secret officially their government can't look into it. No, to do the one-step jump to orbit the way they do, they have to use this stuff." I gestured at the last two cylinders waiting to go down; while Charlie and I had been talking, the job had gotten done. "How deep are we, now?" I asked.

"Thirty-nine meters of shaft left," one of the men on the line said. The last two cylinders nosed up together in their cradle, valve ends pointing up, and swung down into the shaft. The crew of men on the rope came forward slowly, lowering it in, and I turned to Charlie. "Okay, let me check continuity on the electrets."

The continuity lights on the board were all on. "Well, let's get the wadding down, and start bringing up the darts," I said. "Everything's fine so far."

For wadding, we used a big roll of fiberglass insulation—kind of primitive stuff, the sort of thing that vid producers like as "historic ironies." I did some figuring and then decided that no, it had probably not been used as musket wadding in the

1776 American Revolution, but when did probability ever stop a vid producer?

Even with the grease, it took us quite a while to worry that big roll down the shaft. I ended up using four guys and a big rock on the derrick, a sort of primitive pile driver, to get it the last few feet. By now the sun was well up in the sky and the people backpacking loads of darts had gotten almost all of them there. From there on it was just a matter of throwing the darts down the shaft, all eight hundred of them.

"How are these things supposed to work, again?" Charlie asked. "If I saw anything like that in my garden, I'd pull it out." He held one up; the dull lead object didn't really look like much of anything, just a ball as big as his fist tapered to a point on one end, with about eight centimeters of cloth tied to a ring opposite the pointed tip.

"It wouldn't do much good there," I agreed. "The idea is that the cloth helps it fly straight, and it's made out of lead to get the maximum energy transfer. The lead will squash against the target instead of bounce off or tear through."

"But if we're trying to shoot it down—"

"That's the trick. We can't—we'd have to hit it a lot harder to actually destroy it. But they land practically dead stick, at three-hundred-fifty kilometers an hour, and nearly out of maneuvering fuel, even if they could get the maneuvering engines going in time. If we mess up his landing gear, and damage his control surfaces—"

"He'll make a hell of a bad landing, at best." Charlie grinned in satisfaction. "This is the way to do it. Get rid of them wholesale instead of retail."

"Doing what?" I asked.

"You didn't know?"

"I must have missed something."

"One of Jesse Snyder's daughters talked them into paroling her so that she can live in town. Now she spies for us. The Wednesday afternoon shipment this time is troops—about three hundred reinforcements, crack troops that just got done with something over in the East Baltic District."

"The Gagaringrad Volunteers? 27th Cosmorines?"

"That's what she said. Do you know them?"

"They didn't exactly come aboard to do some drinking and talk philosophy, but yeah, I know them." Then I added, "In East Baltic," with a little wince because I really didn't like lying.

They were the ones who had made the surprise landing on Eros during the Independence War. You would not be reading this if they had landed two weeks earlier, but luckily for me, they showed up after I was discharged from the hospital.

The 27th had slaughtered the wounded there—I can still remember the wards with the huge puddles and stench of blood, the bodies strewn everywhere, the faces of the corpses in the unplugged respirators. Mlarik, the officer in charge of that, was court-martialed, but public sentiment prevented breaking up the 27th. In fact, Mlarik was still a hero to some of the extremists in the Republics; you could see posters on their walls with his picture and the caption "Treason's treason and execution's what solves it," what he had said when he gave the order.

Charlie was watching me intently; I realized I had fallen off into the old memories, and that my fists were clenching. "They're good people to kill," I said. "Famous for some really ugly things in that area—and used to swamps."

We got back to loading the darts in; privately, I resolved that, even though we needed some prisoners for exchange, if it was left to me there would be none from the 27th.

11

The sun was well up, and it was roasting hot; half the people with me seemed to be asleep. We were lying in the tall grass, watching the five NF troopers on guard across the river; the river was so low with the drought that it was wadable here—in fact, I doubted that the *Spirit of Monroe* would be able to float through here before fall. It was 2:14.

The man on my right tapped my shoulder; I rolled over on my back and looked up at the sky, shielding my eyes from the overhead sun. A tiny, almost invisible dot swam out there; I borrowed a pair of field glasses to look at it, and that confirmed it. We nodded to each other, rolled over, and tagged the people beside us; in a few seconds everyone was awake and getting ready.

I visualized the thing at the bottom of the shaft. One electret, fully charged, was power enough for four snapper starts, or four 15-second bursts of 3 kw power; there were three electrets down there, adding up to five hundred plus kilojoules, all sitting harmlessly stored at the moment. I could almost imagine the lines of force bending and twisting in there.

I blinked and looked up carefully, scanning the ground ahead of us. Forty meters across the river from our high, grassy bank were the guards; behind them, another fifty meters, were the repair shops and warehouses, and beyond that was the inner compound, the control towers, mess hall, and barracks. Ordinarily there were fifty men or so in the shops, in addition to the skyboy technicians, Earthside laborers, and officers. Usually they were all Native Forces, which in general meant they wouldn't put up much of a fight, but we couldn't count on that.

The plan was straightforward enough from our viewpoint. When the OrbiTransit came down, the crash landing would presumably pull everyone out of the repair shops. We'd fire on the guards, cross the river, and get as close to the inner compound as we could, setting fires and smashing whatever came to hand. Then we'd try to pin down as many people in the inner compound for as long as we could hold; as soon as they got a serious sally up against us, we'd break and run down half a dozen escape routes, and—with luck—all meet up in the swamp afterward.

There was plenty to worry about. We didn't have anything to build radar with; the triggers were a set of electric eyes rigged to homemade telescopes. True, the ship had passed through all their sights at the same time every time for the past two weeks; but they might get smart enough to vary the landing path, or they might even have some ordinary course correction to do a bit earlier than usual—at least last night's wind had died down.

After the eyes, I had the whole electronic setup to worry about; then the possibility of the wind going the wrong way, blowing the plume into places where there were people; and then finally I could worry about the troops staying behind at the shops—our twenty to their fifty, with all the cover on their side.

A mosquito started to gnaw on my arm; I crushed it. The wind had died completely. On the other bank, one of the guards seemed to be telling a dirty joke, the main point of which was a series of pelvic thrusts. Almost as pure intellectual exercise, I wondered if he'd have time to get to the punchline.

Somewhere back and above us, the ship crossed the trigger spot. A whole series of things closed and flipped in less than a millisecond; the caps in the explosives fired, shattering the dielectric films in the electrets. The two immense charges combined in a literal lightning stroke confined to a few cubic meters; the swiftly shifting magnetic fields tore the steel casings of the gas cylinders and the tremendous electric currents superheated the gases themselves. More than three tons of methane and fluorine mixed as plasma.

The ground shook under me as that massive bomb went off four kilometers away; I glanced back to see the white-hot plume going straight up into the sky. Judy, who was watching with binoculars from the other side of the landing field, said the OrbiTransit seemed to actually fly through the plume. That might account for what happened in part, but certainly it was hit by at least fifty or sixty of the darts. It lost three control surfaces, and the extended landing gear was pounded into scrap.

We stayed flat on our faces; when we looked up, the ship was almost down. It was careering out of control, its engines howling in a frantic try to regain control, but the steering engines lacked the energy to lift the ship, and OrbiTransits land with the main engine tanks empty.

The pilot was good or lucky; he landed her on her belly, trailing the smashed landing gear behind as she screeched down the pavement. Still, he had no control; between a maneuvering jet that seemed to stick on and the shattered spars and members underneath, she spun as she hit the pavement, and all four-hundred-fifty tons of her went whirling off in a scream of metal, like a top on a table. She arced off toward the control tower; we heard more crashes as she went out of sight behind the row of sheds.

I kept my voice low and calm; I had some of our best shots with me, and I didn't want to muss their concentration. "On my mark, after three."

I watched the shop; I was vaguely aware that the guards were turned around and gaping at the scarred stretch of runway where the ship had crashed in. Sirens and bells sounded, and the crews poured out of the shops; we saw the detachment of Native Forces pile into hovercars and race toward the wreckage.

"One, two, three . . . now."

All the rifles rang out at once; the guards fell. "All right, forward." We ran down the bank and splashed through the knee-deep water.

The river was wide there; I was more scared than anything of being caught in the open, in the middle of the stream, and several of us fired froggy guns at the guards on the chance that any of them were still alive. In a moment, though, we were running up the bank, past the little pier and through the gates. "All dead," someone shouted behind—we had agreed the last one through would stop to check the guards.

The dash across the pavement was over in a few seconds. We stopped for breath and began the search of the buildings around us.

No one was in any shop anywhere. Matt switched on all the power machinery and poured a mixture of jet fuel and sand into the moving parts; another crew broke into the warehouses, leaving the grocery building alone but setting fires everywhere else. We left charges and set timers, poured alcohol everywhere and ignited it.

It was now 2:25. I blew a whistle, and was oddly pleased to see them come running. "Toward the tower!" I shouted.

The long, low drydocking shed that lay between us and the inner compound was just as empty of people as the rest of the shops had been; after checking to make sure, we went out the side door away from the landing strip, to use the building for cover.

For a whole second, I just gaped at what I saw. The ship had spun right through the fence into the inner compound, bounced against the tower, gone through the fence again, and whirled back out onto the strip half a kilometer away from us. Some faint bangs told me that Manuel's crew were able to cover the wreck with their rifles, preventing the men inside the Orbi-Transit from getting out or rescuers from the inner compound from reaching them.

What drew my attention, though, was that a big chunk of the tower had been knocked out at ground level; the whole thing leaned crazily, and the men in the compound were running around like ants in a spilled hill. Two of the barracks were on fire, apparently from the exhaust of the jammed-on engine. "Matt."

"Skipper."

"You and—you and you—" I pointed at two more froggy gunners—"Give me a count of fifty, then spray them. Try to hit as many, as far apart, as you can. Two clips. Then run around the building and join us. The rest of you, come on."

A drydock shed is long—three hundred meters at least. We were only part way around when I heard the brap-brap-brap noise starting again. By the time we had reached and rounded the corner, the sound had died out. I took a glance and saw Matt and the other two racing for us. "Come on!" I shouted, once more. "Right through that fence gap; head for the tower!"

Dad said once that nothing is as crazy or dangerous as an officer who has gotten ahold of an idea. I wouldn't know—I didn't have one at the time, but I did know that as a safety measure the cosmorines in the inner compound were unarmed, and I thought it likely that the machine guns on the tower were knocked out when the ship hit them. What would have happened to us if they had *not* been knocked out is an interesting question—but as it happened, they were.

When we burst through, we were the closest thing to an organized body in the place. With the blind side of the tower to our backs, we had the whole compound covered. "Hold fire, hold fire, hold fire," I kept repeating. I was beginning to realize I was badly winded, so I sucked in a deep breath as I pointed the froggy gun upwards and fired into the air.

There was a sudden, immediate silence.

"Raise your hands. Pass all weapons forward through the crowd," I bellowed. "Give yourselves up and you'll all get out alive. Pass all weapons to the front and lay them on the ground. If anyone moves fast, or puts his hands below his shoulder, we'll fire into the crowd."

It was basically a back-and-bag, done in two dimensions instead of three; it worked mostly because none of these poor kids was a combat vet. Every cosmorine with a weapon had rushed up close to the corner where Matt's gunfire had come from; we had about sixty unarmed hostages between us and the guns.

In all, we had picked up about thirty guns and seventy-plus prisoners. Hope Sandworth and Matt did a fast check of the buildings; we had the lot of them, except for three badly injured ones we left in the tower. "All right," I said. "Form up into a column, three across. Rest your hands on the head of the man in front of you. No talking."

They were really too stunned to make a break, anyway, but I didn't know how long that would last. I detailed a few of them to carry their wounded; we got them formed up and moving down the river road, toward the swamp, moving as quickly as possible. I sent Hope to carry the message to Manuel; she was off like a rabbit.

I was elated. We had lost no lives from our group; we had gained much more than we had expected to. It was all I could do to keep from breaking into a little dance.

We made good progress on the road. Behind me, I could still hear occasional shots; long columns of smoke went up from the field. It was warm, and despite what I knew the UV was doing to my skin, I liked the feel of it on my face. Maybe back in camp Sam would have a little time and I could get married to Judy officially.

As we came around one turn, we met up with five of our people from Manuel's group. "Captain Proxman wants us to take over the prisoners," the leader explained.

It took me a moment to realize we had gotten to be a big enough operation that not everyone called him "Manuel;" we had called him the captain because it was as good a title as any when we were first starting out. "Er, uh, yeah," I said.

"He also wants you to go back and join him. He said to bring all your people with you, and be quick."

I handed over our prisoners with a wave, and called my crew together. There was a sinister, cold feel to things that hadn't been there before.

Manuel, Mary and Charlie were all together, pretty much in the position they had had during the attack. "What's up?" I said, coming up to them.

Manuel handed me the field glasses and pointed to the wreck of the OrbiTransit. I focussed them and looked closely. There was a big crowd around the OrbiTransit, hundreds of people—

"Those aren't cosmorines! Those are farmers!"

"Yeah," Charlie said. "Can you see what they're doing?"

"It looks like they're—" I saw. Suddenly I turned and vomited, the hot acid running out through my mouth as if it were trying to wash away what I was thinking, the stink in my nostrils almost a relief compared with what I had seen.

They were dragging out the cosmorines, one by one, standing around them in a circle, and beating them to death with shovels and axes. I had just seen them set two cosmorines on fire, cheering as the skyboys crawled a few feet before collapsing and dying in the flames.

"A while ago they dragged out an officer and castrated him before they killed him," Manuel added.

"They showed up right after the crash," Charlie said. "We had driven the rescue party back toward you. They got back and saw the wreckage of the tower and the shops, and just broke and ran, mostly headed for the river. I imagine they'll make it to Rogers City if they don't run into another mob. Then that mob came through the fence and rushed the OrbiTransit. You can see what's happening now."

I nodded. As long as I didn't think too long about that one human head that had been so obviously flattened, I thought to myself, I can live through this, too. "What did you want me for?"

"Council meeting," Charlie said. "The Underhills are back in the swamp and can't make it. We need you to cast a deciding vote."

"Manuel's the commander. What he says—"

"Manuel wants to fire into the mob," Mary said. "And try some of them for murder. We think he's wrong."

I sat there, staring. I knew what Manuel was thinking; he had said, often enough, that the war had to be fought fairly and without bitterness, because Earth and the Republics would have to live together afterward. The poor fool wanted to do justice, and this was plain murder—

"What do you want to do?" I asked the other two.

Charlie shrugged. "This is my idea of what ought to happen. I say, let them do it. If they have to break and run when the skyboys get back, fine. They can run into the swamps and join us."

Mary's lips were tight and thin. "And I say we've got to stop it, but we can't try to punish these people. They're with us. We can't afford to do that to them."

"Whatever gets two votes wins?" I said. They all nodded. "So it's me." I took a deep breath. Mendenhall might have been happier with Charlie's way; I had to live with myself. "Okay, we do Mary's way."

"How?" Charlie said.

For the first time in my life, I saw some use in social psychology. "I think I know how..." I said. "We'll need the biggest men we've got—"

In a few minutes we had put together a pretty good little im-
promptu parade—Manuel out front with an honor guard of
two guys on each side, then Mary, me, and Charlie with a guard
on each side, then six rows of four men each. Even though our
fighting units were made up of anyone old enough to follow
orders and keep his or her own gun clean, I was counting on
large burly males to have their traditional threatening aspect.
"All right, now one more time. Just keep your head up and
follow orders; stay in ranks. We are going to walk slow. Do not
talk with anyone. Don't bother trying to march in step like the
cosmorine honor guards do—that's a hard trick to learn in a
hurry. Any questions?"

"What if they rush us?"

"We have all these rifles covering us, and we have a clear way
of retreat. If they can't be talked to, we'll fight. Just stick close
to each other. As long as you don't get separated from the others, they can't do much to hurt you." I hope, I added mentally. The only mob situations I had ever been in were on Eros
during the early days of the rebellion—and that had been as a
member of the mob, always a lot more fun.

They looked up as we approached. Only then did I realize
that we should have approached with the sun at our backs, even
if we had to walk around. A hot, salty drop of sweat dangled
on my eyebrow, waiting to fall into my eye, then slid down my
nose into my mustache. I blinked hard a couple of times, which
didn't help, and noticed that Manuel really had the bearing for
the job—if we got through this, I was going to nominate him
for king.

By the time we were within ten steps of them, they had
stopped entirely. Two of the cosmorines on the ground moaned
and whimpered; I couldn't quite see them without turning my
head, and I was just as glad. There was a sharp, greasy metal-
lic smell of blood; someone obsessed with neatness had piled
the corpses like firewood in a rough pyramid, but there were
some strays around, including the two charred bodies that had
run a few steps before collapsing. (We figured out later they had
been drenched with ether from one of the shops). Right down
in front of me, unignorable in the bottom part of my vision,
was a half-torn severed human hand.

One of the crowd stepped forward; it was an older guy, white-haired and wrinkled. There were red stains on the blade of the shovel he held, and hair was stuck to it. Nervously, he said, "Most of them have barricaded themselves into an inner compartment, sir."

"I'll take charge from here," Manuel said. "All of you are dismissed."

There was a long silence; then one of the ringleaders, a man I had seen ramming a shovel handle into a man's teeth, said, "You heard the General." And slowly, not looking at us or at each other, they started to drift away in groups of two and three.

"Help me." The sound was more bubbled than spoken. Charlie broke ranks and ran forward; I heard him swear a moment before I caught up with him. The man had one eye hanging all the way out; a good part of his face was simply sausage.

"Murdering bastards," Perry said. "Manuel was right."

"Yeah," I said, "Oh, Jesus, yeah." And yet, sick as I was with the sights and smells, a part of my mind was thinking that it was a shame this wasn't going on the vid in the Republics, because nothing would get cosmorines down here—to leave the orbital cities unguarded—faster than the sight of that young man.

Mary shouted for us from the inside; they had succeeded in opening the back compartment door with a small charge. We ran in.

One hundred fifty of them sat absolutely still in the seats, slumped over, faces faintly blue; most looked peaceful, but a few had evidently had some kind of convulsion. "The capsule wrappers," I said. "Those little bits of plastic on the floor by them. They took poison and killed themselves—those are standard issue for cosmorines."

"I'd have thought they'd have shot themselves," Mary said.

"Cosmorines land unarmed, except on a drop into combat," I explained. "Safety precaution."

Manuel shook his head slowly, surveying the whole thing. "I guess we'll try to save the two outside, though one of them looks pretty gone. The other one seems to have fainted. It probably saved him from the worst of it. And we need to get the supplies from the food warehouse. We'd better send some runners, get the rest of our people, and get to work on this. He turned and went out; the rest of us followed him quietly.

"You know," he said to me, so softly I don't think anyone else heard him, "if I'd been one of them, I'd have killed myself, too. Hell couldn't be any worse."

THE CHAOS WAS EVEN WORSE when we got back to camp; three quarters of the people we'd chased off the field had decided to enlist, for one thing, so the first order of business was to haul even more food from the warehouses and to send back parties to abandoned farms to get whatever else was available. This was half the night, and I was dead on my feet before Judy came by, also exhausted, and insisted that the two of us were getting some sleep. We fell asleep in each other's arms; if I had had the energy to have any emotions, I would have thought it felt wonderful.

It was the next morning, already daylight. There were footsteps on the deck. I started to grope for clothes, then realized I had fallen asleep with them on and laughed. I unbolted the door, and there was Sam Klein with his Bible, with Levi standing next to him, and Charlie, the Underhills, Mary and Manuel, Bea, Matt, Ezra McLaren, Hope—

"Who is it?" Judy asked, still trying to get her hair pinned back.

"It's a wedding," I said. "I think it's for us. You still interested?"

She let her hair fall loose and came right out; even dirty, I thought her hair looked better loose anyway. Sam gave us a short, fast ceremony; then everybody cheered and I kissed her.

Occasionally, now, when I'm tired and unhappy, I think about that moment, and I don't sleep for hours after. It makes me too happy—and too sad.

12

"How do you like that?" Esterhazy was saying. "After all I do for the boy, do I get an invitation to his wedding? No. Does he introduce me to his bride? Of course not. Does he even consider waking up?"

I opened my eyes and looked up at him, his big, muscular frame bent over in the cabin. He had an immense grin.

Judy, beside me, said, "I do believe the gentleman is correct. We have not been introduced."

"Captain Dan Esterhazy, of the *Queen of Long Point*, may I present Madam Judy Pareto, of the *Spirit of Monroe*. There."

"Much better," he said, gravely.

"Then how the hell are you, you old pirate?" I rolled out of the bunk and grabbed him in a bear hug; he hugged back.

"Pretty good except that a crazy spaceman is breaking my ribs," he said—then stiffened for a moment.

"It's okay; I know my husband's a spacesider," Judy said. "Parts of him glow in the dark. Why don't you two go out on deck so I can dress?"

As I closed the door behind us, Esterhazy asked, "Which parts?"

To avoid dignifying that with an answer, I looked out at the river. Moored two bends above the GXS, the *Spirit of Monroe* commanded the only view in the neighborhood not excessively infested with people. In the two weeks since the Battle of the Landing Field—the term still sounds strange to me, but that's what the vid dubbed it—we had been busy, but there was still way too much to do. At least we had gotten quite a few people back to growing food, and without ERACA in force, we were getting a pretty good crop to all appearances—being able to borrow tools and machinery when you need to, without having to certify that market-value barter or rent was paid, helps a lot. A lot of our fighters were rotating in and out, spending a week or so rebuilding their homesteads, then coming back for more time watching the skyboys.

That was how we spent our time now. It turned out that most of the hovercraft fuel had been burned at the landing field, and of course now there was nowhere for an OrbiTransit to land—some log and rock walls across the landing field had seen to that. After a little dickering, we had traded our prisoners for theirs; other than that, neither side had accomplished much.

So we were all out here, and they were all in there; we couldn't get in and they couldn't get out—it was a siege. If we could have cut off their water, we might have won in three days, but in that country, you could always get stuff that was at least distillable five or six meters down. Or if we had been able to cut off their food, it might have been over in a couple of weeks. But they were well-stocked, partly because so many farmers had been driven to such bad trades in the weeks before the fighting broke out.

So we sat behind log and dirt barricades and in trenches and shot at them, and they sat in the old GXS compound, surrounded by plenty of open space, and shot back—less and less often on both sides, as we all got to the point where we could operate without ever exposing anyone to fire.

I was telling this to Esterhazy in probably boring detail, when he interrupted. "What would you need to take the GXS compound by assault?"

"All our troops at once might be able to do it, if we could do something about the five machine guns they still have working. And if we could be sure of breaching the fence when we got to it. None of us wants to climb a chain-link fence with a barbed-wire top, thirty yards from men with rifles."

He nodded in satisfaction. "How would you like four pieces of field artillery and a decent team of sappers?"

"Personally I was hoping for Joshua and a brass band."

"Could be nice," Esterhazy agreed. "However, what I have to offer is the artillery and sappers."

"Where did you come up with *that*?"

"Cast the guns ourselves, actually. Muzzle loading and in-efficient, but at these ranges they'll put an iron ball through any of the buildings in an ordinary GXS. And, of course, you can just keep banging away for a while. If a machine-gun bullet hits the cannon, not much happens, but if a cannonball gets the machine gun—"

"It's gone."

"That's how I see it. And we have a little group of twenty guys, good with explosives and willing to try their luck if there's enough covering fire. You want to help me present the deal to your General?"

"To Manuel? Really it sounds like you should talk to the whole Council. But there's no hurry—one great thing about sieges, there's always time."

Then Judy came out; Esterhazy dropped me a wink, looking at her, and I thought I might explode with pride. We all went to breakfast together, and spent most of the time telling stories and laughing.

There was a Council meeting that afternoon; Esterhazy's offer was accepted at once, of course. What excited us more, in fact, was the news from around the Lakes. "It's going up everywhere," the old Sea Gypsy said. "Nobody's gotten as far as overrunning a landing field anywhere else, but there's fighting everywhere, and there probably isn't anywhere left where a skyboy can walk away from a base by himself. The skyboys've tried to split people along Catholic and Protestant lines, but it hasn't worked. Especially not since that bishop that was preaching no violence got sort of accidentally dead about three weeks ago."

"How did that happen?" Manuel asked.

"A man stood up in the cathedral and shot him at the pulpit. One of those little accidents that can happen to anyone."

Manuel looked a little uncomfortable; the rest of us applauded. "Any news from the rest of the Underground?" Mary asked.

"We're cut off," he said, shaking his head. "They've got Niagara, and the Empire Canal beyond it, blocked and guarded. From the West, we get stories about a great big herder's revolt—apparently there's a running war on the plains all the way from the Mississippi to the Rockies, and to judge from the vid, things must be going up all over the planet. The draft call-ups are a lot bigger than the Sea Gypsy records show them being in 2076—and there are fewer exemptions this time. And, of course, they're using the Packers, this time, too.''

"The Packers?"

"The skyboys call them the Irregular Corps—new branch of the Native Forces. The vid version is that they're 'Loyal Protectorate citizens carrying the fight to the enemy in his own way in his own forest, desert, and swamp.' Unofficially, the same kind of boy that used to join the Native Forces for fun, plus anybody that wants out of a death sentence or a long brig stretch, is now being paid by the ORs to do some raping, looting, and killing, and the skyboys are no longer springing for the cost of a uniform. So far they haven't even tried using them against guerrillas—they're strictly a terror force, to keep the farmers in line in the areas still under Orbital control.

"I don't think they'd be doing anything that would stir up so much hatred if they were strictly rational about it. I think they've been bloodied a lot, and now they're just hitting out any way they can. The fact that the rebellion is world-wide this time is putting a lot of pressure on them—"

"Yeah," I agreed. "It's the old bind for an empire... The more troops they put in the field, the more it's a burden on the civilians they claim to be 'protecting.' So they need more troops to get the same amount of cooperation out of the civilians—and that increases civilian resentment more. They're caught in a vicious circle."

"How do they get out of it?" Mary asked.

"Usually they don't. That's why wars like this have humiliated some of the biggest powers in history."

She nodded. "But they know history, too. What are they likely to try next?"

I ran over every grim case I could think of offhand. "Three ways I can think of. Escalation, tolerance, or atrocity—the empire either tries to overwhelm them with sheer numbers, learns to live with a permanent running war, or tries to frighten them out of the war. Tax-haters like the Republics people don't have the patience for tolerance; escalation is short-run easy, long-run difficult. That leaves atrocity, which, after several months of embarrassment and losses, might very well be popular with the military and with the extremists in the Republic.

So, offhand, we have to be ready for them to do something ghastly.''

Manuel nodded. "And what would we do about it?"

"Keep fighting. Do something big the day after the atrocity. Hit back. Massacres and so forth are supposed to scare rebels, but they normally just make them mad. What they do accomplish is firming up support on the home front. The only response to terror is not to be terrified."

They all seemed to agree; in practice, I knew, if the skyboys did something outrageous, it would only inflame the countryside more. At any rate, other than accepting Esterhazy's aid, I didn't think the situation called for any change of course.

BACK IN THE CABIN I gave Judy a long kiss and said, "Promise you won't be mad."

"Hmmph," she said. "What have you been up to?"

"I've just been appointed ace diplomat, along with Mary. We're supposed to go back with Esterhazy to work out the arrangements for the help from the fleet."

"Will you be gone long?"

"A couple of days."

"Then I guess I'm not mad. This place could use a cleanup, for one thing."

"Like where?" I keep my cabin *clean*.

She grinned, a little sheepishly. "Well, nothing's dirty, but I just never feel like anything's mine 'til I've cleaned it, and now this is my home."

"Sure." I kissed her. "Is that why you insisted on washing my back the other day?"

"Damn straight."

Then we cuddled up together and went to sleep. The next morning I kissed her, whispered a goodbye, and got going.

The sun was just coming up as Mary, Esterhazy, and I started down the back road that would join the river well below the GXS. For once it was actually cool; I realized that we were creeping up on fall. There was a sort of clear taste to the air, and I wished I had brought Judy along—she'd have loved the walk, and it would have been fun to introduce her to the crew.

I don't think we talked much on the trip. It was getting fairly warm, around noon, when we cut eastward again to hit the river. That was a short trip—only about three kilometers—and we had decided that when we reached the river we would sit down and cook some lunch.

Esterhazy was about to start a joke when Mary laid a hand on both our arms. "People up ahead; coming this way." We got off the trail and into the brush quickly; I'm not sure how good the hiding place was, but as it turned out nobody was paying enough attention to notice us.

It was two skyboys, a captain and a lieutenant; the man with them was in civilian clothes, carrying one of the little pistol-like cameras that screamed "VidCorp" almost as much as his silly campaign hat.

"So this is where you're going to introduce me to some authentic rebels," he said, grinning. "Pretty stretch of country."

The captain nodded. "You have your camera on?"

"Always do; direct transmission right back up to orbit."

"Look out!" the captain shouted, pointing off into the swamp.

As the reporter turned, pointing the camera, the lieutenant swung his rifle, bringing the butt against the camera. The reporter dropped it, clutching his hand; the captain calmly shot the camera.

"What are you—"

The captain grinned, showing a lot of tooth. "Special orders. You bastards have been running all over with those things too long. No more of your pigfucking spying. We're gonna do what we need to do out here to get Earth back under law and order. We aren't going to have you taking pictures for all the weepers and moaners back home.

"You bastards don't have any loyalty, you know that? We have a successful raid, and one of you takes pictures of some fucking kid that got shot and his mommy crying over him, and never mind that these dirtsiders don't fight with all that code of honor shit, probably Sonny was working for them, yeah, and Mommy, too—they won't even wear a uniform or an armband or something so we can see who they are. Or we finally get something out of a prisoner and you make a big deal of what we did to get it. Well, drycake, buddy! These assholes change the passwords and everything once a day, sooner if one of them gets captured. If he doesn't tell us inside two hours it's no damn good.

"That's what I mean, you shitfingered genetic leaving. This is the kind of people you ought to be with down here, cancer-eaten bandylegged leatherskinned whores and killers. These are really your kind of people, aren't they?" By now the captain was almost screaming; the lieutenant was keyed, bouncing on his toes.

The reporter started to back away. "Let me just ask if—"

"You ask too many questions. Lieutenant!"

The lieutenant brought up his rifle.

"No, please, I—"

The lieutenant shot him in the face. He fell dead on the trail. The captain turned his own rifle on the lieutenant. "Hold it right there. You're under arrest for murder."

The lieutenant stared at him.

"Drop the gun."

"Captain, I only did what we agreed on."

"Drop the gun."

He did.

"Turn your back. Now, run."

"Captain, I don't understand, what is this—"

"Run." The captain fired a shot just over the lieutenant's head. The lieutenant ran about four steps before the captain shot him in the back of the head. He walked up and kicked the body a couple of times to make sure he was dead, and then returned to the trail. As we watched, he set his knapsack down and began to get undressed.

We glanced around at each other; all of us nodded. Esterhazy raised his carbine and shot the captain dead.

The knapsack turned out to contain a complete NF uniform, plus papers with the captain's picture and prints that billed him as an NF corporal.

"What was he doing?" Mary asked.

"Slit his wallet edgewise," I told Esterhazy. Inside the hidden compartment there was what I expected; a thin flexible wafer with a few numbers seemingly painted on it. I stuck my knife through it several times.

"What is it?" Esterhazy asked.

"Transmitter. For talking to a low overhead satellite. This guy was in intelligence. He was going to come and join us—god knows for what reason. To kill Manuel maybe, or just to spy. Anyway, it's taken care of; let's go."

"Why'd he kill them?"

"The lieutenant so there'd be no talk; murderer killed while trying to escape. And the reporter because they're up to something they don't want people back home to find out about."

We hurried on toward the river; it was getting to be time for lunch.

THE STRIPS OF DRIED GOAT had just begun to soften in the boiling water, and I had just peeled the last potato, when we heard the faint rattle of gunfire, off upriver. "Another sortie," I said. "Sounds like a big one."

"It's the first one you and I will miss," Mary said. "I suppose we should just relax and enjoy lunch, but I'm going to indulge in a little worrying anyway."

"They're trying to get out?" Esterhazy asked.

"Yeah. They try every few days," I explained. "I think they're trying to capture a big enough perimeter so that supplies, and maybe reinforcements, can be parachuted in. But all their advantages work against them when they try—they have to cross all that open ground, being shot at the whole way. And remember, those are garrison troops—old hacks plus bottom-of-the-tank draftees doing their Required Service, rounded out with a few NF troopers they can't entirely trust. Half the time they start the covering fire and then nobody charges."

"Have you ever tried counterattacking when they open themselves up that way?"

Mary shook her head. "I've wanted to, but Manuel won't take the losses. I can't blame him. He never thinks of them as so many troops to use or save for this advantage or in case of that problem. He still thinks like they're his neighbors and friends. They love him for it, and he's probably the only one who can keep them all fighting through the winter—but it's not a very efficient way to run a war."

She sat brooding as the guns soared and banged in the distance. I noticed a couple of plumes of smoke, indicating that they had gotten far enough this time to fire some of the barricades, and pointed that out to Esterhazy.

"Aren't you worried?"

"Not really. They can't hold a perimeter like that. Even if they take it, we can take it back the next day—especially since they'll be up close to the cover. And if they break out of the base, they won't have much of anywhere else to go—the nearest station is South Ontario, and that's a long hike for people who never walk if they can help it. No, my guess is that the commander there, whoever it is now, is just trying to cover his ass with his superiors up in orbit—show the right spirit and so forth."

"How does getting them killed show the right spirit?"

Mary shrugged. "They're all crazy. The stew smells great, by the way."

"Thanks. It needs another few minutes." I leaned back against a rock. "Actually, it makes sense if you realize that the top officers are all veterans of the Independence War—space fighters. In space, if you're Navy there's never any cover at all, and if you're cosmorine there's nothing but. Inside the cities, battles are all fought up close, and they tend to be won by the bloodthirstiest, most reckless types. So the top officers back in the Republics just don't have much understanding of sitting out a siege—they expect their troops to attack. I suspect the guy in the field is more afraid of them than he is of Manuel."

Esterhazy had listened carefully the whole time; he turned to Mary and said, "You're right, they're all crazy."

We all laughed, and I went to stir the stew.

And all hell broke loose.

Fortunately we were out of direct line of sight, so when the flash lit up the landscape none of us reflexively looked into it. Eight or ten seconds later, everything around us blew over, trees crashing in the woods. Places in the drought-dried grass were on fire; thin lines of smoke were rising everywhere.

"Up the bank!" I shouted to them, and we scrambled up. Within seconds, a boiling flood crashed past us, filled with bodies and debris, smelling sickeningly like soup. It wasn't 'til then that I realized that we were all bleeding from the nose and ears. "What was that!" Mary shouted at the top of her lungs. She sounded like she was far away.

And I finally realized. "Nuclear bomb!" I shouted. "Tactical job—one of the little ones!"

"They hit their own men!"

"Why?"

"They're all crazy!"

And we turned and started to stagger toward the disaster. Our hearing came back a little over the next hour; sometime after that we met the first shocked, staggering survivors, but they couldn't tell us anything.

The vid has done revoltingly accurate depictions of the scene much too often. I won't bore, or annoy, you with that again.

I will only say the bare things that we learned from one of the refugees who had somehow not gone into shock: ground zero was the GXS. Manuel Proxman and Charlie Perry were personally commanding the defense against the sortie, and along with everything else in the vicinity they had simply vanished into vapor.

And we found a pile of charred wreckage that turned out to be the *Spirit of Monroe*. Mary and Esterhazy wouldn't let me see what was inside, and Mary took me off to cry, and cry, while Esterhazy did the burying.

13

"Nobody home," Esterhazy said, peering through the doorway. "To judge from the looks of things, nobody's been for a few days, maybe a couple of weeks. No sign of the animals, and the windmill is running free, not driving anything."

"That's not uncommon anymore," Mary said. "There's at least one thing I can see that we need. Does that vid set work?"

"What for?" I asked, stupidly. "We need to get to the ships." They looked a little startled. I hadn't spoken since we started out.

"We won't get there tonight," Esterhazy said. "It's dusk. And we can cook that rabbit."

I was going to ask what rabbit when he raised his carbine and shot it; it had been nibbling grass by the fence. The vid set was working, but it was playing nothing but Republic patriotic music, plus warnings of an impending attack on the Republics from a "conspiracy of dirtsider terrorists" who had supposedly stolen nuclear arms from a Republic arsenal. At least it confirmed what I had guessed; the bomb that hit the GXS compound had been one of the little tactical ones, less than five kilotons. Citizens were warned that there was no reason to suppose that only one such weapon had been stolen; attack might happen at any time, but the "gallant armed forces" were "unleashing the full array of their modern warfare capabilities to exterminate terrorist, Prattist-led banditry."

"Pretty obviously, that's us." Mary was staring into the fire, waiting for the rabbit to finish cooking.

"Yeah." I didn't have more to say than that, so I just turned the rabbit again. It wasn't searing very well—the dry summer again.

"Why'd they do it?" Esterhazy finally asked.

I shrugged. "The cosmorines have this idea of being invincible. It's part of the mystique. I guess they wouldn't want to admit to the viewers at home that a whole garrison of them got captured—I'm sure that was part of it, anyway. And the outrage over this will let them do more, give them a freer hand. Cosmorines, and Navy too for that matter, are never all that popular in peacetime. Now they've got an outrage and a list of martyrs, and they'll be allowed to do whatever they want, with the blessings of the public."

"Big effect down here, too," Mary said.

"We saw," Esterhazy said.

She shook her head. "Not like that. I mean, if we had captured a District Office, we'd have made the cosmorines look real bad. A lot of places that are ready to go up, would have gone. But now, instead, we've beaten them with a dirty trick, a fission bomb—"

Esterhazy nodded. "In India and South Asia—anyplace direct downwind from the Nuked Belt—that will make us look pretty bad. Hoang's old country won't be much help this time."

I caught myself thinking I'd have to talk it over with Judy. "This rabbit is about as done as he's going to get," I said. "Let's eat and then get some sleep."

We left the vid on as we were eating; there were three more "emergency announcements," all calculated to scare the brains out of civilians in the Republics, followed by an interview with General Somebody who hemmed and hawed about trying to win a war with one hand tied behind his back. We finished up the rabbit, and Esterhazy went to toss the garbage into the manure pit.

"Saul! Mary! C'mere!"

There, in the barn, was the explanation for the deserted look of the place; the family was in there, dead. The father was nailed to the studs in a spread-eagled X, crucified. The wife and the two daughters were nailed on the floor; their clothing was ripped and their skirts were pulled up around their waists; their throats had been cut, and the father had been left there to look at them until he died.

"Suffocated," I explained to Esterhazy. "When you slump forward, you can't breathe. Sooner or later the muscles give out. If the poor bastard was smart, he just leaned into it 'till he passed out."

On the floor, between the woman and the two girls, the word "WHORES" had been painted. On the wall, there was the slogan "ONE PLANET, ONE LAW, ONE LOYALTY."

"The Packers did this," Esterhazy said. "That's their motto. I see a shovel over there. Anyone remember the burial service?"

We didn't, but we found two more shovels, and we got them far enough under to be out of reach of coyotes. Working in the dark was inconvenient, but not really a problem; the worst of it was pulling out the nails.

We were bone tired—it must have been past midnight—when we staggered back to the house to get some sleep. Since there were Packers in the area, Esterhazy volunteered to guard; I drew second watch. Mary and I stretched out on the floor on blankets; I was dead to the world 'til Esterhazy woke me for my turn.

The trouble with the second watch is that it's perfectly quiet and you have all that time to just sit and think.

MARY SHOOK ME AWAKE; beside me, Esterhazy was stretching and blinking. "Hurry," she said. "They said they'd repeat it constantly 'til they were forced to shut down."

I don't think either of us knew what was going on at all—it was half an hour 'til dawn—but she sounded so urgent that we followed her immediately to the vid set. "I had it on to keep me awake," she explained, "you know, the noise in the background. Here, it's starting again." She turned up the volume.

There were a few seconds of stray music from an entertainment program going off; suddenly an announcer appeared, an ordinary face looking off to the side of the camera the way the reporters in the old, twentieth-century "newscasts" did. "The next voice you hear will be that of Retired General Constantine Yamato, president and chairman of the board of VidCorp."

There was an abrupt, artless camera switch, and Yamato was looking at us. "I must report the following news with a heavy heart. I assure you it is absolutely true; I shall be brief and direct. We have learned from unimpeachable sources and from military documents that the recent nuclear explosion at the South Erie District Office, Protectorate of Earth, was launched from the Navy facilities at Gagaringrad, deliberately, at the express order of the Protectorate Military Command.

"Let me repeat that. The nuclear weapon used against our troops, the cause of some six hundred deaths of our cosmorines and Native Forces and of uncounted enemy and civilian casualties, was aimed, fired, and detonated at the orders of those in the highest levels of our government.

"We urge you to switch on your faxers and receive copies of the relevant documents for your own examination. Document Channel transmission will begin on my mark; turn on your faxer, now. Five, four, three, two, one, and—mark.

"As you can see, the primary and apparently unquestioned motive for this act was the preservation of the present government. The Prime Minister's initials appear on two of the specific orders, one of them authorizing the removal of a fission bomb from Graham Arsenal and the forging of the records necessary. The stated goal is to maintain the present government; it was felt that, and I quote, 'the capture of a District Office and the GXS and landing field associated with it, along with several hundred troops, might well bring about a vote of no confidence, perhaps bringing to power other parties which would not prosecute the war with sufficient vigor to insure an eventual return to law and order. It is believed that a terrorist attack, attributable to enemy forces, with a large loss of life, will have the opposite effect—a rallying of support to the government and to measures necessary to secure swift and complete victory over collectivist bandit activities.'"

Yamato's voice quavered; he looked down for a moment. "Citizens of the Republics and of the Protectorate, I have weighed my responsibility carefully in this matter. It is our duty, as the newsgatherers, to bring you the truth. I have done so; at what cost, I don't yet know.

"I ask only that you hear the truth and act on it as you see fit."

There was another abrupt cut back to the announcer; he said simply, "Company guards are defending our facilities with their lives as we speak. We will stay on the air as long as we can, broadcasting this message continuously. Tell your friends, your neighbors, your co-workers, anyone who didn't hear us! Tell them now!"

Suddenly we were back to those last few seconds of the entertainment program; then the same announcer came on to announce Yamato again, in the same words—

And the screen went blank. A moment later, the blue and silver banner of the Orbital Republics hung across the screen, and a voice announced, "Viewers of the System. Your attention please. Enemy propaganda has been disseminated through our legitimate news channels, apparently with the connivance of high-level traitors. Constantine Yamato, formerly of Vid-Corp, has been placed under arrest, as have nine of his employees. VidCorp has been placed under temporary government control—citizens are assured this is a temporary measure and no threat to the right of private property. Vocator William McHenry, and members of the self-styled Prog clique, will be detained for questioning in relation to their role in promulgating slanders on the armed forces, in a direct abuse of the privilege of office and the right of free speech. These are the critical facts to which we can safely call your attention.

"The security of the state has been gravely compromised by a number of slanders. Do not believe people you hear bearing tales to the discredit of the Navy, the cosmorines, or your elected government, especially if they have shown evidence of Prog sympathies in the past. If they persist, report them to the proper authorities at once. It is only through your efforts that the rights of free speech and press can be maintained for loyal citizens—remember, when in doubt, report it. Someone's son's life may depend on you!"

Patriotic music came thundering up, and Esterhazy flipped over to the Public Affairs channel. "They should be carrying Convocation debate right now, and they only said that McHenry 'will be' arrested—"

Then McHenry's face was up on the screen; for the next few moments we were all mesmerized. The resemblance to the son was uncanny; the delivery was masterful, and the cold fury of the words burned through to the pit of your stomach. We sat and watched, Mary and I clenching and unclenching our fists. Somehow McHenry was saying what we wanted to hear, calling those who had killed Manuel and Judy and all the others to account like an angry Old Testament Jehovah. "Yes, oh, yes," I heard Mary breathe.

I glanced at her, but couldn't see her expression through the tears streaming from my eyes.

Suddenly it was over. There was a crashing noise and something that might have been a gunshot in the background; the screen went blank, then came up with the flag. The same message as before came on. Esterhazy flipped the dial around, but that, and the patriotic music, was all that was on.

Esterhazy switched it off. "Well, if they'd ever let me vote, I'd've voted for him. McHenry preached 'em a hell of a sermon. Called the Prime Minister a murdering bastard, which is reasonably accurate but not polite in the Convocation."

"His son was at the GXS," Mary said.

"He was going to be shipped—" I began, then realized. Linsmann and Voorbeck wouldn't have committed their decision to paper. When they died, the case against Billy went with them. "No. You're right. Unless he was killed earlier, Billy McHenry was there."

"A lot of people have lost sons, but not all of them got to tell the Prime Minister about it, and I'm glad he did," Esterhazy said.

THERE WAS ABSOLUTELY NOTHING standing at anchor in Sandusky Bay. "Well," Esterhazy said, "what do you know? Looks like my boy Calvin had a little more imagination and initiative than I ever gave him credit for. Probably took the fleet elsewhere right after the bomb fell—better yet, scattered it to present less of a target.

"Anybody have any suggestions?"

"Will they be back?" I asked.

"Sooner or later, sure. But we could spend a long time sitting here, and there's still a war going on." Esterhazy scratched his head. "The next anchorage of any size is just this side of Cleveland Ruin. That's bad country, but it's bound to have some Sea Gypsies in port if anywhere does—it's the biggest port in the Lakes for unloading ganjj, and where there's skyboys, there's a demand for ganjj. We could all ship out there as distressed seamen, and sooner or later we'd link up with Cal and the war fleet. Might take a few weeks."

"Anything could happen in that much time," Mary pointed out.

Esterhazy shrugged. "I know. For me, I'm more interested in getting back to the *Queen of Long Point* than in getting back into the war...but Saul's got orders, and you might have something of your own—"

"Revenge?" she asked. "Yeah, I'd like that."

"Well, your way to that is inland, away from the river—maybe southeast at first; there's a couple of big skyboy bases on the Ohio, one up near Pittsburgh Ruin and one down toward the Mississippi, at Delta-town. Probably before you got to the river you'd hear something about which way the action was going, but if you don't you can always just follow the Ohio 'til you either find some trouble or start some. You're both pretty well known by now, thanks to VidCorp—you shouldn't have any trouble enlisting, if that's what you want to do."

"Suits me," I said. "It's about a six-to-ten day walk on the old highways, but call it two weeks if we stay off them a lot. We might be able to make for the Scioto and raft it partway."

"We're going to kill some skyboys?" Mary asked.

"Oh, yeah."

"Then I'm coming with you."

The next morning Esterhazy set off toward Cleveland Ruin. About a year later I got a letter from him; he made it back to the ship without any special trouble. I've always been glad he didn't stick around.

THIS PART WAS A LOT WILDER than the western reaches of the lake, and the few little settlements were mostly deserted, but there was a broad pack trail that followed an old highway south to the Ohio, and we followed that after hitting it the second day. There was plenty of game, and it was warm and pleasant during the day; without much to be afraid of, we built a fire every night and enjoyed the warmth. Three days went by without either of us saying anything much.

That night, as we sat staring into the fire, Mary asked, "Saul, do you think about Judy much now?"

"No."

"I don't think about Manuel much either."

I shrugged. "I guess we have other things in mind."

She leaned against me. "I was wrong about you," she said. "You've been decent enough. You've done your share and taken your own risks. I thought you were just visiting, just getting your fingers into the Earth like all the other skyboys, only from another side."

"Maybe I was. Seems to me I was expecting a lot of Earth—more than I'd expect of any place in space."

"What do you mean?" She threw another log on the fire; sparks went sailing up, and I watched them until they vanished.

"I don't know. I guess I wanted the war to be fought with only the other side doing the bad stuff. I can still see that unarmed kid Wes cut down. I try not to think too much about what happened on the landing field."

"People are angry."

"Yeah."

"You want Christian forgiveness? We should love them, just hate what they do, all that stuff?" she asked.

"I'm not even a Christian."

She laughed and rubbed against me. "Neither am I," she said. "Church was fun, getting to see the neighbors, but God is a pile of shit."

I was quiet; I let an arm fall around her, which felt good. "Did I shock you?" she asked.

"No. I was raised in the Great Rationalization. I don't believe in God, either. But I'm surprised—"

"At me? Maybe Voorbeck just beat God out of me at a tender age." She shrugged. "All I ever saw God do was keep people from doing what they wanted ... or make them do things they didn't. Don't kill the skyboys, they're God's children, too. Don't fuck when you feel like it . . . God doesn't like adultery, never mind what he was doing with the blessed virgin, who was engaged to somebody else.

"And I started to notice how it worked out. If you didn't kill skyboys, things went smooth and people got to keep their land. If you didn't fuck around, people knew which baby inherited which piece of ground. God didn't give two shits about what you wanted, but he sure was interested in land and property." She was sitting with her knees drawn up, huddled close against me. "What do you think?"

"You feel like God's in your way," I said, feeling like an idiot.

"Yeah. Would he bother you?"

"I said I don't believe in him."

She nodded. In the firelight I could see how old and burned her skin was, like dried-out leather. At the same time I could feel that her flesh was firm and warm. I felt very strange.

"Ever since I was about twelve, I haven't been able to tell the boys no," she said. "I wasn't faithful to James. I used to take guys on the side, besides Voorbeck . . . who probably managed to be the only man in the world I didn't want."

"I was faithful to Manuel, except for what Voorbeck made me do. I loved him a lot."

"He was a great man," I said, and flung another log onto the fire, harder than I needed to. I felt disgusted . . . but I didn't move. Instead, I let my hand creep up 'til it was lightly touching the firm, warm underside of her breast.

"He was a big kid," she said. "Everything he believed, he believed all-out, like there was no question. He had faith. He saw things different than what they were, and he could make you believe them. I was different while I was married to him."

Her face was so brown, so old, so wrinkled. There were scars under her eyes where cancers had been cut off, and her hair was flat and dull, besides being dirty from the trail. "He's gone," I said. I let my hands come all the way down onto her breasts, cupping them, running my thumbs over the stiffening nipples.

She got up and pulled off her shirt, then stepped out of her pants. Her breasts were big but flaccid from all those years of high gravity; her crotch was a mass of dark hair, and even her nipples were hairy. Except for her arms and legs, her skin was as white as a spacer's, a white patch that began at the neck and went down to the shoulders and knees.

I brought her to the ground gently, lowered my trousers, and mounted her. The harsh leather of her scarred face rubbed against mine as she gave me one wet, slobbery kiss after another; between kisses, she panted against my neck, spraying me with hot breath and saliva.

It was over in a few seconds, she hugged me to her. "Thank you," she said.

I nodded, holding her, trying to remind myself that this was Mary, that I had always liked her and now we were friends. Her hair in my hand was oily, but I imagined mine couldn't be much better.

"Why don't you admit it?" she said.

"Admit what?"

"You wanted to. You enjoyed it,"

"But I did!"

"Admit it to yourself," she said. "If you can do that, I might just love you someday. But I'm not going to love some asshole who thinks he doesn't need it. I'll leave that to God."

Oddly, I realized that I did feel better; we slept in each other's arms that night. I found I wanted to be next to her.

I dreamed of Judy, and woke the next morning miserably guilty. Mary, on the other hand, was cheerful, more than I'd seen her in a long while.

WE HAD CONTINUED ON in silence; I was being morose, but I didn't see much reason to inflict it on her, so I tried to be as cheery as she was. It was a poor act, but she didn't probe it and after a while I felt better, telling myself that anyone could get carried away, and besides Mary was one of my best friends and she had wanted to.

As we came over the ridge, we saw the plumes of smoke. "That's people, anyway," I said.

"Might as well take a look," she agreed.

From the next ridge we could make out that it was a GXS branch, one of the little trading stations with a half-dozen skyboys at most, and it had been set fire to. The hovercars outside were also burning, and there was a woodpile that I decided not to examine too closely through the field glasses . . . it was giving off really oily smoke from something that had been thrown on top of it.

As I was lowering the glasses, I heard the noise.

"Singing," Mary said. "They're singing a hymn."

As they got closer, we discovered that the hymn was "Fairest Lord Jesus." We got down into the undergrowth on the north side of the ridge and watched them come up the trail.

They were led by ten men holding up crosses on tall poles; in front of each cross-bearer, a man with a machete cleared a path so that the cross-bearer would not have to turn aside or watch his feet. Behind them came rank on rank of marching men, farmers mostly to judge by their clothes, but well-ordered, carrying their rifles and shotguns proudly; they weren't perfectly trained by any means, but they looked like companies of soldiers, not like the ragged militia we had put together. A troop of makeshift cavalry on mules followed them; mules being what they are, that was much less orderly. Behind that—

"That's a litter." I said, amazed. "The kind of thing Julius Caesar travelled in."

Mary was about to say something, but I didn't find out what because that was when we were jumped from behind. Whoever the guy in the litter was, he wasn't anyone's fool.

From the way they were muscling us along, I was pretty sure we were going to meet him. They got us pushed down the hillside without either of us actually falling; by then the column had struck up another tune. At first it seemed unfamiliar; then I realized it was the old church words to "Solidarity Forever," the words that Lincoln's troops had sung.

Then we were flung down in front of the litter. "Prophet, these watched from above," one of the men behind us said. "They carried only a carbine and a froggy gun."

"Set down," one of the guards bellowed. "The Prophet must judge."

The litter was brought to the ground quickly, but without a bump. The white curtains parted; the cross-bearers ran, a little undignified, to stand beside it. The one nearest each side of the litter extended an arm; two hands emerged to grasp them.

As the bent and scarred figure stepped through the curtains, I gasped. He was blind and burned, but there was no mistake. It was Billy McHenry.

14

For a moment I didn't realize I had gasped his name out loud; but his face turned toward me, and he said, slowly, "No one here knows me by that name. Who are you?"

"I sold you the life of Saint Francis," I said, trying to think of some peg he could hang my memory on. There was a lot of whispering among the crowd at that. "I'm here with Manuel's widow."

"Pitch a tent. Give us privacy," he said, calmly. His followers were suddenly running all over the place; in a few minutes, a tent made of three old blankets was in the clearing by the roadside, and we were being ushered in with guards standing around.

The little tent was musty and too warm, but it beat the direct sunlight, and we'd been going long enough that we were glad to sit down. They gave us water and some boiled potato, and that was good, too.

On the other hand, there were a lot of big men with froggy guns standing around, and it was plain we wouldn't be leaving soon.

Billy sat impassively while all this went on, nodding and smiling at nothing. Eventually we were alone.

"All right," he said. "If we keep our voices low, only the people I trust will hear us. How did you get here?"

"We were on—I guess you'd call it a diplomatic mission. To the Sea Gypsies. So we were away from camp when the bomb came down. We've been heading south to the Ohio ever since. I had the idea we might get down into the Ohio Valley and get some action going there."

He nodded; then he looked around, a little bewildered. "Mary?"

"I'm here."

"Thanks. I'm not used to being blind yet." He took a sip of water carefully. "Was Manuel—"

She started to nod, then flushed. "He died."

"I'm very sorry." He sounded desperately sincere.

"Saul lost his wife there, too," she added.

"Saul's—" he looked startled.

"I married Judy Baker, the day the OrbiTransit was shot down." I said it calmly, thinking of her and realizing how much she'd have been fascinated with being here—and again, the weirdness of the whole thing hit me. "Actually, if you don't mind—"

He laughed with no humor at all. "Yeah. How did a cosmorine officer get elected Prophet? I wish I knew. I didn't see the whole process. That's not a pun, by the way."

His arms came down to his sides; he had been sitting with his legs crossed in a half-lotus, as most spacesiders usually do, but he spread and extended them. He was absolutely naked to assassination, I realized, that was what the body language was—but on the other hand, we were shorn of weapons. He breathed deeply twice, and I realized that he really wanted to be believed. I said so.

"That's right," he agreed. "You're the first ones I can really talk to, and you're the only way my family will ever learn what really happened. So I want you to remember and report everything.

"The day before the attack, my father came in through the scramble channel, max secure, contact only to me. He told it to me in short terms—the bomb was coming down. He wanted me to get out, somehow, and tell Manuel to pull back from the base—he told me to 'find Manuel's advisor Saul and say to Saul Pareto that he should convey my greetings to the Chancellor.' He said if I did that I'd be believed. Does that mean anything to you?"

"Yeah. Quite a lot. It's a good reason for me to believe you. What happened?"

"The bomb was nine hours early." He let his head hang for a moment. "I'd gotten past your frontline troops, dressed in some clothes I stole from a Native Forces Trooper. I was trying to find my way around your rear lines, looking for Manuel's HQ, when the fighting started. Nobody inside had any idea that Manuel and Charlie always commanded from right up at the front, by the way—it was a good thing the skyboys didn't know, I guess, though it doesn't seem to matter much now.

"Paul Klein spotted me. All of a sudden I was crashing through the swamp, trying to get away from him and about ten other men, mud rolling in over my boots, things in my face, pissing my pants because I knew they'd hang me for a spy without my ever getting to you or Manuel—and there was a bright flash.

"My head whipped around, right where I was in the middle of the creek, to look at it. That's the reflex, you can't help it. An instant later I realized I'd looked at a nuclear flash and that I was blind; my clothes were bursting into flame, but I didn't quite have time to feel that—a convulsion got me, maybe from the blinding flash and maybe from the radiation, I'm not sure but I think that thing was a neutron bomb.

"I fell right into a pothole, and went all the way under water. I was thrashing around, drowning, and then I passed out.

"I have some memories of getting hauled out of the stream— it was somewhere downstream, not far. I think the people that pulled me out were fishers or trappers. All I remember is that I wanted to talk to God, and I had him all mixed up with my father, and there was the idea that I'd had for a long time that my father was wrong, there was no way to reform the Protectorate, and that was all mixed up with some stuff from Revelations, and I know I started shouting—and I heard a lot of people yelling 'Amen,' and I kept shouting louder. After that it's all just confused images, except that the crowds kept getting bigger.

"I woke up yesterday. By then we'd been marching east for two full days. I have a bunch of officers, I guess you could call them—rebel leaders from all over this part of the continent. I don't make decisions as such. I'm their symbol, sort of a living flag. Apparently they found they could plant suggestions in my mind and I'd then make them direct commandments, right from God himself. I suppose what happened spaceside is just as well. I'm not sure I could have faced Dad, not just a convert but a real live prophet.''

"I'm not sure what—" Mary began.

"You didn't know? Of course, where would you have found a vid? Sorry. Dad was killed 'while trying to escape' three days after the bomb was dropped. Dad's old friend, Connie Yamato—"

"We heard him. And that your father had been arrested," I said. "That was as much as we'd heard. What's going on up there?"

"Well, Connie's dead, too. And there's a news blackout. But nobody from the government, and hardly anyone from Vid-Corp, has been on the air. My guess is a coup."

"But I thought the bomb was dropped to preserve the government—" Mary began.

Billy snorted rudely, from the bottom of his throat. "It probably was. But there are limits to what a legal government can do; VidCorp's lawyers would have gotten subpoenas, injunctions, habeas corpus from the courts, and tied the government in knots—and closing the courts would have triggered a no-confidence in the Senate, sure as death. No, the civilian government was cooked as soon as their cover blew. That's what Dad and Uncle Connie were counting on. What they didn't realize was that bringing down the government was going to mean throwing the whole high command out the shitport— they backed them against the wall, and when it was kill the state or kill the generals, the generals preferred the former."

"I'm sorry," I said, again, not knowing what else to say.

He shrugged. "We need to get on with business. I just needed somebody to talk to a little. Most of my officers know I'm lucid and so on; though they don't know that I'm losing hair and probably developing some strange-looking bruises."

I sucked in my breath, hard. "Radiation sickness."

"That's what they call it," he agreed. "Assuming that being submerged kept me from catching more than a fraction of the neutron pulse, there was still a good load of prompt gamma— and I think I probably did get some neutrons, too. I've noticed that a little electroscope I've cobbled up drops like a brick when I get near it. I figure I'm a day or two from the point where they catch on that I'm dying. They already should be suspicious, considering I have to wear diapers and change them a few times a day, but they haven't seen much of this before.

"That's why it was such a relief to have you turn up. They need you."

"Need us? For what?"

"To replace me. Not only are you famous, it doesn't hurt that both of you have had a lot more experience at this than I have. Or that you're not prophets, either."

We were both sitting there, a little stunned. He went on relentlessly. "Apparently when I was raving, I got them going. At least I only brought along the able-bodied. The trouble is, there are at least twenty rebel groups out there, not all of them on good terms. I'm what holds them together, and they know it. Twice when they've deadlocked, I've broken the tie by being a divine oracle. If they're going to fight together as one army, they need a single command. I can't anoint one of them without destroying my shaky authority. The losers would decide maybe I wasn't the Prophet after all, and even though I'd love to step down—"

"You can't. Unless you can appoint some outsider as a successor." Mary said it flatly.

"Even better. You're not outsiders. In fact, you're legendary—the only person who might have been better would have been Manuel himself. So—"

Mary shrugged. "Looks like we're elected. Where's this army going, anyway?"

"First to Monangahela District Office; then Niagara, then Quebec Regional Office. That's about as much as we can hope for before winter hits. If we don't get that far, we just stop wherever we get to. There might be better plans if we had communication with other forces, but we don't. I've got messengers and scouts out trying to set that up, but it probably won't amount to much 'til we're all dug in for the winter and have time for that stuff." He took another couple of swallows of water. "You'll forgive me, I hope, but dying people are impatient. Let's go."

I remember Sam Klein once said, offhandedly, about the Apostolics, that there's nothing more dangerous than a former heathen who's gotten ahold of the Book of Revelations. That was certainly the case here; Billy dragged us out, introduced us to all the captains and leaders and chairmen and whatever else they called themselves, then got us up in front of the crowd—and went into the most frenzied, maniacal, screaming act I've ever seen. It was like the old flat films of Hitler or Mussolini, except that those can't possibly catch the smell, the insane feel of things, like a crazy New Year's party gotten out of hand—people screaming and crying, falling on the ground in convulsions, leaping and waving, as if they had been touched by fire. It was like someone had shot the Apostles full of amphetamines and hallucinogenics just before the Pentecost—and then put them in an amplifying echo box.

It was like my personal vision of hell.

At the end of it, we were "anointed," as Billy put it—actually that meant he smeared some muddy water on our faces and screamed "these then shall lead you 'til the dragons of space burn the holy planet no more"; the whole effect would have been a lot more impressive to Mary and me if he hadn't used his one good eyelid to wink as he did it.

They wanted us to speak. Mary looked at me, skin pale and shaking, and I suddenly recognized stage fright—which finally explained to me why Manuel had been the leader. I stepped forward.

"I enjoin you," I said, "to be warriors, and to be holy." Good going so far; they were cheering. Actually I'd rather they were just warriors, but in present company it didn't seem wise to say so. "Therefore, I will lay upon you the commandments to keep you on the path." It would really have been easier to call them orders of the day...

"First, obey your commanders in all things." I've always hated barracks lawyers. "Second, harm no one except the skyboys and their allies, and then only as long as they fight. When they cry for mercy, show it to them." Maybe that would help—though from the look of things, it wasn't popular; they were awfully quiet. Let's see, that didn't sound like enough...

What I really wanted to tell them was to settle down into a revolutionary army, instead of behaving like a Crusade-bent gang of barbarians out to murder Saracens. Somehow I didn't think that would play at all.

Inspiration hit. "In token of the high purpose of our cause, I lay the following commandment upon you. Except for the things necessary to run our army, you shall not speak from now until we storm the gates of the New Babylon." Nice touch there, I thought. "You may sing on the march—" I always did like the music "—but you shall speak only when the army requires it; we shall be silent except when we praise God or serve our commanders. Return now to your camps in silence."

They did. It was the eeriest thing I ever saw, thousands on thousands of them getting up and quietly moving away. "Reflect on the Lord and on justice!" I added, for good measure, as they went. "God be with you." I put down the microphone and switched the amp off.

"Good trick," Billy said quietly, at my side. "I wish I'd thought of it."

As we walked back, Mary said, "Saul, I'd have thought you'd want to free them of this."

"I thought so too," I said. "What choice did I have? I couldn't just tell them to quit believing in fairy tales and act like an army."

"Not much," she admitted. "But I wish you'd thought of something."

She didn't say anything at all after that; we ate the noon meal, washed a little, and set off, walking beside the litter. Occasionally we'd hear a hymn start up somewhere, and that would last for a while, but for the most part there was no sound at all. We moved through the winding trail in the forest like an army of the dead.

Late in the afternoon, well toward sunset, we dispersed to camps. They set Billy's litter down, but he didn't come out. "Come on, wake up," I said quietly. "You need to drink a lot of water, anyway—then you can go back to sleep."

Finally I looked inside. He was dead—and there were three empty bottles of synthetic heroin beside him. It made sense, of course; with all that burned skin and his intestines tearing themselves out, he must have kept himself doped to the limit all the time anyway. As soon as he could, he just took the long dive into euphoria and never came up again.

There was a long delay that night as the whole army filed past to look at him, there in the torchlight. If I hadn't known about the heroin, I would have been amazed at the sleepy, relaxed, peaceful smile on the ravaged face—though not, I hope, amazed enough to believe the stories about the halo some people claimed to have seen over his head.

And I was there. I could never have believed the popular story that after his death the litter smelled of roses. What it did smell like, I'd rather not describe. It took us a lot of fast scrubbing to get him ready for the bier, and if he hadn't been Catholic we'd have cremated him. As it was, I made sure he was deep under the cairn we raised for him.

I MIGHT HAVE EXPECTED several days of marching in mostly dead silence to have been eerie, but in fact it was restful. Mary came to my bed every night; I still didn't know what I felt about that, except that I couldn't really see any reason to turn her away, and it seemed to make her happier. Sometimes she would lay back after we were done and talk until she fell asleep; one night she came around to the subject of Manuel again.

"It wasn't just that he was like a little kid," she said. "It was more what he could make you believe in; I think I even believed in God, sometimes, in church with Manuel. And I couldn't hear the neighbors anymore . . ."

"Hear the neighbors?"

"You know, you take a boy back in the woods, have a good time with him, it's nice, but as you're walking home with him you realize somebody's bound to see you and you know what they're going to say. Or like the things I could imagine the other women that worked at the GXS saying when I'd have to go around in uniform there. It was like I could hear them 'til Manuel turned up, and then all of a sudden it wasn't just I didn't give a shit. I never did. It was that I just didn't think of them saying it. Which is the way Manuel was, too. There were a lot of rumors about him and every girl around Rogers City." She giggled suddenly. "They were true, too."

"Sam said something about that—"

"Yeah, he would. For Sam it was okay for men to be that way. It was okay for women, too, as long as they admitted they were sluts...but it wasn't okay for a woman to just get what she wanted, if and when she happened to want it. Sanctimonious old pigrapist."

I was a little shocked; he had been my friend. She must have seen that somehow.

"Saul, when are you going to figure out we're just people? You see all these people fighting for justice and freedom and all that shit, and of course they look noble to you. They're doing the biggest, most important thing they'll ever do in their lives. If they win, or when they lose, they'll go back to their regular life, and they'll be the same shits people always are. Sam didn't really give two shits about women, and he'd cite the Bible to back him up. Wes Perry was a slimy little killer. Charlie was an old brute that beat up both his kids and never smiled in twenty years—long before he got into trouble with the skyboys. And Manuel—"

"I'd rather not hear."

"Ha. You know how I got Manuel? He came in from the fields one day and I was in his house, with the curtains pulled and without any clothes on. I knew about him from what the girls had said; I gave him a good time, then and at least twice a day from then on. First girl he'd met who wanted it as much as he did, so he married me..."

She started to cry.

"You meant more to him than that," I said.

She shook her head. "I know. I know I did. I just didn't expect I'd miss him or any man, but I do..."

She cried 'til almost morning; I didn't sleep either. I felt dead for a day or two after that, just going through the motions as we marched along by the Ohio; it was easier, anyway.

15

It took us almost three weeks to reach the Monangahela District Office. The great mystery to me was why we didn't get nuked on the way; the answer was something that came out only when the war was over. The military government wasn't sure of its footing, and every inch of the earth between the 85th parallels was constantly visible from one Republic or another. After Yamato's announcement, they couldn't risk the rumor of another nuclear shot—they avoided even using the Iron Ball. There had been riots in at least four of the Republics and three mutinies Earthside; if the cosmorine generals wanted to carry on this war, they would have to do it without offending people.

Much of the march was through real wilderness; the population in some of those areas peaked before 1900, and they had been in decline for a long time even before the big die-offs of the 1990s and 2030s. Forested hills like those would have been perfect for a guerrilla war, and I mentally marked the place as a possible area for retreat, but at the moment I didn't see any way to lure the cosmorines into it. Leaves were beginning to turn, and there was something beautifully peaceful and soothing about all of it, but I realized that McHenry had planned with a skyboy's sense of distance, and we'd be lucky if we took Monangahela, let alone got any further, before winter set in.

The scouts had reported that the District Office was abandoned and burned; the commander at Monangahela had been smart enough to dig in at the landing field, preserving his supply lines. There were dugout forts, connected by trenches and tunnels, in a string around the field; brush had been burned for a half-kilometer all the way around, and fence strung in the burned areas. We were an easy day's march away now, but we still didn't quite know what we were going to do when we got there. Mary and I, along with all the various group leaders, were having an extended, frustrating meeting about it when the excited sergeant burst in and saluted.

"Colonel Nakagawa-Gratiski, of the Monangahela District Office, requests parley, sir."

"Parley?"

"Yes, sir. He and some of his officers came out with a white flag and turned themselves in to the scouts. He says the war is over and he needs to arrange terms of surrender."

"Tell him we don't surrender, whatever the other armies do."

"No, sir. He wants to surrender to us."

MY MEMORY of the next few days is of unending craziness. We accepted the Colonel's surrender, of course, and took over a thousand of them prisoner there; just quartering troops and guarding prisoners would have been enough of a problem without having to adjust to the rest of it.

Confederation troops had boarded all twelve Orbital Republics within minutes of each other; a nice little piece of planning and navigation, since they hadn't taken a setting-up orbit first. Of course, thirty-six-thousand kilometers out, that's not as tough as the landing a drop boat makes on Earth, on paper—but when you figure in having to match velocities with the Republics, and doing it in fleet formation, on a timetable, twelve different spots at once, it's enough to make you give up twitting the Navy.

The Revolution, from a Confederation standpoint, was an overwhelming success—almost all the cosmorines had been down on the ground, bottled up in sieges, chasing guerrillas, or patrolling areas they still held. Before even one troop transport could be loaded onto the catapults, the Republics were in Confederation hands and their missiles and lasers were trained on the launching sites. At Tsukubanichi and Tereshkovagrad, the local governments had actually welcomed the Confederation troops as liberators; only at Bothasburg, Gagaringrad, and Von Braunsburg was there any real resistance at all. All over Earth, cosmorines and Native Forces were giving up their arms and turning themselves in; makeshift prison camps were springing up everywhere. I suppose we might have had trouble with jailbreaks—except that there really wasn't anywhere for the cosmorines to go.

With victory, Mendenhall's role had been revealed, along with our names. I vaguely remember sitting in a shack with a tall, blonde woman, answering question after question, telling the whole grim story as if I were reciting a nightmare. That, anyway, is all I remember of the "famous" Clara Bly interview.

I'll tell you the first thing I do remember; for some reason it's never been made much of in the popular accounts of the Revolution. I was in the main HQ in Quebec, formerly the offices of the Protectorate Command for North America, pushing papers around and trying to figure out how to integrate some of the militia units down in Georgia into the North American forces—we hadn't gotten the integrating done in the course of the war, and it shouldn't have been necessary now, except that we happened to be the only government the benighted continent had.

The problem in this particular case was that the Georgians had done a perfectly good job of seizing the trading stations around Atlanta Ruin and had taken the surrender of the Savannah River District Office and GXS; since they had the only armed force in the area, and they had beaten their own skyboys, they had the idea that they should run their own affairs. Again, it wouldn't have been a problem—except that they wanted to put their whole ragtag army onto permanent pension and support it with taxes that were easily twice what the skyboys had charged. Somewhere along the way the point of the whole business had gotten lost.

What I was trying to do was to decide between threatening them with a military expedition we couldn't mount or bribing them with privileges we couldn't deliver; I had about six layers of officials over me to report to on this one, so I was also trying to get the paperwork done, too. Three weeks before there hadn't been any such thing as a "Forces and Resources Request"; now failure to fill one out was a big offense.

My other big project was killing flies. The heat pumps had wheezed and died a few days before; Indian summer had promptly descended, and the large number of open pit latrines and garbage dumps we'd had to set up had brought more flies than I'd ever seen in my life.

I had just finished killing one on the outside edge of my desk when a kid came running up. I kept my head down, hoping he was going somewhere else or that someone else could handle it, but he came straight to me and said, "Message for Colonel Pareto."

That title was one of the sillier effects of winning. "Yes," I said, holding out my hand.

He nodded. "Colonel Proxman requests you at the max security stockade immediately, sir. Fast as you can make it, she said."

I got up and pulled on my froggy gun in its sling. "Anything else?"

I realized why the boy looked strange—he was terrified. "It's...there's a crowd..." he said.

"Get me all the Superior Carbines you can muster," I said. "They're—"

"Barracks Three, first floor, sir?"

"Right. Get them quick. See if you can find me some Plains cavalry, too." I turned and ran.

The max security stockade had no skyboys in it. Even on dry ground like this, they had no desire to run for it. After all, their only chance to get home was to stay and wait out the negotiations. What was in the max security was Packers, the Earthsider irregulars who had spent the war murdering, raping, and torturing for the ORs.

They were being held because we figured if we let them out they'd be murdered, and nobody wanted them to sneak home and avoid trial, either. A lot of us, including Mary, were in favor of just killing them; not all of them, however, and not all at once.

When I got to the stockade, the crowd there couldn't have been less than three thousand people—and what was keeping them out was Mary and two very scared guards.

The stockade wall was simple chainlink fence topped with wire, around what had been the drydock for the big hover-buses. Inside the fence there were four big metal-walled sheds; at night the one guard-tower with its spotlight was manned and a few men with dogs walked the fence. During the day, we simply relied on the six hundred bare meters in all directions, the guard posts at the corners and the gate, and the prisoners' awareness of what would happen to them if they were caught outside the compound. It hadn't really occurred to us that we'd need to keep anyone *out*.

There was only one gate in the chainlink fence; Mary and the two guards stood with their backs to it. The mob formed a rough arrowhead pointed at them; the people up front were about ten meters from Mary. I made myself walk slowly and deliberately, but it was an effort not to run straight to her.

She looked up and motioned me to stay back where I was, near the corner of the stockade perhaps sixty meters from her. Then she turned to the crowd again and shouted something I didn't hear. Whatever it was, it quieted a lot of them in the front rows. She took about three steps forward, hands extended and open, speaking quickly and quietly, her face impassively calm. For a moment, the crowd seemed to waver.

Then one of the guards saw his chance and broke and ran. he charged off, dropping his rifle, heading along the stockade back toward the barracks. We never did find out who he was.

Mary turned at the clatter of the dropped rifle; I saw one instant of plain, naked fear on her face, but the other guard was standing firm, his rifle at port arms. She took an instant to take a breath, looking more annoyed at the interruption than anything else, and turned back to the crowd, opening her mouth to speak.

Somebody shot her. It was a shotgun, I'm sure, because her whole face caved in and the back of her head blew out, spraying the pavement with blood and brains. She was dead instantly.

The guard whipped his rifle up and fired once into the crowd; someone fell. I've always hoped it was the one who fired the shot, but there's no way of knowing that, of course. The mob recoiled back a second, then rushed forward. The guard dropped to one knee and shot two more of them before they got to him; I think he was simply trampled in the press of bodies. I'm going to put his name in here because we never did find his family: Ishmael Etrangere, and he was from somewhere right around there. If you're reading this Earthside, and you know his family, I'd appreciate it if you'd let them know that they can claim his medal and some money through the Vets Bureau.

The mob broke the gate down in an instant and swarmed in on the unarmed prisoners.

Quite a few of the Packer prisoners had families; some women and children were voluntarily in there. Mostly, unless they fought, they were just shoved aside in the crowd's rush to get as many Packers as they could. One teenage girl tried to shield—her brother? her father? I don't have any way of knowing—and a man shoved her up against the fence; it looked like intended rape, but in fact he disemboweled her with a butcher knife. I didn't even realize I had brought up my froggy gun and fired until he fell across her.

Right then the Superior Carbines got there; I had sent for them because they were mostly Sea Gypsies from the Northern Lakes—tough, well-disciplined people I could depend on to take orders. "We've got to stop this massacre," I said. "One volley over their heads."

Their sergeant nodded; they fired.

Apart from a couple of stray shots back at us, nothing much happened. There were just too many of them, and they were busy in the stockade, where the screams and shots were an overwhelming pandemonium.

They looked at me. "We'll have to go in and push them out," I said.

"Excuse me, Colonel, but there's only twenty of us, and no bayonets."

I looked again. The sergeant was right, and furthermore, some of them were unarmed. The kid must have gotten whoever he could snag from the barracks.

There was a cheer from the crowd; a squirming body was being hoisted on a rope. "Better send runners back and get some help," I said. "There's not much we can do here."

There was a sudden thunder of horses' hooves, and two companies of Plains cavalry rode up. A hand clapped me on the shoulder, and I turned to see who had done it. Kwanza was standing there in a perfectly ridiculous-looking outfit—calf-high boots with built-up heels, baggy blue canvas pants, and a bright green jacket, with what looked for all the world like a baseball cap. "We're here, sir," he said. "Permission to clear the stockade?"

I nodded, numbly, and the plainsmen thundered in. There were shrieks and groans, and in gratifyingly little time the crowd was streaming back out the gate, helped along by the clubs and pistol butts of the cavalry. I looked sideways at Kwanza again. "We're not needed here anymore," he said. "Do you want to dismiss your men?"

I did, and they went, shaking their heads and shuddering. In the compound, a few of the mob were being rounded up by the riders; the rest had fled. There were more bodies on the ground than I could count. A few of them were moving.

"I'm glad I found you," he said. "It's time to come home."

MENDENHALL'S OFFICE hadn't changed; after the trip there I was accustomed enough to low grav—Navy cruisers only boost at about a tenth of a gee on a long haul, though they can hit six full gees on sprints and turns. Still, I felt strange, as if I had come around a corner in Team Pareto's Common Hall and found my xmothr and xfathr there; Mendenhall belonged to another time, as far as I was concerned.

He set out the coffee, smiled, and said, "Has Kwanza told you much?"

"Only that we won, and Earth gets self-government in about a year."

He bobbed his head. "That's the basics. We're getting a temporary government together to draft a constitution and so forth; that should be interesting. Except for the Sea Gypsies, most Earthsiders haven't travelled much and don't really know what's over the next hill."

"The plains nomads travel a lot," I pointed out.

"Yes, but it's all in big loops—seasonal migration. Often they don't even see much of the inside of the loop. No, this should be a big event. The people of Earth will get to meet face to face, with vid carrying it to every home, for the first time since the UN collapsed in '34.'' He spread his hands. ''Anyway, since you got cut off from us and were a little more deeply involved, I thought I might tell you what our future plans for Earth are.''

''If it's self-government,'' I said skeptically, ''how do you have plans for them?''

Mendenhall laughed. ''Saul, you've certainly learned to cut the cards. And of course that's exactly why I have you here...I could have had your debriefing report to read, or for that matter watched the dramatization on the vid—''

I blushed. ''I never intended—''

''Easy, friend. You talked to a reporter while you were in a state of shock. It may not have been wise, but it's one of those things that can happen to anyone.''

''It's the way they portrayed it. They made it sound like I planned and carried out a whole master scheme to liberate North America. I just rode along and did what I had to do, when it was there to be done. I lost most—''

He raised a hand; he looked strangely sad. ''I'm sorry. I was unkind. The wounds are still raw—I shouldn't have touched them. I meant only to say you've become famous.''

''I didn't ask to be.''

''You didn't,'' he agreed. ''But you are. You're one of our few heroes this time. You and the other agents, of course, but your exploits were the ones that made it into the popular media first. Other than that, there were the few kids that got killed at Gagaringrad and Von Braunsburg. One of them was a student of yours, by the way, Goddard al-Ghirad.''

I winced. ''What happened to him?''

Mendenhall looked a little startled. ''You knew him well?''

''He was very promising. We'll all be a lot poorer for the loss.''

He cleared his throat. ''He was the first off a clampon lander, jumped out right as the panel fell away from the lasers. It was airlock B, by the way. There's a fund being set up to install a monument there. Anyway, there was a late OrbiTransit load of cosmorines that hadn't quite left yet sitting around waiting there, and in the four minutes warning they got they managed to get armed. Al-Ghirad held them off for the few seconds that his buddies needed to get gas in there..."

I nodded. The poor kid had been doing what he had to do; it was what I had expected.

Mendenhall let the silence get cold for a while, then finally said. "Now, if you're ready, I could tell you what I brought you here for."

"Sure. Go ahead."

"You're not very eager."

"I lost my eagerness with my innocence. It was a package deal."

Carefully, he poured coffee for each of us, before speaking again. "I want you to know that none of this conversation is off the record, unless you want it to be. You're free to run out and shout this into a vid camera for Solar System-wide broadcast. If you decide to keep anything confidential, it's your decision, and you can revoke it any time.

"All right, it's like this. Strictly speaking, of course, we have plans for Earth. We fought the war to get access to the volatiles. The question is what the terms will be.

"First fact: we need the Earth. The ORs have eighty times our population, and we'll be returning local sovereignty to them soon. We just don't have the troops to occupy them. Therefore, we're going to have to live with them, within the framework of what we're going to call the Council of Humanity. Votes based on population, and this time Earth gets to vote. That gives us a majority as long as we keep Earth happy.

"I assume how happy they are will depend on the deal they get, so here's what we'll give them:

"First of all, no more OrbiTransit flights within five years. We're building four skyhooks."

"Four what?" I asked.

"Four towers 30,000 kilometers high. So that the top is actually in geosynchronous orbit. An elevator to space, if you will. The idea was actually quite common among the engineers in the decade before the first space cities were built; popular enough that even after independence thirty years later, Orbi-Transit went to the trouble of securing a permanent patent on everything related to it. Since then it's been mouldering away, but OrbiTransit is going to be broken up and abolished, along with the other private monopolies, and one thing we will *not* have again is permanent patents.

"Anyway, the relevant point is that skyhooks don't destroy ozone. And while we're building them, we're going to set up ozone generating plants and, if the engineers come through for us, put the OrbiTransits on an oxygen diet. We'll probably have to go back to the old low-orbit system with a ferry between low and geosynchronous orbit. So, by our figures, we should have the ozone layer back to its old self in five years, self-maintaining in ten."

"That's a lot of ozone," I said skeptically. "Are you going to set up another orbital power station to run the plants, or what?"

He smiled. "There's a lesson in systemic evil for you, Saul. There was always more than enough power to do it, just in the reserve capacity of the Republics. Solar Electric, though, wasn't going to give it away free, and the Republics weren't going to get involved in anything as 'socialist' as buying the power and using it for a public good like that. Hell, they never built one kilometer of public road in almost eighty years of the Protectorate. There was no replacement ozone because nobody could make a profit selling it. And it wouldn't have taken much—a few million cubic meters a year even with the full OrbiTransit system running."

It made perfect sense; of course, I knew how the Republics looked at things, but I was still just about speechless. "You mean they didn't even consider—"

"The Progs, and their friends, must have proposed it a hundred times, except they never made a point of how cheap it was, and they never talked about what was in the way of doing it. If they'd done that, they'd have had to give up reform and take up revolution. You should recognize the pattern, Saul. Remember Pratt's *Letter to the Social Democrats*?"

"Liberal reformers down through the ages," I said, hoisting my coffee in salute. "May the nonexistent gods fry their hypothetical souls."

"Now, that's a toast," the old man said, grinning at me. You want to hear the rest of my offer to Earth?"

"Sure."

"Complete domestic self-government, funded mostly by a tax on the volatiles they sell us."

"What happens if they try to stick us, like the Republics did?"

"Then the Republics move in and get us both. They'll figure it out, Saul. I have faith in them. I'm an old Earthsider myself."

Mentally, I revised his age at least another three decades upward; the past few months had made me pretty well shockproof.

"One more part of the offer," he added. "They're going to start selling us food again."

I gaped at him. "Unless you've repealed all of economics since Ricardo—"

"Nope. It's a straightforward economic problem that's been thoroughly analyzed already. You're the Pratt scholar, you should remember what got his books banned in the Republics."

"Collectivism and opposition to space development, I thought."

"Nope. That was the official version. I was quite a bit younger at the time, but I was already on a faculty committee at the University of Tereshkovagrad. It was a political suppression, the same thing that happened to your thesis. Pratt had written an unpublished manuscript called 'Social and Economic Roots of the Present Crisis.' A couple of years after Pratt was missing and presumed dead, a copy found its way to orbit; it was read by the censorship board, and they decided to ban all of Pratt, just in case such ideas might be implicit in his other works."

"Why didn't you tell me this when I was writing my master's thesis?"

"It wasn't really germane. And I thought you knew. It's a common enough anecdote. Anyway, we were talking about the Earth's balance of trade problem. Pratt's point of view—and don't quote me to the Regents, but he was often dead right—

was that the problem was always purely physical. You can't compete from the bottom of a gravity well *if* you have to use a reaction engine to lift with. But the skyhooks will beat any rocket ever built by a factor of twenty, at least; maybe as much as fifty if they amortize them according to a little scheme of mine for which I hope to take all the credit. Oh, sure, there's still a little difference between orbit-grown and Earth-grown in initial hauling cost, but it's more that offset by what Earth has: free leak-proof enclosure, free or cheap volatiles, a complete array of minerals with hardly any preprocessing. If all of us were up here, we'd be sending colonists down to build a sky-hook and grow food anyway."

Shaking my head, I almost blushed. "It sounds obvious now. Every time we expand a farm up here, we have to expand the bubble it lives in, and the water and air supply, and the power hookups for the pumps...so the balance of trade problem has been repealed?"

"Oh, god, no. Rural areas always run chronic debts to the cities, which both sides resent. Think about the chip most Titans have on their shoulders. But we'll give them a fairer shake than they've gotten, and their smarter kids will move up here for the bright lights and fast times."

I was going to ask about why anyone would want to look at a bright light when a thought came to me. "All right," I said. "Where do I come into this?"

"I'm not going to catch you napping twice, eh?" It was amazing to see him flip up onto the desk, swinging his legs.

My arms stayed folded; I let my fingers drum on one arm.

He looked at me intently for a minute. "Sorry," he mumbled. "I know this won't be easy for you. What I want you to do is help me make Earth fashionable."

"Do *what*?"

"I want to get as many young people up here as possible to develop an Earth fetish, a desire to go down there to study, work, tour, see the home world. If the old fascination with the conqueror holds, they may very well lure a lot of the Republics kids down with them, too."

"Why? And how am I going to do it?"

"We're coming to how. As for why, well, the family of man has had eighty years of civil wars, and sixty millennia of one gang exploiting another, and we're all going to get to know each other and learn to live with each other. Don't you know what we've done this time?"

I sank back into the chair. "We've abolished war," I said. "As long as the Confederation itself doesn't torpedo it in the next few years, we're going to have just one sovereignty."

"At least until some other species turns up looking for the same niche in the ecology. Yes, we have abolished war; except for civil war, which could erupt around half a dozen issues in the next century." He pulled out a printed report.

"Copy for you. Sociodynamic model I've been running a lot in the last few weeks. See if you agree with it, but do me a favor and don't hand it to the first reporter you see, since I'd have to recalculate the whole thing if it became public. The conclusion, anyway, is that if we can hold peace for one lifespan—say two-hundred-plus years—it will hold for all time, minor police actions and riots excepted. What we need is a generation to get going in the right direction. Which means you, as the great hero of history's last war—"

"Hero?"

"As I said, that's what it's called. You're a hero, Saul. The Facilitator is going to shake your hand, make a big speech, and hang a lot of fruit salad on your shirt next week."

"But," I sputtered, "I didn't do much of—"

"Did I say you were deserving?" Mendenhall asked. "Among other things, if you'd been a little more foresighted, we'd have Manuel Proxman alive today, and he'd be worth more than you can imagine in getting a planetary government going. While you were down there you apparently married a girl no older than most of our freshmen here—I'll tell you right now you're not teaching at Confederation University again. And the final straw is that I've had to go to a great deal of trouble and expense burying an autopsy report that shows that Manuel's widow was carrying *your* child at the time she died. If it were up to me I'd bury you some place sorting mail or cataloging field reports.

"But you were the first agent that a reporter got near—so you're a hero. Now, If you don't mind, I'm going to take you down the hall and introduce you to the public relations people, who will teach you when to say what to whom. And if you don't cooperate—"

"I'll cooperate." After all, it was what I had been doing all my life.

THERE WERE EIGHTY of them at the school, all between fifteen and eighteen. The first question I got asked, by a little, fat, dark-haired kid, was, "How many people did you actually kill, personally?"

"As few as I could," I said. It was the prepared PR answer, and it was a great one.

The next was a girl, tall and blonde with odd-shaped pointy breasts that I found myself staring at for a moment. "How do the dirtsiders—"

"Earthsiders," I corrected.

She nodded, flushing a little. "How do they plan to spend the money we're giving them?"

"I wasn't aware that we were giving them money."

"We'll be paying for water—"

"Oh," I said.

"—and I just don't see what farmers are going to do with money. I mean, are they going to put extra vid sets in for the *chickens* to watch?" There were a few nervous giggles. "We won the war. Don't we have a right to that water? Why can't we just take it?"

There was a smattering of applause, but I practiced my cold stare, like the PR woman had showed me. The blonde girl cringed a little and sat down, and the room got very quiet. Now all I had to do was think of something to say.

"For every life we lost, they lost two thousand," I said. "Is that enough?"

There weren't any more questions. The reception committee hoped this wouldn't prejudice me against Ganymede; the guy who was steering me around said afterward that I might have overdone it, but I'd get the hang of it soon enough.

ROGET HAD FOUND ME a great corner where I wasn't terribly visible; after six months of touring, with three days 'til I went back out on another swing through the Confederation, it was nice to have a place to just sit and read. It was brightly lit—there was a fixture just over my head—and very comfortable, and Roget had set me up with a nice big drink from the bar. I was reading Pratt's *Criteria* and enjoying it more than ever; I was down to the last few paragraphs:

Ultimately, then, there is just one question for the conservative political theorist in the wake of the Third Industrial Revolution. Given the certain capability of feeding and sheltering every human being in a physically adequate way, with no more than one in four of the adult waking hours committed to labor at another's service, and without degradation of the environment or restriction of civil liberties, by what right can anyone stand in the way of the realization of such a world? Let him draw his support from the Bible or from what he takes to be natural law, the conservative is faced with a challenge opposite that of his progenitors; he need not justify the continuing existence of wealth, but of poverty.

For the radical, there is only the answer. That which stands in the way of the world of plenty that our technology is capable of is evil. He who defends the system that continues unnecessary poverty defends murder.

And given that stark choice, let us act as if we were moral, in the hope of deceiving our descendants into following our example.

I closed the book with some satisfaction; it's a good thing to read when you've overdosed on public speaking and people in general.

I'm still not sure how the boy found me, but he was standing there when I put the book down. I took a big gulp of my drink and looked again, but he was still there.

"You're Saul Pareto," he said.

"Yeah." He was about ten years old, and a little dirty look-ing, not an easy thing to manage in space. Maybe he'd just come from the Sand Park that was our kraal's biggest boast.

"Could you . . . I mean . . ."

I knew the routine by now. I pulled out a picture and signed it. His eyes lit up, and I talked with him for a minute about the Confederation no-grav basketball tournament and the general unpleasantness of math class.

As he took the signed paper, he said, "What's the most guys you ever fought single-handed?"

"YOU SHOUTED at the Interplanetary Club," the PR guy said. "I think you offended them. And you shouldn't have stormed out."

"They kept saying 'dirtsider.' Every pigraping question it was 'dirtsider.' "

"It will take them time to learn."

"Let 'em learn on their time. Not mine."

"I think you need a vacation. There's a faxgram for you." He handed it to me.

I opened it and read it:

SAUL: AM BUSY SAVING THE REVOLUTION. COULD USE HELP, HEROES PREFERRED. WANT TO COME DOWN AND GIVE ME A HAND? DE-TAILS TO FOLLOW. YOURS. KWANZA.

It took the details three agonizing days to follow; it only took me an hour to pack.

16

"What is this thing, anyway? It has to mass fifteen kilos." I set it down on the desk as gently as I could.

"Only a hair over ten, xtove, you're just not used to high grav anymore," Kwanza said. "It's called a word processor, a computer designed to be dedicated to text work."

"I thought it might actually be a typewriter, like you see in museums. It's eighty years old if it's a day."

"There's a jack here to hook it to the dynablock interface," he said. "That's more recent, anyway."

"You mean this thing is so old—"

"Yes, it originally took disks." He sighed. "The budget could be a little higher, I admit."

I had been going to ask him if it read punched cards. The contraption sat on the table for a minute while I caught my breath. Kwanz' was right, it's amazing what a few months in low grav will do to you if you don't work out regularly. Then we got it unpacked and set up—or rather Kwanza read me the directions while I did it. His Japanese was rusty, but better than mine.

"Will you look at this?" I said. "They put the keys on wrong."

He looked over my shoulder at the keyboard I had just plugged in. "Nope. We'll be hunt-and-pecking, I'm afraid— that's the old QWERTY keyboard. You push the keys one at a time, one key per character. This machine was at least ten years before the Ergonomic Standard Model; must've been one of the first ones built after the Troubles."

I sat down and stared at the thing. "I don't suppose we could interface it to a standard multikey?"

He shook his head.

"And we're going to do legal work and research on it?"

He nodded.

"How did I get here?"

"You answered my faxgram."

He had me there. I changed the subject. "Okay, now I'm unpacked and the office is set up. You said I was perfect for this job. What am I doing?"

Kwanza grinned, and I suddenly felt that, despite the fast, hard drop in a Navy ship's space-a cabin from Apollo, and running all over East Africa Landing Field all morning getting the papers straight, and then having Kwanza drag me everywhere . . . just maybe it was going to be all right for a change.

"Why don't I just say you'll be reading fine print for the Earthsiders?"

"Good. Why don't you say that? Now what does it mean?"

That was a great laugh to hear. "Touche, I guess. Okay, the deal, summarized with no diplomatic politeness, is this: any thirty-thousand Earthsiders who can get their signatures together can send someone to the Constitutional Convention, which everyone seems to be calling the ConCon. All of these miscellaneous people whose sole qualification is a combination of popularity and persistence, or maybe just the brazenness to annoy thirty-thousand people into signing a petition—all of these clowns are supposed to draft a constitution for Earth. When they get done, they submit it to his nibs the Temporary High Commissar, General Johann Sheridan, an old mossback who took me four weeks to break out of the habit of calling his citizens 'dirtsiders' and who still won't shake hands with one unless he's wearing gloves. He seems to be part of some complex deal Mendenhall worked out. I don't know what the boss got in exchange for this, but it wasn't worth it. Where was I?"

"Sheridan looks over the draft constitution."

"Unh-hunh. Then he approves it, *pro forma*, and the people ratify it, and the troops go home and everybody lives happily ever after."

"What if he doesn't approve it?"

"Then we rewrite until he does. But he will. His signature is his passport out of here."

I could understand the feeling. "So where do I come into this?"

He sat back. "The Commissarate has submitted a suggested draft document for the ConCon to consider. One look at it told me that I needed someone with a knack for the formal side. Unless I'm completely crazy, what this thing will do is create the worst governmental structure since twentieth-century Italy—maybe since the Byzantine Empire."

"And you want me—"

"To prove it. Full-fledged math treatment, static and dynamic. And explain it to our Earthsider friends. I can spot half a dozen booby traps in that thing, but I've already got money down with Veblen that you can find at least twenty."

"*Henry* Veblen? Is he here?"

"Yep. He's out beating the bushes with his volunteers, teaching them how to gather signatures. If we'd stuck with Sheridan's idea—just announce it a couple times on the radio and wait for 'em to come in—I doubt we'd get a hundred attendees."

"A big group will make it tougher—"

"But the small one would have been a handful of well-educated half-orbitalled types that probably quietly collaborated their way through the Revolution. With a little luck we'll have two thousand, from all over the planet. That was Henry's last announced goal. Anyway, deadline is next week, and they start showing up ten or fifteen days after that, most of them getting the first rides in a rocket they've ever taken. They'll be all excited and nearly impossible to talk to. By then we need to be ready."

"Who is 'we'?"

"You, me, Henry, Katrina Hayakawa, Cynthia Levi-Strauss, Yoko Beard. The ones that really went native on our little jaunt for the boss. Officially we're all here as requested advisors to the ConCon; we're all just military enough to eat in mess halls and sleep in officer quarters. Welcome back, Colonel."

"Let me guess," I said. "You're coordinating, Henry's doing grassroots, Kat's working conflict resolution—"

"As a prophylactic, yeah. Mostly she's trying to come up with a three-hour course in semiotics that'll confine the fighting to real issues. That should pull the rug out from under a bunch of stunts Sheridan's people want to pull. It had better work, too. If the Earthsiders divide among themselves they'll get stolen blind; I'm hoping she can at least keep them civil to each other."

"Okay, so then Cynthia must be doing the ecosocial modelling—"

"Plus she's the closest thing to a development economist I've got."

"—and Yoko—you've got me there. Thought she was a pure historian."

"Her dissertation was on the evolution of extraconstitutional institutions in written constitutional systems. Besides, she went to Earth four times with the HHRF and this last time for the boss."

"Perfect," I said. "Do you have a copy of this abomination of a document? I can already tell this will be fun."

NINE HOURS LATER I had twenty pages of scribbles and a whopping headache. Finding the problems here was trivial; the thing that mystified me was who or what had written it. I said as much to Kwanza, who agreed, and suggested coffee and some supper; it turned out that Yoko and Katrina were going, too, so we made a party of it.

I had met Kat, because some of her work had been on stabilization of semiotic-exchange systems, quite close to Kari's work. Yoko had been teaching Gymschool while she waited for a place to open up at Confed U; I only knew her papers. Both were sharp as razors; I was probably at one of the best colloquia I had ever attended, enhanced by the absence of a set agenda.

Mess hall food too, is conspicuously better than the nasty little sandwiches that are the food of discourse at universities.

"All right, Saul, you're the entertainment for tonight. What've you got so far?"

I shrugged. "Thirteen things I can prove. Some of them are trivial, like that self-interest would virtually require the districts to be hostile to their nearest neighbors, no matter how arbitrary the original boundaries are—the first four provisions of Article Six practically say as much, and the proof is just nine fast steps, no dynamics to it at all. But take a look at this integration of these seven predicate transformers here—''

The sheet of notepaper probably wasn't that easy to read, but they all pored over it for a minute or so. Finally Yoko said, ''My math is rusty and I don't quite understand your notation. Where did these three implications come from?''

''Article one, section four. Together they work out to being a minimum liberalism constraint on each house in the tricameral setup—''

She whistled and moved in, almost sitting on my lap; that was rather pleasant. ''I hadn't seen that. And section six has a clause that virtually enforces acyclicity...'' She looked at me, shaking her head. ''Under rules like that, they won't be able to agree on what time it is if there's only one clock in the room.''

''But they will,'' Kwanza added. ''That's the point of these last five statements. Article three. The President can break deadlocks arbitrarily under section nine. He's practically a dictator, unless all three houses agree—''

''Which they won't,'' I said. ''Look at the dynamics. Farmers will dominate the Debate Chamber and herders will dominate the Senate. And the water projects rule in Article Five will put them at loggerheads all the time; a lot of bitterness there. Whoever controls the House of Selectors won't be able to dominate enough to overbalance the President, unless both factions can get together.

''Further...'' I pulled out another sheet ''...look here. Just a rough estimate. I think that the Sea Gypsies are going to dominate the Selectors anyway. That house is appointed from the bureaucracy, right? And who else has the education to be bureaucrats?''

Kwanza shook his head. ''Saul, you've already paid for your ticket down. This is enough to get them to tear it up right off the bat.''

Kat had been sitting quietly through all of this; she finally spoke. ''I'm not so sure. This is a carefully designed little travesty here.''

"Somebody perverse did it," I said. "It's senseless."

"Not if you realize its purpose. This is supposed to hamstring Earth for good, and get them to do the knifework. Look," she said. "We know that those clauses interact to paralyze the legislature and limit the President to administrative duties; the whole system will freeze up like a dry engine three weeks after the first swearing-in. The point is, every single clause here has a powerful constituency. Herders aren't going to give up the Senate or the water rights provisions—they'd be gobbled up by the farmers' numbers. Farmers will dominate the Debate Chamber, so they'll want to keep that, but the proportional representation system there will get them too fragmented to ever form any kind of coalition except a purely negative one: they won't be able to push anything through, but they'll be able to block everything. And the Sea Gypsies aren't more than a twentieth of the population, but they're well-organized. They'll easily be a quarter, maybe a third, of the ConCon; so the House of Selectors stays, too. Requiring the assent of all three houses—and having them dominated by three different interests—well, right there you've got a guarantee that cyclicity will rear its ugly head system-wide—"

"Ouch," Kwanza said. "And there has to be something to break it. Namely the President, which the farmers won't give up on because it's the only globally elected office—and the SecGen is the Speaker of the Debate Chamber, so both the Head of State and Head of Government will be from a majority constituency—"

"In a minority position in the state." Yoko scanned the page again. "Classical formula for paralysis, or bureaucratism."

"Paralysis, in this case," I said. "Last two sections of Article Three. No extra Cabinet bureaus and it takes a majority in all three houses, plus the President, the SecGen, and the majority of consuls to create a new Ministry. Nope, Kat's right. This is a formula for complete immobility. But it's an immensely popular one. That argues that it's deliberate."

Our spirits were sinking as we headed back to Kwanza's office to talk further. No matter how we looked at it, none of this was going to be easy.

"DIDN'T YOU SPEND the war with farmers?" a tall cattleman demanded.

"Yeah, but my ass got saved when he turned up with the plainsmen," I said, jerking my thumb at Kwanza.

There was a little laughter, but not enough, and the place stayed tense. I went on through the presentation; I'd have preferred a class one-fifth that size, but with nine days 'til the session opened, all we could hope to do was expose everyone to the theory once. And since doing it right meant starting from set theory and working up to impossibility theorems and interfaced difference equation structures, I was stuck doing it wrong: trying to show verbally what the proofs worked out to.

There were no fewer than forty-two boxes and traps concealed in that little masterpiece of treachery, and I had ten hours per presentation to get them pointed out and to sell the delegates on a cleaned-up version with only six sticky spots, three of which were biased—about the practical minimum in a constitution.

This was the third such ten-hour day in a row; I had four more coming. After me they went to Kat and Cynthia, but if we had done our job properly, the two women only had to answer questions and supervise discussion. (*Only* is a relative term. It was only about as exhausting as running a daily marathon).

Yoko Beard, backing me up, was giving an example from the 1830's USA—the Bank of the United States fight. "Look," she said. "It's the same thing. A big institution has become critically important by doing the unpopular-but-necessary dirty work. It has, however, no protection against an arbitrary attack launched from elsewhere in the state. The first time a populist farmer gets the Secretary-Generalship, the Water Ministry will be in danger, and god knows whose ox will be gored. Could be herders, could be farmers, might even be harbor users. If you don't give it some ability to fight back, or at least to shelter behind another institution, that Ministry—any of the Ministries—will go right out the shitport."

Unfortunately, what they got out of all that was another reason for herders to distrust farmers, and for farmers to hate herders. The place went berserk for the third time that morning; people were yelling, shaking fists in each other's faces, swearing, and screaming. It took Kwanza twenty minutes to get order.

The only consolation was that Katrina said her side was going okay; some friendships were even forming across bloc lines. We had all agreed that if this one pulled out, we were going to present her with a life supply of Bordeaux—the one luxury she'd acquired a taste for while stirring up the rebellion in western Europe. At the moment, I was dead certain that my money was safe.

THE ROOM WAS DEAD QUIET, except for the Secretary calling roll. With each "Yes," Kwanza hit the tally button again; there had been relatively few of them in the last hundred. We needed 824 votes to carry, and for the sake of popular support and decent PR it had better be more than that. With 522 votes recorded, we had only 138, which did not project going over the top.

The six of us sat close together. Henry's long skinny shanks stuck over my shoulder; Cynthia, barely a hundred-and-thirty centimeters tall, was perched on Yoko's knee on the other side of Kwanza, and Katrina was leaning so far over me that her stomach was almost on my knees.

The place had once been a theater; it was probably the only standing building on Earth with enough seats for 1647 delegates.

The counting went on for hours, as each individual vote was requested, stated, and recorded one-by-one; optionally that included a one-minute speech, and about one in five of them was exercising the option.

Toward the seven-hundredth delegate, we got a long run of fifty nos. We all sat silently, tense as coiled springs, trying not to jinx it by shouting aloud, but then just after one thousand, there were thirty nos in a row. Sometimes one of us would get up, go to the restroom, get a drink of water, and pace off some energy in the hall. One delegate who had been friendly with Kwanza came up at about the 1100th vote and crouched in front of us.

"Getting to the tail end," she said. "Those that are last in the alphabet get to show their patriotism, I guess." She went back to the floor.

"What did that mean?" Henry asked, pulling his beard.

"Quite a few of them are convinced that our way *is* better for the planet," Kat explained. "But they plan to run for the Debate Chamber or the Senate. They'd rather have voted against it as part of their record...it will play better with their constituents. So the people who voted first had lots of reason to vote against, whatever they actually thought. Now that it's getting close, the ones voting now have to choose between the public interest and their self-interest. I'm glad I'm only watching."

Something was bothering me—had been for days, I realized. I got up, asked them to call me if anything happened, and went out. I had to look around for a while before I found a pencil and some scrap paper; I spread out my copy of our new version on my knee and started scribbling. At first I had no idea what I wanted to write as the "To prove." My first guess was that I wanted to prove there was an undetected flaw, but I quickly realized I was actually working toward something specific.

The thing that concerned me most was the number of sections whose formal equivalents I was using; this was easily six times as complex as anything I had done, an estimate I revised to twenty times before I was done.

But it was easy. When you do proofs for a while, and perhaps more so when you demonstrate them, you get sharp, and suddenly you can just let go and jam, leaping from line to line of icy logic the way a bop trumpeter steps cleanly from note to note, not knowing where he's going but letting the trumpet follow the melody. In thirty minutes I covered four pages, with nary an erasure or crossout, and when I sat back I was strangely pleased with myself; something had finally fallen into place.

Then I realized what it meant. Before I knew it I was running down the halls, clattering and panting through the old theater.

The count stood at 759 of 1322, almost a hundred higher than when I'd left. A good projection was that it would go over the top in half an hour. The group was relaxed and smiling.

"There's a terrible mistake," I said. "I just found something worse than all the others rolled together."

I must have been louder than I thought I was because the Secretary glanced my way and my colleagues shushed me. "You've got to understand," I whispered, crouching beside them. "If we get word out, we can stop this one and draft another. If this passes—"

"Too late," Yoko said. "We'll have to go with what we've got. We can't stop now."

Henry chimed in. "Lots of theoretically unworkable states have done all right. If it was so subtle that you only just found it, it can't come up that often."

"Not often! *Constantly!* What I didn't do was figure in the economic relationships to the Republics and the Confederation—taken together with this constitution, they practically doom Earth to being a tributary backwater—and any efforts they make to get out of that are going to make matters worse."

Katrina looked a little worried, but she just said, "You're getting loud. Kwanza, I can run the tally. Why don't you take Saul outside and talk to him?"

"We're losing time," I said.

"You can't do a thing without the rest of us," Cynthia whispered. "If you can convince Kwanza, we'll play along. But not until you convince him. We've worked too hard this past month to throw it away because of a few scrawls on the backs of some old forms."

The rest nodded, almost in unison. Kwanza and I headed for the hall.

"What's the matter, roomie?" he asked, almost lightly, but I could see how tense he was.

"This," I said, spreading out the four sheets. "I don't expect you to follow it all in the time we've got, but let me just point out the major features and ask you to trust my detail work.

"Let's start with this section here. $Y = C + I + G$, the classic definition of aggregate income, okay? Now, assume the sky-hooks are up. Then transit cost each way is a fraction of what it is today—heat shielding and soft landings cost money too, right? So agriculture and herding take off like a shot, according to this system here...and aggregate income goes up with them. Government won't grow because of this vacuum-blown constitution. Investment is minimal and slow-growth because these are labor-intensive industries, so what takes off is the C term, mostly in light consumer goods. That gets supplied from the Republics and to a lesser extent from the inner Confederation. Earth runs a debit, right, but not a big one? Big enough, however, that the derivative here—growth in investment—all goes offworld. The small crafts, everything right down to shirts and shoes and pots and pans, all move up into space for good. Earth trades nothing but food, and probably pays to get dry-cake back to use as fertilizer.

"That could all be avoided with some simple government measures to increase import substitution. Normal sort of thing to do in the situation, right? Only that's the rub! *This camel-raping constitution prohibits import substitution policies of any kind!* That's what the last two pages show.

"You have to track it through all eight articles, but it's there: any policy with the tendency to cut imports and boost domestic production is going to turn out unconstitutional in operation. And because of the jury nullification provision in Article Two, we couldn't even count on the Selectors' good sense—any little jury in any little village whose ox was gored could strike down the whole programs at one fell swoop.

"I don't need to tell you what that means. Earth is never going to have another big city. It's unlikely that there will even be a town of ten thousand. No cities, no culture of its own, just a quiet backwater stagnating in its own juices...the best brains will all go off to orbit."

"Except the ones that like it quiet," he said.

"Exactly!"

"Like farmers and herders?"

"I don't know what you mean." Suddenly I was confused.

"Look," he said. "Historically, do farmers and herders like or trust cities?"

"No. And this thing here is a prime example of why they shouldn't!"

He nodded vigorously. "I agree with you. But look at it this way. What kind of future do people want their children to have?"

"Well, a better one—"

"Unh-hunh. But better how? Typically, like their own, but less insecure and more prosperous. True?"

"Well, sure, but—"

"And what does this thing give to the Earthsiders?"

"Well, okay, but it still amounts to freedom to rot in a backwater and to sell their children into that."

"Rot?" He grinned at me. "You know as well as I do, we both drink a lot less and sleep a lot better when we're doing field work. Ask the average farmer whether he wants life to speed up. In fact, suppose you could put this kind of future to a vote, against a more urbanized one—"

"That's not the point," I said. "They have the same right we do to try to make a real civilization—"

"Who does?"

"The Earthsiders!"

"You're not talking like it's a right. You're talking like its mandatory."

I was taken aback at that; he had a point. "Were you in on this?"

"Me? In on what?" Kwanza looked at me as if I'd gone crazy.

"Somebody designed this. It couldn't have been buried in that constitution so subtly by accident. If you ask me, all those other flaws were just a smokescreen for this one. And you're right. The Earthsiders would *rather* have things this way.

"This was a defense in depth, Kwanz'. First, we had to catch all those original bugs, then find this one—and two of the key clauses for it are results of our fixing other bugs—then convince the Earthsiders that they didn't want it. Which would probably have been impossible in any case."

He nodded slowly, scratching his head. "You realize there's only one possible suspect for who did this?"

"Yeah."

"Do we tell the others?"

I nodded firmly. "They're entitled to know. Besides, we need their help. As Yoko likes to say, after the rules are written the game really starts. We aren't done yet. You're right—this might not be so bad. It might even have been what Earth would have chosen for itself. But they were tricked into it, and that smells."

He was about to reply, but then there was a wild, roaring cheer from the auditorium. The door opened and the rest of our little group ran toward us. "Passed!" Katrina shouted. "With one hundred twelve votes to go!"

They crowded around us. "What about that thing you found, Saul?" Henry demanded.

"Tell you at the party tonight," I said.

"What party?" Yoko asked.

"In my office," Kwanza said. "We have a lot to talk about."

17

It was close to time; after everything we'd been through I wouldn't have expected us to be scared, but we all were. Yoko, Henry, and Kwanza were hanging all over each other; Kat, Cynthia and I were talking a little more—mostly about being scared.

"Time," Henry said. All six of us got up and went out, setting up in the order we'd agreed on: Kwanza first, then Kat and Cynthia, then Henry, then Yoko and me. We were hoping this would work; a lot depended on getting there at just the right moment, and on nobody else getting off schedule.

The problem was that the arsenal at Ganymede Orbital was max security—not surprising, considering what was in it. We had spent a lot of time working this out, trying to minimize the role of luck, but in something like this we ended up leaning on it heavily, and the biggest piece of luck we had going for us was surprise. No one had tried anything like this in a long time. We would never get a second try.

Especially not one with the vid there.

The vid reporter was just there for one of those routine visits they do to any sizable government facility, the sort of classic "where your taxes go" story. It had taken some fast and fancy lying by Kwanza to get the exact time when the reporter would be in a warhead vault, and a little more prevarication by Yoko to find out which vault and what the route to it was. Not that she'd made any big deal of it. "Why," she had asked, "would you expect a historian to have any more regard for the truth than a societist?"

We came around the blind turn to the Arsenal entrance and flashed our faked badges; the guard let us go right by, though from the nod and gulp it was obvious that he knew who we were. He must have simply assumed anyone he'd seen on the vid was important enough to have a security clearance.

We knew that the next guard would have a badge scanner and would insist on using it. When we reached that door, Kwanza walked up, holding his ID, then threw his arms around the guard. Kat hit the door button; we went through, and Kat hit the emergency close, then lay down under the door.

As we hurried on, I could hear the guard yelling at Kwanza, who was quite calmly lying on the floor ignoring the orders to get up. The door, of course, programmed not to crush a human body or to let one go, had jammed down on Kat, uncomfortably, she said later, but not painfully.

Around the next corner, there was a gun operated by a guard in a booth. "I'm unarmed. I surrender," Cynthia said, and walked up, pushing her chest against the gun port. She held up a bunch of roses—a neat little trick she'd found in some obscure history book. "I brought you some flowers. Please don't shoot me."

The guard stared at her, unable to make up his mind; then he got into an argument with a voice from a loudspeaker in there. It appeared that neither the guard nor his boss wanted to shoot or order the shooting. The rest of us walked on. "One to go," Henry said.

By the time we got to the gate at the mouth of the weapons vault, sirens were going off everywhere and we could hear loudspeakers crackling. The metal detectors and explosives sniffers had, of course, confirmed that we weren't carrying anything lethal, but I'm sure the administrators were not particularly comforted. It simply meant they couldn't legally shoot us, which meant the potential embarrassment was that much greater.

Yoko and I went through the gate; Henry closed it, grabbed the handles, braced his feet on the lower lip, and waited for the guards to turn up; he would offer no resistance, except that he would not let go until they pried him off.

The vid reporter, accompanied by several Naval officers, was starting to come out of the vault when we came in, walking past him. "Hey," one of the Navy men said, but the reporter had already turned.

Like any good reporter, he was trained to point that camera as soon as something happened. It was what we had been counting on.

"My name is Yoko Rosaparks. I cannot participate any longer in maintaining these warheads, which are the physical manifestation of the brutal threat of genocide by which we coerce our fellow beings. In token and reminder of their deadly purpose, I cover them with my own blood." She raised the 500 cc jug over her head, broke the seal with her thumb, and poured it on a warhead. The camera shifted back and forth between her face and the trickle of blood running over the warhead.

A Naval officer whispered something to the reporter; he shook his head.

"My name is Saul Rosaparks," I said. "They have said there is peace, yet after more than a year they still keep these tools of war. I call on the Confederation to renounce their weapons and to completely demilitarize, as the Orbital Republics and the Provisional Government of Earth have done, turning over whatever small forces may be needed to the direct control of the Council of Humanity. To retain these is to threaten murder, of which we are all victims; as a victim, I give my blood."

One of the Navy men rushed at me as I raised my jug, so I smashed it on the warhead rather than pouring it. The blood sprayed everywhere, on me, on him, on the warheads, even a little on Yoko. He stepped back, wiping his face, stunned.

Yoko and I joined hands. "You may do with us what you will," we recited. "We will accept any penalty, but we will no longer assent to your keeping these weapons."

One of the Navy men suddenly grabbed the vid reporter's camera, but another one, with a keen sense of what news organizations can do when they're thwarted, stopped him. Still, they hustled the reporter out pretty fast when he started trying to ask us questions. We stood there and waited for the cops. "Think the others are okay?" Yoko asked.

"I hope so."

"Are you scared?"

"Yep."

"Me, too."

Then there were footsteps in the corridor. We lay down, went limp, and let them carry us out.

"I'D LIKE TO RIVET your scrotum to the bulkhead," the cop said to me, almost pleasantly. "We won the vacuum-blown war. You fought in it. And now you think it's just too terrible because we want to keep some of what we fought so hard for. What've you got against freedom?"

"Why do you want those bombs?"

"Just stick out your hand. I need to take your prints." He pushed my hand down on the plate; the printreader hummed and printed out a digital description, followed by my police record. "Eight counts of subversion."

"All from before the Independence War."

"So?"

"So, if you were in the PRA, and you got caught, you got some counts of subversion. There's supposed to be one for sabotage and one for unauthorized possession of weapons, too."

"Yeah, there is. Why'd they give you those counts?"

"I got caught running guns for the independence fighters."

"How old were you, then?"

"Six. I don't remember much. I was in this last war, though. But they didn't make a hero out of *me*."

"I'd trade you if I could."

"Very funny. Okay, retina charts." He was a little rough putting the clamp over my head, and the light flashed a bit longer than I'd have thought necessary.

"Why'd you do something stupid like this?" he asked me. "You one of those Pratt people? It says you wrote a book about him or something in the printout. In the Republics they knew what to do with Prattists—out the airlock, no more questions."

"Why do you want to keep those weapons?" I asked again.

"You know, I did the other two men in your little group. They kept asking that."

"What did you tell them?"

"Shut up and bend over. You're a seditionist and you were in a max security facility. I think we better do a rectal check for concealed weapons."

After that he wanted me to dictate a full confession, with prompting on some technicalities that would let them get me a longer sentence, and there were some more physical measurements and body-probings. In all, it went on for two hours. He never did tell me what he wanted the bombs for, though I asked him often enough. He probably didn't tell Kwanza or Henry either.

"HELLO, Saul, mind if I come in?" he said. He looked, if anything, older than ever; I suppose the war had taken its toll on him, too.

I didn't take his hand, and I didn't say anything as he came into the cell. He gave me a very nicely printed copy of my dissertation; I thanked him. "It's been selling like crazy—the 'Earth-mindedness' campaign is off to a flying start, no thanks to you. Kwanza gave me a copy of your proof when I visited him yesterday. Elegant," he said. "I think he was angry with me about it—"

I nodded and sat down. "You were always 'the boss' to him. Of course, he feels a little betrayed at not being trusted enough to know what dirty work he was supposed to do. It's not such a big deal for the rest of us." I let my deep breath out slowly. "It's going to take some effort to learn to think of you as Lemuel Pratt."

"What?" he said sharply, not really a question, as his hand slid into his jacket pocket. I wasn't sure what he had there, but I was sure he already had a credible story to explain the wounds on my corpse if he needed to.

I shook my head. "You're in no danger, Dr. Pratt. I'm not going to rat on you. I don't care. I just wanted to say I know—and to ask you why."

"I suppose," he said, "I could accuse you of paranoia. It might get us both some interesting publicity. You and this illegal Team Rosaparks of yours have already lost a lot of popularity with that stunt of yours at Ganymede Arsenal."

"The only blood spilled was ours," I said. "A little trick Yoko pulled out of twentieth century history. And I didn't damage the warheads by pouring it on them, either. It was the authorities that decided to make a production of the whole thing..."

He smiled warmly. "No doubt you're right—though any government that ignored people like you would eventually have to cease to be a government, so perhaps their range of choice was limited."

"Their limits," I said, "are their problem. The weapons are there to kill. If they don't like the smell of blood, they should get rid of the weapons."

"This won't help your Team's appeal any."

"We're within our legal rights to form a team in free association. We'll get recognition in court, or we won't. We're a team and we're going to live as one. And the grounds for denying the petition were specious in any case. Working for peace is a single project."

"Peace is already achieved, dammit!"

"Freedom from war is," I said, shaking my head. "Part of your problem, Dr. Menden—Dr. Pratt, is that you can't tell the difference."

"Why don't you just use Mendenhall? We're both used to it. And what makes you think I'm Pratt? Are you sure I'm not Karl Marx, Adam Smith, or Pope Peter the First?"

"How do I know? Well, I spent a lot of time doing formal proofs. That really improves your concentration and especially your sense of where a chain of logic is leading you. All of a sudden I started to wonder why so many of your orders and requests had so little to do with winning the war—especially after I compared notes with the rest of Team Rosaparks, the night after the Constitution passed. We got suspicious, of course, because it was obvious you were behind that scam at ConCon.

"As Dr. Mendenhall, you wouldn't have been interested at all; I suppose a secret Prattist might have been, but the whole reason that there probably aren't any real Prattists left is that Pratt absolutely condemned concealing one's beliefs. So that left one possibility, which fit in very well with your unknown origins and your talents and interests in the social sciences.

"Especially when you consider how long-lived we are now. There are still some people born before the Second World War alive in the Republics, I understand. The assumption was that Pratt died shortly after he was last seen, on Earth just before the Collapse. Or if not then, certainly within twenty years—he was fairly old by 2034 and Earthsiders don't live long. But if Pratt got to the Republics—"

He thought about it for a moment. "Still a bit of a jump, Saul. You got the rest of the way to your conclusion with a leap and a guess, even if it did turn out right. Anyway, as for why . . . you did your master's thesis on my work. Why do you think?"

"The Lemuel Pratt I read argued that the way a civilization produces its goods and allocates its work is the most sincere expression of its moral character. I'm not sure I *can* reconcile that with assassination, dabbling in wars, and running a spy service that I suspect includes some kind of secret police."

"That Pratt," he said, "was almost a century ago. Twenty years after that, in the middle of the Troubles, he found himself temporarily without ID and with a chance to get on one of the last refugee flights to Port Armstrong. He took it, and as soon as possible he moved to the outer settlements in the hope of never being recognized. He worked at several honest trades, including fax programmer, and at that occupation, managed to make himself a Harvard doctoral diploma in his next alias. Fair enough, he'd earned one in his real name, and Harvard was by then a pile of bricks under a greatly expanded bay . . . I was obviously a social scientist, the University here was terribly short of them, and so the credentials check was not extensive.

"I even managed to take up some of my old research, but with a new angle. I had come to realize that the moral vision of the future, in my early books, was much closer to our grasp than I had imagined. A world without hunger, ignorance, war . . . where people suffered no more from exploitation than they did from smallpox.

"But if these were pursued by 'moral' means—without violence or guile—they might take centuries to achieve. I was letting petty scruples stand in the way of the human future. Certainly, peaceful evolution might have worked eventually, but it's not nearly as easy to win over every last opponent as it is to exterminate their ancestors.

"And there it was: Paradise physically within our grasp, and all of us kept out by our collective greed and stupidity. When a few simple steps, things that were a distant possibility anyway, might bring us there overnight. A set of worthwhile ideas had informed my vision; if I wanted to realize it, perhaps it was time for realism to inform my actions."

"'When anyone with principles opts for realism, he is no more than five years away from doing the unspeakable,'" I quoted.

He smiled again; not much seemed to rattle him. "I wrote that line when I was younger than you are now. Let me know what you think in another century. With the life-extending effects of low grav, you should still be alive, and I might be.

"So, to finish the story, I did what I could to get the War for Independence started and to win it; and I did the same with the Earth Revolution. Technically, I suppose, neither was necessary. The cooperative lifestyle of the outer colonies would almost certainly have gradually influenced the culture of the Republics into more humane directions. As that happened, the opportunity for leaders in the King or Gandhi style to achieve freedom and dignity for Earth would have expanded as well . . . and in a few centuries we might have seen what we see today, a united human race in a united solar system preparing to abolish want and suffering."

"But today we see it after two bloody wars," I said, doing my best to keep him to the point.

"Exactly. After two bloody wars. But within my lifetime."

"That was it, then," I said. "Within your lifetime. If you were going to live two hundred years, you wanted everything to happen in that span . . ."

"Phrase it as selfishness if you like," he said. "I don't much mind. You're part of my game now, you know. The kind of no-compromises nonviolence Team Rosaparks practices is part of the next step. You can't avoid working for me. In fact, let me add, I've already taken steps. Your appeal is going to succeed, despite the monkey wrench you almost threw into my path with that stupid stunt at the arsenal. Several reporters, including the egregiously sentimental Clara Bly, will be doing favorable stories about you. You're going to have success, a lot of it—and you'll owe it to me."

"Success is irrelevant in this kind of thing," I said, "but I'm glad of your help, I suppose. So we're still pawns on your board?"

He looked wary, but he couldn't help a small smile.

"There's a difference," I said. "You wouldn't care what pawns thought of you."

"Obviously I don't, or I wouldn't stick to my course. And you're not entitled to be that smug." The old man's eyes flashed. "The early Christians hated Rome, but they travelled its roads under the protection of its legions. Modern pacifism developed as a theory during the long peace in Europe between Napoleon and the First World War, because a bloody war had made that peace possible, and the idea of permanent peace conceivable. And supposing that Hitler or Stalin had won out, there'd be nothing like your little band of dreamers possible. Every culture stands in a river of historical blood up to its neck; all you can do—"

"All we can do is keep more off our own hands. Which begins by refusing to go along with other people's violence. When are you going to get rid of those warheads?"

"When we can trust the Republics to keep the treaty they've signed. As soon as the Council of Humanity is secure."

"And how will you know you can trust them until you get rid of the warheads?"

"You," he said, "have given up practicality. I must remember that."

"It's practical to seek trust at gunpoint?"

He grinned. "You won't rile me that way. I admit, groups like yours are what will eventually bring a permanent peace. But it was those of us willing to spill some blood who paved your way. You don't have to accept that, but it's true."

"Is it relevant?" I asked him. "Spaceborne society is what really makes abundance feasible. That could only grow out of industrial society, and the first industrial revolutions were capitalized out of slavery and genocide. All right, fine. We can't restore the dead. What we can do is refrain from killing. Here's another quote from you: 'The only crime of legitimate interest to society is one that may yet be prevented.'"

"Look at all that has been prevented—"

"Look at all that hasn't," I said. I expected some reply, but in fact he just sat with me quietly for about half an hour until the guard came to take him out. I tried to talk to him, but he didn't respond—just looked at the floor.

I had a letter from him yesterday; he told me my message was important and he could help me spread it. Unaccountably, it irritated me; I haven't written back yet, but I will.

There are fifty-two days left in my sentence, and I want him to come back; especially since he said, in his letter, that he'll bring coffee if he does. It's strange how I miss little things like that almost as much as I miss Kwanza, Kat, Henry, Yoko, and Cynthia. I really am looking forward to getting out of this damned jail; I miss them.

But my big hope right now is to get that old man back here for some long talks; he really seemed unhappy after that last one, which I think is a good sign. If I'm careful with him, gentle but firm, there might be hope for him yet.

ISAAC ASIMOV PRESENTS

AGENT OF BYZANTIUM

HARRY TURTLEDOVE

"Engrossing, entertaining and very cleverly rendered... I recommend it without reservation."
—*Roger Zelazny*

The Byzantine Empire is about to be destroyed! An elite agent to the emperor learns of hostile threats from rising enemies and becomes swept up in a dangerous and desperate struggle to save Byzantium from utter collapse.

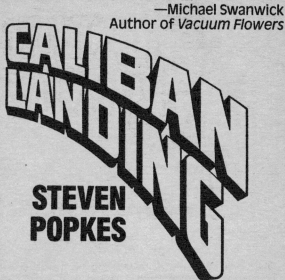

Chilling novels of international espionage, intrigue and suspense

Chilling novels of international espionage, intrigue and suspense

		Quantity
PROSPERO DRILL—Carl Posey An airborne scientific team becomes caught in a spine-chilling clash between the superpowers.	$3.95	☐
WAR MOON—Tom Cooper Russia has launched the ultimate weapon and the United States wants it. The genius behind the weapon becomes a pawn in a dangerous game of international cat and mouse.	$3.50	☐
THE MAN ON THE TRAIN—W. J. Chaput In 1941 a German spy with orders to assassinate Winston Churchill puts his deadly plan in motion.	$3.95 U.S. $4.50 Canada	☐
DZERZHINSKY SQUARE—James O. Jackson Captured by Nazis during World War II, a Russian soldier becomes a reluctant spy in his homeland in order to save his life.	$3.95	☐

Total Amount	$
Plus 75¢ Postage	.75
Payment enclosed	

Please send a check or money order payable to Worldwide Library.

In the U.S.A.	In Canada
Worldwide Library 901 Fuhrmann Blvd. Box 1325 Buffalo, NY 14269-1325	Worldwide Library P.O. Box 609 Fort Erie, Ontario L2A 5X3

Please Print

Name: _____

Address: _____

City: _____

State/Prov: _____

Zip/Postal Code: _____

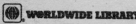 **W RLDWIDE LIBRARY**

ESP-2